HARPER'S TEN

PREQUEL TO THE FRACTURED SPACE SERIES

J G Cressey

Harper's Ten
Prequel to the Fractured Space Series

Copyright © 2015 by J G Cressey
www.jgcressey.com

All rights reserved. This book or any portion thereof may not be reproduced or used in any manner whatsoever without the express written permission of the publisher except for the use of brief quotations in a book review.

This is a work of fiction. Any resemblance to actual persons, places or events is purely coincidental.

First Printing, 2015

Edited by Amanda Shore
Cover art by Linggar Bramanty
Cover design by Andrew Hall
Formatting by Polgarus Studio

For my family and friends.
You're a good bunch, I'm a lucky guy.

CHAPTER ONE

Lieutenant Callum Harper woke with the back of his head rattling against the metal restraint. It seemed smart-gel, or even basic padding, had been overlooked on this ship. The violent shaking meant that nap time was well and truly over. They'd be touching down on Capsun 23's surface in a matter of minutes, and he had to get his act together. Sometimes, it was easy to forget that he was the one in charge. He'd only been a lieutenant for a little under a year, and the role still felt strange, as if he were donning someone else's ill-fitting armor.

Cal glanced at his team. Five men and two women in full Corrain armor were nestled in the flight seats around him, and Sinclair and Malloy were up front in the cockpit. Nine soldiers, most of whom had proven their combat abilities countless times. Some had been on the team for years, some just a handful of missions. And then there was one who was fresh out of the academy and green as hell. Peter Coutes, or *Couter* as the team had begun calling him, was a fit, strong young man with exceptional grade rankings. But somehow, his unblemished face and wide, eager eyes made him seem little more than a kid. Cal studied him for a moment and did his best to get the measure of the young man. Right now, he was brimming with jokes, smiles, and bravado as he talked to Wilson and Oshiro, the grizzled old veterans sitting on either side of him. Cal thought the smiles genuine but the bravado not so much. Couter had been chatting away when Cal had fallen asleep, and now, an hour later, his mouth hadn't lost any velocity. It was a sure sign of nerves. Cal didn't blame him; anyone who wasn't nervous on their first mission was either lying or a nut job—especially when that first mission was to an uncharted planet.

Cal rubbed the sleep from his eyes and stretched his arms as best he could beneath his flight restraints. He had to admit to feeling on edge himself on this particular outing. Annoyed too. In fact, the mission brief had made him damn right angry. That pathetic excuse for a starship captain, Laurence Decker, had probably made the order on a whim or perhaps distractedly muttered the go ahead between drinks in the officer's club. It wasn't that the mission was a dud but more that it could turn out to be the exact opposite. And if that were the case, Cal and his team wouldn't have nearly enough muscle power, or indeed fire power, to dig themselves out of the hole they'd be in.

"You think the new kid'll hold up, boss?"

Cal turned to Sergeant Becker, who was sitting by his

side. She was roughly snapping point grenades to the side of her ten-click pulse rifle. "He'll be alright," Cal replied semi-confidently.

She nodded and reached for another grenade.

Upon seeing the sergeant's fine features, long eyelashes, and silky blond hair, a person might be forgiven for labeling her as a lady of delicate pursuits, a *debutante* even. The sight of her muscular, battle-scarred arms, however, quickly killed the illusion dead. Becker was hard as nails. In fact, after working with her for the past five years, Cal could think of no one he'd rather have backing him up in a fight. That was one of many reasons he'd been quick to recommend her in the role of sergeant when he'd been promoted to lieutenant.

Cal winced as she snapped another of the little explosives into place. "Of course, you keep bashing those point grenades around like that, you might just blow him and the rest of us to hell before we even touch down."

Becker shook her head. "You're such a pussy, boss," she replied, handling the next grenade with extra vigor. "Besides, I've seen you juggling with these things when you're drunk."

"Oh yeah," Cal said, disengaging his flight restraint and climbing to his feet. "When this mission's over, remind me I've given up drinking."

"Sure thing, boss," Becker said with a smile. "Then we'll have a round of shots to celebrate the fact."

Cal returned the smile and had a quick stretch, his armor adjusting easily and smoothly to his movements.

Having now broken through the planet's atmosphere, the turbulence had diminished, and the metal grating beneath his feet felt as steady as a rock. Bringing up his wrist, he activated the comm on his data pad. "How we doing, Sinclair?"

"Not much to see yet," the flight officer answered. "Low-level cloud cover. Should see more in a few minutes. We'll be touching down in ten."

"Okay. Keep your comm open; I want you and Malloy to hear the brief."

"Sure thing."

Cal walked to the back of the deployment cabin, took hold of an overhead grab-bar—more out of habit than necessity—and looked back at his team. They only filled a fifth of the available flight seats. *Not nearly enough,* he thought grimly, *not by a long shot.* "Okay, listen up. Time for the brief." This got a little cheer from Corporal Franco, the team's one and only smart ass. Cal ignored him and continued. "Capsun 23's in stage one of its colony compatibility trials. Three data drones touched down on the surface five days ago, but all three went dark shortly—" Cal paused mid-flow. The new recruit had raised his hand like he was on some sort of school outing. "What is it, Couter?"

"Sorry to interrupt, sir, but haven't we all already studied the mission brief?"

Cal raised an eyebrow. "You read it?"

Couter nodded, looking a little confused.

"All twelve documents?" Cal asked.

Couter looked about at the rest of the team. "Of course, sir, didn't…"

Franco whistled. "Looks like we've got an officer in the making, people."

"Shut it, Franco, and keep it shut," Cal said, ignoring the wide, Italian grin that he knew the corporal would be shooting his way. "I want you all to take note of young Couter's enthusiasm and dedication. There was a day when you all had some. And maybe even a day when you all read your mission briefs back to front. The details could save your life and, more importantly, mine. *Brief* doesn't mean you briefly glance at the front page. Especially this mission."

"You suspect a hellhole, Lieutenant?" Veteran Wilson asked. He was a hardy, thick-set man who looked as though he'd spent a long lifetime pulling fish from a rough ocean—quite the contrast to the fresh-faced Couter by his side.

Cal found himself nodding even though he had no hard evidence to support the theory. "All three data drones went offline shortly after touching down. None of them sent out much info before going dark. Only the basics; gravity's a touch on the heavy side but well within acceptable limits. Atmos and temps are friendly."

"So we're a goddamned tech retrieval crew." This came from private Poots. She'd joined Cal's team a year ago. She was a good soldier but cranky as hell.

"No. Primarily, we're here to rescue," Cal replied. "A small, non-military research team touched down on the planet shortly after the drones went offline. Twenty-eight civilians in a Class Three Base-pod. Contact with them was lost before their first report was even sent. Intel believes pirates or scavengers are involved. A small, unregistered vessel was detected in the area around the time the drones died, so it could well be that we're looking at a simple scavenge crime…" Judging by the faces of his more experienced team members, Cal was starting to feel more confident in his own suspicions. At least ninety percent of scavenge crimes on data drones failed within a few hours. The thieves either gave up upon discovering the level of drone's protective shielding or they attempted to disengage it and got vaporized in the process.

"…Or it could be that the planet's wildlife is responsible," Cal continued. He looked around at the team and noted that Couter's confident expression was starting to wane. The change on his young face was only subtle, but Cal could spot it a mile off. He felt an urge to tell the recruit not to worry, that maybe Intel had the right of it and they'd find nothing but the remnants of a simple scavenge crime. But he didn't believe it. Besides, this was the life the young man had signed up for; mollycoddling him definitely wouldn't help.

"I'll be honest with you," Cal said after a moment. "So far, we don't know anything about Capsun 23 other than it has abundant water, and we'll be able to breathe and walk around. Three things that encourage life. My gut feeling… We could be looking at a hellhole."

There were a number of mumbled curses.

"Or we could be looking at a paradise full of sweaty Amazon women," Corporal Franco suggested.

Orisho, the big Japanese veteran to Couter's left, let out a booming laugh. This was a common occurrence; Orisho found most things that Franco said amusing. This time, Cal looked at Franco. The corporal was a ridiculously good-looking man who knew it only too well. Cal also suspected that his thick, Italian accent was emphasized for effect. They were about the same age, mid-thirties, and Franco had been part of the team for four years. Despite the corporal being a bit of a dick at times, Cal couldn't help but like the man. He was tougher than he looked and a hell of a lot more capable than he acted.

"Come on, people," Franco continued. "We're living in a vast soup of infinite possibilities. Don't deny me the hope that all my future wives could be waiting for me down there."

Cal headed for the cockpit with the continued sound of Oshiro's big laugh echoing off the walls.

There wasn't much to see through the flight window other than thin cloud cover. Cal laid a hand on the pilot's shoulder. "Sinclair."

"Lieutenant," she replied, briefly turning to look up at him. "Still not much to see yet. But the clouds are breaking up fast."

Out of all his team, Cal had known Sinclair the longest. She'd been his advanced piloting tutor back in his Academy days as well as a mentor. Despite being advanced in her years, Sinclair was still as fit as they came, and she had the intelligence and experience to back it up. Strictly speaking, she wasn't actually part of the team—not on a long-term basis anyway. Having left the Academy, Sinclair now enjoyed a Class One Flight Officer ranking, meaning she got to pick and choose which teams she worked with and when. It also meant that she technically outranked Cal while they were off the ground. Cal didn't mind that one bit. He was just glad she was with them; he had a feeling that experience was going to be a godsend on this particular mission.

As they neared the clouds, Cal felt his gut tighten. For a single team to be landing on an uncharted planet was bordering on insanity. They didn't even have one of the new synthetics backing them up, just an aging combat robot that Cal suspected was nearing its cybernetic retirement. God knows how the civilian research team had felt touching down without a heavily weaponized escort. It seemed the military weren't the only ones with rash incompetents dishing out orders. But in truth, it was more than the lack of intel and idiotic orders that was causing Cal his unease. A primal instinct was welling up inside him and encroaching the rational part of his brain. It wasn't a feeling he could explain, but it was there and was growing in intensity. As they entered the clouds, he gripped the back of the flight chair hard, knuckles turning white. He'd been to plenty of hellholes in his time, often filled with beasts straight from a child's nightmare—or an adult's for that matter. Planets where even the ships were attacked. And others where the flora demonstrated a larger appetite than the fauna. On all of those occasions, however, data drones had already dished out comprehensive intel. They'd always known what they were getting into and were as prepared as possible. Not only that but his team was usually just a part of multiple squads, all armed to the teeth.

"It's not like you to be so tense, Cal."

Despite his anxiety, Cal smiled. Sinclair only used his name when she was worried about him. "I'm fine. Just a bit frustrated. I'm not sure our superiors have been diligent enough on this one."

"Captain Decker?"

Cal's smile morphed into a grimace. "None other. It's not the first time he's been responsible for a bullshit mission, and I suspect it won't be the last." Cal had tried to confront the captain before departing the starship, but the man had supposedly been indisposed—no doubt filling his belly in the officer's club. Cal felt annoyed at himself. He should have tried harder, found the man, and forced some sense into him. Cal's team was a tough, capable lot, but they weren't infallible. They were his responsibility. They relied on him to minimize the risks. Dangerous missions were part of the job; suicide missions weren't. He couldn't help feeling that he'd let them down on this mission before it had even started.

Leaning forward, he peered through the cockpit's window. If it was that bad, he could always abort the mission, retreat out of the atmosphere, and demand reinforcements to aid in the rescue. He'd happily take whatever reprimand Captain Decker dished out. But then again, if it truly were that bad and the civilians weren't already dead, they'd no doubt be in dire need, and time would be of the essence.

Finally, they burst through the last of the clouds. Cal leaned further forward, holding his breath as he did so.

Then, he slowly let the breath go, his eyebrows rising. Through the window, as far as the eye could see, were far-reaching views of green, rolling hills peppered with vast patches of vibrant flowers, and calm, glittering lakes.

After a few moments, Sinclair turned to him with a smile. "Looks like a peaceful paradise to me."

Inclined to agree, Cal stood up straight and rubbed the back of his head.

Weirdly, he felt almost deflated.

CHAPTER TWO

"Yep, I wouldn't wish this lethal, dark pit of a planet on my worst enemy."

Cal turned to see Corporal Franco nudging what looked like a large daisy with the toe of his boot. Cal shook his head and tried to remember exactly why he considered the man a good friend. "You might just make *me* your worst enemy if you keep that up, Corporal."

Franco shrugged. "I'm serious, sir. I'm not sure all of us are gonna make it this time." He nudged the flower again and looked down. "Maybe none of us."

Cal turned to Becker. "Sergeant."

"Yes, boss." Becker sidled up to him, pulse rifle nestled firmly in her grip.

"When this mission's over, remind me I need to kick Corporal Franco's ass."

Becker smiled. "Delegate that one if you would, sir. Be nice to do it under orders for a change."

"Good, then consider it an order. As long as you

promise not to pull your punches." Cal walked forward a few paces and continued to take in the surroundings. They'd landed by the first drone, which was situated at edge of a small lake, its surface rippling in the gentle breeze. The clouds overhead had mostly dissipated to reveal a neighboring planet, large and pale in the vibrant, blue sky. Having risen from the east just like Earth, the light from two suns beamed down and glittered on the water. Cal had half an urge to strip off his armor and take a dip. The water was crystal clear, and Malloy, the team's science officer, had already tested it and deemed it safe. But there was work to be done. He'd sent the veterans Orisho, Wilson, and the eager young Couter scouting for signs of pirates or scavengers. With any luck, the two older men with their wealth of experience would be a good influence on the rookie. They had been for him—still were to a large extent. So far, Cal wasn't overly worried about the wildlife. The most dangerous creatures they'd spotted as yet had been a small flock of white birds swirling through the bright blue sky, which Franco was quick to observe had quite pointy beaks. No matter how pleasant the surroundings, however, he knew it wasn't smart to become complacent.

Turning, Cal strolled toward the big, solid block of dark metal that towered over the rest of his team. The drone had traveled vast distances before entering Capsun 23's atmosphere. It and its two identical kin had then detached from each other and gone their separate ways, spreading out over the planet's surface. On reaching its designated sector, the drone had anchored itself into the ground, where its single-minded AI immediately began to drink in the unsurveyed planet's secrets. Cal looked down to where the drone's multi-jointed, spiked legs had pounded down and twisted into the earth. The legs looked as though they'd been pulled from some sort of giant, mechanical arachnid—a hard, ugly beast mercilessly seizing the soft, serene landscape. Cal hoped that whatever colony ended up here was a damn sight prettier in design than this metallic monstrosity.

Heading to the drones before the research base had been a decision dictated in part by protocol but mostly by Captain Decker's insistence. The captain had clearly marked the retrieval of all three drones as priority, and his orders were clear without an ounce of room for misinterpretation. During the briefing, Cal had told the team that rescue was their primary objective, and if it were up to him, it would be. But he doubted if any of them, bar perhaps the rookie Couter, were fooled. The research base was privately owned and therefore had no monetary worth to the military. The fact that there were twenty-eight living souls running the base didn't seem to enter the equation. The rescue of the civilians was of course part of their mission but only once all three drone assets were secured. In the end, it was one more piece of idiocy that made Cal sick to his stomach. Right now, he had no idea what sort of trouble the civilians were in, and the recovery of each drone would add up to a hell of a lot of time.

Shortly after touching down, Sinclair had picked up a

simple, short-range SOS signal emanating from the research base. The signal wasn't unexpected—they'd already known that the researchers were having difficulty—so it stood to reason that they'd send out a local distress signal. But it was unusually weak and intermittent with a puzzling frequency. Sinclair had described it like something a kid would have sent out after rigging up a simple beacon using old spare parts. The assessment had been all the reason Cal needed to send a message to Captain Decker requesting immediate retrieval of the civilians. As yet, no reply had been received.

"Malloy, how long?" he asked, looking down at the man who was crouched between two of the drone's hideous, spiked legs.

"Fifteen more minutes," Malloy replied, pausing for a moment to look up. He had stripped bare a section of the drone's base and was wielding a couple of complex tools.

Cal shook his head in frustration. They'd already been here well over an hour. "Any way to hurry it along?" He asked the question even though he knew it was futile. Malloy was as fast and efficient as they came whether you asked him to be or not.

The science officer shook his head. "It would usually have taken far longer, but the drone's shields were already offline when we arrived."

Cal's brow creased. "Signs of tampering?"

"None whatsoever," Malloy said as he returned his attentions back to the job at hand. "I'll need to ensure that the other defenses are inert before we delve any deeper."

Cal nodded approvingly. Malloy was a damn fine science officer, something that was hardly surprising considering he had a T-tech augment fitted inside his skull. The augment enabled him to instantly access and process an unfathomable amount of information. Not only that but his eyes had been enhanced to a level almost matching that of a synthetic combat soldier. It made him privy to a host of details that normal human sight couldn't hope to discern. On their first meeting, Cal had found the golden sheen covering Malloy's eyes disconcerting, but he'd soon become used to it.

Stepping back from the drone, Cal glanced at Franco. "Corporal, stop caressing that flower, and get Max up and running. We'll need him to shift the drone into the ship."

"Sure thing, lieutenant," Franco replied. "That drone looks his type though. Might get unprofessional." The corporal took a moment to appreciate his own joke before jogging up the ship's loading ramp.

"Cal, we've had a reply from the starship." The voice was Sinclair's, emanating from the comm on his wrist.

Cal gritted his teeth. He could tell from her tone that it wasn't good news. "Do I want to hear it?"

"Probably not. Captain Decker wants the mission followed precisely as was ordered. Absolutely no deviations."

God damn that prick, Cal thought angrily. The man was a bona fide idiot who'd not once set his own feet out on the field. How could such an ignorant, inexperienced person be expected to command? And how the hell could he have reached the rank of *captain*? Unfortunately, Cal knew the answer, and it was a woefully simple one: Decker's father was the admiral of the fleet, and the truth of it was admirals could pull any strings they pleased.

"At least the communications seem to working fine," Sinclair commented in way of conciliation.

"True enough," Cal replied as he pondered his next move. "Send the message again if you would, Sinclair. And if the same reply comes back, then send it again." Cal doubted if this approach would do the least bit of good. Decker was a blinkered, stubborn idiot, and pushing him only made him more so.

"Consider it done," Sinclair replied. "If nothing else, it will be a good way to keep a check on the comms."

"Thanks, Sinclair."

Cal stared up at the ugly hunk of drone that towered over him and tried his best to simmer his frustration. He was starting to find the rank of lieutenant a bitch of a position—to be in charge but at the same time really *not* to be in charge. In an attempt to distract himself from thoughts of his inept superior, he planted his foot on a mound of churned up soil that surrounded one of the drone's legs and leaned forward on his knee to get a better look at Malloy's efforts. He didn't know why he bothered; he couldn't make head nor tail of the ridiculous maze of circuitry.

"What could have caused this malfunction, Malloy?"

Again, Malloy shook his head. "Sorry, right now, I have no answer for you."

"You heard of this happening before?"

"There're no similar occurrences in my database. And like I said, there's no sign of damage. Bottom line, it should be working just fine. You want me to keep digging?"

"Yes…but not now," Cal replied. "Best we get on the move. We'll get Max to load it onto the ship, and you can puzzle through it later."

Cal left Malloy to finish up and walked to the lake's edge. Dipping the toe of his armored boot in, he swirled the crystal clear water and took a moment to consider the situation. His gut was still telling him that humans weren't the problem here. And despite his science officer not being the most communicative of fellows, Cal suspected that Malloy agreed. Even the most sophisticated of scavengers, or even pirates, would have left their mark when disabling a drone in such a way. And even if they had managed it, to what purpose? Why just leave it? He rubbed his jaw and looked up to the sky in the hope it might trigger some miraculous insight. Now that the clouds had completely cleared, the suns were beating down, creating a pleasant warmth.

"Nice place this, sir."

Cal turned to see that Couter had returned from his scouting. He eyed the new recruit for a moment, trying to decide if he was taking a mocking leaf out of Franco's book. But the young man's smile as he looked out over the lake seemed one of genuine appreciation. "It is indeed."

"We did a full local sweep, sir. There's a fair amount of

wildlife. Some quite large herbivores but no signs of anything particularly dangerous."

"Good." Cal retracted his boot from the water. "It seems you might have to wait a little longer before you enjoy the pleasures of a true hellhole."

Couter shrugged. "Looks that way… I guess my mother will just have to wait too."

Cal shot him a questioning look.

Couter's smile faltered slightly, making Cal suspect that he regretted having let the words slip out. He shrugged again. "Captain Maria Coutes is looking forward to bragging about her son's unparalleled skill and cast-iron will in the face of overwhelming odds."

Holy shit, Cal thought, almost blurting the reaction out loud. "Your mother is *Captain Coutes*?"

"Yes, sir," Couter replied, his expression suggesting that he'd heard that kind of response far too many times in his short life. "Revered hero of the Terron sector moons," he said with a lackluster wave of his arm.

Cal suddenly felt a little star struck. He was pretty confident in his combat abilities and had beaten a fair few odds in his time, but Maria Coutes' achievements were legendary. Seeing the look on his recruit's face, Cal did his best to swallow his enthusiasm; he suspected that the young man would prefer that his commanding officer didn't ask for his mother's autograph. "So…a lot of pressure being her son, I'd imagine?" he said, deciding that Couter probably didn't want to hear that he had a crush on her either.

Couter nodded. "Let's just say my mother's victories cast one hell of a big shadow. She'll be going down in the history books, and she won't be satisfied until her son's right there next to her. Don't get me wrong; I want to be a soldier…a *great* soldier. I did well at the Academy. I wouldn't have made it into your team if I hadn't. But living up to my mother's expectations… Sometimes, it just seems beyond impossible."

Cal hadn't known his own parents and felt ill-equipped to give Couter any advice. Still, as his commanding officer, he felt it his duty to at least try. "My advice: Just concentrate on your own expectations." *Nice and simple.*

Couter looked out over the lake then nodded.

"And mine of course," Cal added. "I am your boss after all."

Couter nodded again, but this time, a smile appeared.

The two of them continued to look out over the lake for a time until Couter broke the silence. "So what's next, Lieutenant? We heading for the civilians?"

Cal turned to him and found himself swallowing the automatic answer he was about to give—some extra bullshit to cover up the bullshit he'd already been ordered with. Christ, what had happened to him? When had he turned into such a…mindless machine? Had it been after his promotion to lieutenant? He liked to think there was a time he'd have told his superiors to shove their idiotic orders where absolutely nothing could be retrieved, no matter what its monetary value. But up until a year ago, he'd always admired and respected those he was answering to. But then Captain Lawrence Decker had been appointed.

Cal found himself nodding at Couter. Maybe it was recruit's youth and enthusiasm reminding him of what he was once like himself: a headstrong young man who wasn't afraid to give the rules a little bend when it was needed. He activated his comm. "Sinclair, keep checking the communications for me, but forget about sending Decker any further messages, and ignore any replies."

"You sure?" Sinclair asked after a moment.

"Quite sure," Cal said, shooting Couter a quick smile. "The drones can wait. Set us a direct course for the civilian research base."

CHAPTER THREE

Cal stood at the front end of the deployment cabin. Now that they were traveling within the planet's atmosphere, the flight was smooth, especially with Sinclair at the helm. There were no windows in the cabin, and if it hadn't been for the takeoff, one could have been forgiven for believing they were still on the ground. It had taken them a good hour to load the data drone onto the ship, and Cal had been close to just abandoning it. Max, their combat robot, wasn't as young as he once was, and on this particular day, he seemed to be struggling more than normal. Cal looked to the back of the cabin where the big robot stood motionless and wondered if this would be his last outing. The more advanced synthetic combat soldiers were about to be integrated into the specialist teams, and he imagined one would be replacing Max before the year was out.

Max was much bigger than the modern synthetics and possibly a good deal stronger. The new synthetics were designed to replicate a human in appearance, but no such efforts were made with the older combat robots. Max was eleven feet tall—a giant of solid, cybernetic muscle. But compared to the new synthetics, it was relatively clumsy muscle. The synthetics were incredibly fast and precise with far more ability to learn, their AI systems teetering on the very edge of the limitation laws. But even in Max's soon-to-be outdated system, Cal thought he occasionally detected something akin to life behind the robot's glowing eyes even though he doubted it was truly possible.

"You realize this deviation could have harsh consequences, Lieutenant."

The statement had come from Veteran Wilson, who was sitting close by. Cal nodded while still staring at Max. "I'm keenly aware."

"Captain Decker's not the sort of man who takes even the smallest deviations lightly. And his orders were quite clear."

Cal turned to look at the older man, to assess his expression. As usual, it was a stony mask, entirely unreadable. Cal suddenly wondered whether either Wilson or Orisho might try and overrule his command in an instance like this. The two veterans were, after all, his *unofficial overseers*—highly experienced team members entrusted to keep an eye on the uninitiated. Cal could understand the need for such a role—it was one thing for a new officer to perform well in training or even on a more straightforward mission like a scavenger flush on a first world colony—but it could be a whole different story when trying to dish out orders on a fringe world, waist deep in swampland while point grenades rained down. But Cal had never considered that the role may also be to keep a new officer on the straight and narrow, to keep them from bending the rules or breaking orders. Now that he thought about it, however—and was faced with Wilson's stony expression—he thought it entirely possible, perhaps even likely.

"Those civilians could be in real trouble, Wilson," Cal reasoned.

Wilson gave the smallest of nods. "I'm not denying that... But orders are orders."

"They are, I'm in total agreement, but Decker—"

"You mean *Captain* Decker?" Wilson interrupted, an edge to his tone. "The man who is not only in charge of our team but our entire starship."

Cal wasn't liking the way this was sounding. Despite being in Wilson's company for many years, he still felt he couldn't truly read the man. Was he really that steadfast to his superiors no matter what the situation or possible consequences? And would Orisho be the same? Cal suspected that with Becker at his back, he could possibly retain control over the team should the two veterans end up opposing him, but that could get very messy very fast. Deciding that complete honesty was the only way forward, he said, "Decker is indeed a captain, but it doesn't stop the man being a damn fool who dishes out orders on a whim..."

Wilson raised an eyebrow at that—only very slightly, but it seemed a lot on such an unyielding face.

"…Orders that can get a lot of people killed," Cal continued. "Civilians and soldiers alike."

Wilson dropped the eyebrow and sat still and silent as if he were carved from rock.

"Come on, Wilson, you know me," Cal said in an attempt to chip away at that rock. "You know I wouldn't ignore an order unless I thought it was for a good reason. Something's happened at that base, and it's not a simple scavenge crime or comm malfunction."

Wilson still didn't reply, but he seemed to be considering.

"You really think I'm making the wrong call here?" Cal asked after a moment.

The veteran continued to stare at him, that damn weathered face of his still unreadable. Cal stared right back and was about to push his argument further when Wilson turned to look at Orisho, who was sitting further down the cabin. The big Japanese man was deep in conversation with Private Forester, the team's medic, but as if somehow telepathically linked, he suddenly paused in his conversation to look toward his comrade. Cal thought it a strange bond that the two men shared, which at times seemed to border on supernatural, but perhaps it was simply decades of watching each other's backs that attuned their senses past the norm. Seeming to read a lot more in Wilson's expression than Cal could, Orisho gave his fellow veteran a nod before reverting back to his conversation with Forester.

Cal was encouraged by the nod and was further

encouraged when Wilson turned back to him and offered him a hint of a smile. It was subtle but genuine.

"As it happens, I do think you're making the right call," Wilson said. "But I guess only time will tell."

"I guess so," Cal replied, taking a deep breath and nodding his appreciation.

The flight continued to be uneventful, and the whole team took the opportunity to eat and hydrate. As they neared their destination, Cal moved to the center of the cabin to address the rest of the team. "Okay, it won't be long now before we arrive at the research base," he said, looking around the group. "Time for another quick brief."

"You think this touchdown might put us in as much danger as the last, Lieutenant?" Franco asked. The corporal was slouched over two flight seats, his feet on a crate of food packs. "I realize you've won the Federation Bravery Award three times, but the rest of us aren't quite so fearless."

Cal winced. "I'm considering you for a solo mission, Corporal. And if you bring up those bloody awards one more time, I won't bother to land the ship before I send you out."

This got a few laughs that were mostly drowned out by Orisho's booming guffaw.

Cal waited until the big man had simmered to a quiet, sporadic chuckle before he continued. "Just because this planet's fallen a little short of hellish, it doesn't mean we can all ease off the trigger. We still don't know the reasons behind the malfunctioning drones and the loss of communication with the research base. And it still could be that we have to deal with pirates. Even scavengers can be a bitch if—"

Cal's words caught in his throat as the ship suddenly lurched, causing him to stumble. He quickly activated his comm. "Sinclair, what's with the turbulence?"

"*Everyone, grab on to something.*"

Sinclair's tone held an urgency that encouraged Cal to lunge for the nearest restraint. Unfortunately, he didn't make it. The ship took a sudden, dramatic dive, causing the entire team to go airborne. Cal let out a curse that was knocked out of him as the back of his head slammed into the cabin's metal ceiling. Then, a second later, the side of his face bore the brunt as he was reunited with the floor. There was a moment of disorientation as his head spun, and his vision protested. "Sinclair, talk to me," he shouted as he wrapped his arm around a smart-strap that was securing a nearby crate. The ship was shuddering violently, and he had the distinct impression they were heading down fast.

"Hold on tight," Sinclair replied, her voice sounding blessedly composed thorough the comm. "Emergency touchdown in three…two…one."

Cal was pressed hard into the floor as the landing gear blasted out what must have been a maximum thrust. Despite this, the ship still hit the ground hard.

Moments later, Cal heard the engines power down, and the ship became still. "Sinclair?"

"Okay, we're stable."

Sinclair's words had barely finished sounding before Cal pushed himself up onto unsteady feet. He could feel blood trickling down the back of his neck, but his vision had mostly cleared. "Anyone injured?" he asked the team in general. He knew it was likely they'd all have sustained injuries, but he also knew that inconsequential bumps and scrapes would be brushed aside.

"Looks like Forester's out cold," Poots said as she leaned over the injured man to examine a wound on his head.

Cal silently cursed. None had had their head protectors activated during the flight. The hard, overlapping layers ejected from the neck of their armor with the touch of a button. Although impeccably designed to fit the user's head and obey every movement, it was still uncomfortable and was never generally used unless necessary. On this occasion, it hadn't been necessary because ships like this never simply fell out of the sky; it just didn't happen. And any possible hostiles would have been picked up on the scanners long before an attack was launched.

Opening a nearby locker, Cal pulled out a med kit. "Here, see what you can do," he said after removing a small healing pad for himself and passing the kit to Poots. Forester was their one and only medic, but all of them were trained in trauma basics. The team quickly got to work checking the onboard stores for damage. There was no need to dish out orders in situations like this; they were all well-trained, and even the fresh-faced Couter was efficiently filling his role.

Satisfied that Poots had her new medic role in hand, Cal exited the cabin and, pressing the pad to the back of his head, made his way down the corridor to the cockpit. He wasn't surprised to find both Sinclair and Malloy unhurt—both would have been strapped in while piloting. Malloy was already out of his seat and was running diagnostics on the rear console. He paused briefly to nod as Cal entered the cockpit, but he didn't look his way. Cal accepted it; a nod was about all one could ever expect from Malloy unless you directly asked him a question. He suspected it had more to do with the T-tech implant than any real lack of social skills. Behind the golden sheen of the science officer's eyes, there was a vast ocean of information and enough augmented processing power to help him dive to its deepest depths. A person could be forgiven for getting lost in such an ocean from time to time.

Cal headed straight for the flight console. "What happened, Sinclair?"

"One of the rear thrusters cut out," Sinclair replied with a brief glance in his direction. "It took a couple of seconds for the others to compensate. Then, the main stabilizer failed."

Cal shook his head in confusion. "That seems—"

"Impossible."

"What the hell caused it?"

"I wish I could tell you. This ship was thoroughly checked before we left the starship. It shouldn't happen.

Even for *one* of these to fail without pre-warning is incredibly rare, but both in succession…"

Cal looked to the rear of the cockpit. "Malloy?"

"Right now, I have nothing for you," Malloy replied, his golden eyes remaining locked on his screen. "I've just started running a more thorough diagnostic."

"How long?"

"Eighteen minutes. While it's running, I'll begin a visual checkover of the ship," Malloy said as he finally broke his gaze from the screen and turned to face them.

"Let me know how my thruster's looking," Sinclair said.

Malloy gave another small nod. "Anything else?"

"Not right now," Cal replied. Before the science officer left the cockpit, Cal gave him an appreciative smile. Despite his social shortcomings, Malloy had an incredible ability to instill confidence when it came to solving problems and fixing malfunctions.

"At least the terrain still looks friendly," Sinclair pointed out.

Turning back to the flight console, Cal peered out of the window. Despite having traveled a good distance, the scenery hadn't changed a great deal. They'd landed on relatively high ground, and the rolling hills before them still appeared serene with a patchwork of thick, flowery shrubland. A wide, slow-running river divided the landscape a few clicks to the east.

"How far to the research base?" Cal asked, well aware that a malfunction this severe would likely result in them having to finish the journey on foot.

Sinclair took a few moments studying her readouts before answering. "You could walk it in a day and a half, maybe two."

"A day being?"

"About the same as Earth."

Cal grimaced. That was a good deal further than he'd hoped. Unfortunately, the look on Sinclair's face suggested there'd be little choice in the matter.

"Everything okay back there?" she asked.

Cal nodded. He knew the question was asked more in concern for her friends than the mission. "Forester took a knock to the head. Poots is seeing to him. Everyone else is fine."

Cal could see the relief in her eyes. When they were in the air, they were her responsibility.

"Looks like you took a battering yourself." She indicated the bloody healing patch in his hand. "Using your head to break your fall again?"

Cal shrugged. "You know how I like to tinker with the shape of my skull. So how's the rest of our paradise looking?" He leaned forward and tapped on the window, manipulating the smart-glass to zoom further into the distance. "Did you scan the landscape ahead when we were airborne?"

"Of course," Sinclair said, shooting him a look. "If you'll remember, it was me that taught you that."

Cal smiled. "You sure that was you?"

"Quite certain."

Shifting the view with a splayed hand, Cal focused in on a dense patch of distant forest. The trees were evergreens, similar to some of those seen in the conservation sectors of Earth but a good deal larger. The trees were dense enough that very little light penetrated them. "I'd appreciate it if you could chart me a route to the research base. Perhaps one that avoids those forests."

"You think there's something unpleasant in there?"

Cal shrugged. "There's a lot of prey out there; I'm assuming there must be something that likes to snack on it. Otherwise, the balance seems off. Perhaps I'm just being paranoid."

"No point going into the big bad woods if you don't have to. I'll plot you the nervous tourist route."

"Appreciate that," Cal said as he straightened up and headed to the exit. Before he reached it, he stopped and glanced back. "Oh, and, Laura, thanks for getting us on the ground in one piece."

CHAPTER FOUR

With time of the essence, Cal had kept the farewell with Sinclair and Malloy brief. The diagnosis of the ship's malfunctions had not gone well, and for the first time, Cal had seen Malloy at a total loss to explain it. As always, Sinclair had insisted on staying with the ship and Cal had ordered Malloy to remain with her in the hope that time might afford the two of them more success. Unwilling to wait for a repair that might never be achieved, Cal had set off on foot with the rest of the team on a near enough direct route to the research base. They'd already made good time, which was not surprising seeing as the toughest terrain they'd encountered so far was a slight incline covered with patches of low-lying shrubland. Assuming they didn't encounter any problems, he was confident they'd reach the base well before the second night.

As he walked at the head of the group, Cal found himself doing his best not to like this planet—not an easy thing to achieve when the air was fresh, the suns were warm, and the grassy ridge that he was walking along offered a spectacular view of a wide, lazy river, the pristine water of which beautifully reflected the myriad of vibrant flowers lining its banks. The ground seemed impossibly soft beneath his heavy boots, and in the far distance, tall pillars of intertwining, richly colored vines spiraled up from the ground toward the azure blue sky like the fingers of an alien mother earth. He couldn't deny Capsun 23's beauty. Unfortunately, he also couldn't shake the feeling that if he started to like it, it would inevitably turn and bite him on the ass.

"Is it me, or is Max suffering a slight limp?"

The question had come from Sergeant Becker, who'd been walking by his side since leaving the ship. Cal glanced at her and then looked back at the rest of the team. All of them were well-armed with either a ten or a five-click pulse rifle and sidearm of choice. As always, Wilson and Orisho walked close together at the rear of the group. Corporal Franco was deep in conversation with Couter, no doubt teaching the young recruit bad habits. Poots walked on her own, looking as glum as ever. And Forester, despite his recent head injury, had recovered well and was looking strong on his feet. Then there was Max. The battle robot carried no obvious weapons—his strength alone would have been enough—but there were a few deadly surprises concealed within that metallic chassis. Despite being such a large brute, the robot somehow managed to negotiate the terrain as easily as the others. After a few moments of study, however, Cal saw that

Becker was right; his big, mechanized left foot seemed a little off-kilter. It was barely noticeable, but the sergeant had an eye for that sort of thing. She was almost as good at identifying damage as she was at causing it.

"Okay," Cal called out. "Time for a quick break."

As the rest of them settled on the river bank, Cal made his way over to Max, who'd remained standing on the ridge, diligently surveying the area for potential threats. "How's it going, Max?" he asked as he approached.

"No threats detected." Max's voice sounded as mechanized as his appearance—something that had always puzzled Cal as the tech was there to make the voice as smooth as silk.

Cal smiled. "I was actually wondering how *you* were doing?"

"I am functioning within normal parameters."

"You're sure?"

Max paused, his round eyes softly glowing. "Yes."

"Your leg's okay?"

"Yes."

"Both of them?"

Max paused again, this time tilting his domed head slightly like a dog listening intently. Cal couldn't help feeling that the designer responsible for this particular AI system was a touch eccentric.

"Yes."

Cal nodded and decided to leave the interrogation for now. "Do me a favor, will you, Max?"

"Yes."

Cal turned and stared into the distance, toward the direction they were headed. "Keep a close eye on those forests, will you?"

Max swiveled his head to match Cal's line of sight then turned it back to look down at him.

"Yes."

Giving his legs a quick rest, Cal took a seat next to Becker.

"Max okay, boss?"

"According to him…yes."

"Uh huh. So what d'you think's wrong with him?"

Cal leaned back on his elbows and gazed up to the vibrant blue sky. "What's wrong with the drones? What's wrong with the communications? …Our ship? The real question is, what's wrong with this ridiculously pleasant planet?"

"It doesn't seem overly tech friendly," Becker replied, digging her fingers under the joints of her armor and massaging her thighs as best she could through her smart-webbing.

"Must be something in the atmosphere," Cal suggested. "Remember that moon off Kathlom, how that black swamp screwed with our electrics?"

"How could I forget? I was a dark-skinned brunette for months after that sludgy rock." Becker gripped her rifle and laid it across her lap. "There's nothing even close to a swamp here though," she said, angling her face toward the warm rays. "And if there was, it would probably be the cleanest, sweetest looking little swamp you could imagine."

"Probably," Cal agreed. "But there's something off about this planet, and it's not just the malfunctions."

"Sure you're not just having an attack of the heebie geebies? Happens to the best of them from time to time."

Cal raised an eyebrow at her.

Becker smiled. "I'm serious. There's probably just a bunch of idiot scavengers out there screwing things up. Or at worst pirates." She picked up her rifle and checked its readouts. "Nothing we can't handle."

"I'm not denying that there could be a human threat involved," Cal said. "But there's something else."

"We talking monsters here?"

Cal shrugged and let his expression do all the talking.

Becker chuckled, but it lacked gusto—perhaps he'd got her thinking.

Becker shook her head. "How is it that someone who spent a whole year of his teenage life in the Big Game Sector of Mars can be so paranoid about dangerous beasts?"

"That's exactly *why* I'm paranoid."

The sergeant climbed to her feet. Raising her rifle, she peered through its sights and scanned the horizon. "You're probably right. You usually are…well, a good forty percent of the time." She lowered her rifle, a slight curl at the corner of her lips. "I guess we'll find out for sure when we reach the base?" Reaching down, she offered Cal a hand up.

Feeling a little unsatisfied by the lack of insights, Cal

reluctantly nodded and let her pull him to his feet. "I guess so. Let's hope for a warm welcome with hugs and happy news."

"Yes, and a drink with a nice kick to it."

Cal bent down and snatched up his rifle. "It's only a gut feeling," he said, straightening up and shooting Becker a serious look. "But I'd appreciate it if you stayed your usual, vigilant self."

Becker's expression became earnest, all signs of sarcasm vanishing as she looked back at him and nodded. It was the very look that always reminded him how lucky he was to have her watching his back. "Thanks, Sergeant."

They had managed two more hours of walking before the larger of the suns sank below the horizon. With the weaker sun soon to follow, Cal had instructed Franco to set up their shield for the night. Shaped like a dome, the energy shield gave them a thirty-meter bubble of adjustable warmth and light while simultaneously preventing anyone or anything of the wrong dimensions, heat signature, or retina code to enter. Despite this protection, Cal had made sure to set up camp as far from any forested areas as possible. He'd also moved a good distance from the river, reasoning that potential threats could just as likely be aquatic. The shield beamed up and over them from a small, central device that also emanated heat. It was around this device that the eight of them now sat like scouts huddled around a campfire. Max stood apart, near the shield's perimeter, his round eyes glowing a little brighter in the increasing dark.

Cal looked at Wilson, who was sitting opposite him, busily cleaning his sword. Even in the dim light, he could see that the veteran's ancient weapon was already spotless—and he suspected it had been in that state even before cleaning had commenced. The sword's immaculate condition made it appear new, but this was far from accurate; it was an original samurai's weapon, and Cal couldn't even begin to guess how old it was. The sight of it always amazed him how something so ancient could remain so well-preserved.

As he looked around at the rest of his team, Cal noticed that he wasn't the only one admiring the lethal relic. Sitting at Wilson's side, Private Couter stared at it, seeming almost mesmerized.

"Is that your sword, Orisho?" Couter asked.

Orisho, who was sitting on the other side of Wilson, leaned forward, the deep lines on his chiseled face full of contrast in the glow of the shield. "And what makes you say that?"

"Because…well it's…you're Japanese, right?"

"I am. So because I'm Japanese, that means that I should own a sword, does it?" Just like the relic, Orisho's voice had an edge to it.

"No, I…I just assumed—"

"You *assumed*?" Orisho leaned further forward to get a better look at the young man. "You think I'm some sort of sword freak just because I'm Japanese?"

"*Freak*…what? No…what?" Couter frowned, a mask of

awkwardness and confusion. "That's not what I—"

Pausing in the cleaning of his sword, Wilson also turned his gaze on the new recruit. "That's a rather stereotypical viewpoint."

Couter shifted uncomfortably. Cal suspected that if it wasn't for the monochrome glow of the shield, the young man's face would show red. "I didn't mean—"

"I was under the impression that you were more sensitive than that," Wilson continued with a small shake of the head.

"I am, it's just that Orisho looks like—"

Before Couter could get his words out, Orisho got to his feet. Cal was always impressed how fast the older man could move.

"I look like what?" Orisho's deep voice rumbled as if it came up from the earth itself. "Are you suggesting that all Japanese look like sword-wielding assassins?"

Couter understandably flinched and held up his hands placatingly. "Please, you're hearing me all wrong. I—"

"What, so I'm deaf now too?" the big man took a step forward, his rising temper mapping new lines on his face. "I'm starting to get the feeling that a lesson needs to be taught."

"*Hey, what the…*" Couter sprang to his feet. "Look, I didn't mean any offense. And the last thing I want is to fight." His tone was apologetic, but his jaw was set, and there was a hint of anger. "I won't fight a teammate."

Orisho stood stock still. The low light from the shield didn't reach his deep set eyes, and the dark shadows only served to enhance his threatening countenance. "And why would I want a racist kid as a teammate? Go learn some manners, and come back in ten years. I might consider you a man by then. Right now, you're a boy, a soft-skinned whelp who needs to be disciplined." Although they were of the same height, Orisho seemed to tower.

"What the hell is your problem?" Couter asked, his anger finally emerging.

"*Problem,*" Orisho boomed. "My problem is that we've been saddled with an inexperienced, snot-nosed pup who doesn't even know when or where to piss. Probably get half of us killed. You don't have a clue, green as cow puke. You're a bug, and I'll squash you like one."

"You can bloody try," Couter practically growled back. Once again, he seemed to match Orisho's height.

Cal watched on, impressed by his new recruit. The young man might have been easily flustered, but it seemed he wasn't easily intimidated—and few were more intimidating than Orisho. Despite the big man's looming proximity, Couter hadn't retreated an inch. Quite the contrary, he'd even shifted toward him, and not once had he looked to Cal or any of the rest of the team for help.

"Maybe I'll just put you over my knee like a troublesome little kid deserves," Orisho suggested, his barrel chest seeming to expand his armor.

This time, Couter didn't answer; he just raised his fists, jaw clenched, and took a fighting stance.

"Those fists won't do you any good," Orisho said, his voice dropping to a harsh whisper. "This isn't a damn schoolyard. We don't settle such things with bare hands." With that, the big man reached behind his back and in one swift, clean motion unsheathed a gleaming sword that had been concealed within his armor.

Couter reacted instantly, leaping sideways, his eyes briefly darting toward Wilson's sword.

There was a long, silent pause, as if everyone had been frozen on the spot. Then, Orisho's face cracked into a wide grin that instantly extinguished his menacing aura. Pointing the tip of his sword toward the ground, the big man let loose his familiar booming laugh, which abruptly filled every inch of the shield.

Reluctantly, Couter dropped his fists, the anger in his eyes gradually subsiding to be replaced with confusion. He looked around at the rest of the team, who, bar the ever glum Poots, all wore wide grins. Finally, he looked at Cal, who gave the bewildered young man an approving nod.

"Good lad," Orisho said once he'd gained control of his mirth. "I think we've got a good one here, Cal." He sheathed his sword and stepped forward to give Couter a hard clap on the back.

Still looking a little unsure that the big man wasn't about to try and twist his head off, Couter flinched and hesitantly smiled. "This was some kind of test?" he asked, looking around.

"Of course," Orisho said. "You think we'd trust the Academy to tell us what you're made of?"

Sergeant Becker stood up and looked at Couter as if for the first time. "I thought you might have a duel on your hands this time, Orisho. For a moment there, it looked like our new recruit was going to make a grab for Wilson's sword."

"How many times have you done this?" Couter asked, still looking perplexed.

"More than a few," Orisho said as he moved back to his original position and sat back down.

"You should have seen Corporal Franco," Becker said. "Damn near wet himself."

"Hey, what you talking about?" Franco said defensively. "I did alright. At least until he pulled that bloody sword out."

Becker smiled. "The way I remember it, you were trying your best to hide behind Max."

"It was… I was trying for a tactical…"

Becker just continued to smile.

The corporal scowled. "I need to get some bloody sleep," he announced and began disengaging his armor.

Cal looked at him and shook his head. Keeping armor on at all times when out in the field, even when sleeping, was a rule that he happened to agree with. When Franco had first joined the team, he'd been ordered to keep it on. But after countless nights filled with complaints that he couldn't get comfortable, the order had been retracted. If Franco didn't sleep, none of them did.

Before he settled down himself, Cal turned back to Couter. The young man seemed rooted to the spot, looking lost in thought and deflated. Bewilderment still lingered. "Sorry about the test, Private."

Couter snapped out of his brooding and stared at Cal for a moment. Then, he shrugged. "It's fine. I understand its purpose."

Cal wasn't sure how he felt about the young man's response. He was usually met with anger after the test. But Couter seemed more of a calm contemplator—which in this line of work could turn out to be a good thing or bad depending on how deep it ran. Only time would tell. "You did well," Cal said sincerely. "We're all glad to have you on the team."

"Glad to be on it," Couter replied and managed a tight smile. "I think."

"Don't worry; someday, you'll get to enjoy watching some other poor bugger go through it," Cal said. "And they'll be lucky to do half as well as you."

"I don't know about that…but thanks," Couter said, his tight smile loosening up some.

Cal was glad to see it; he didn't want his new recruit up all night fretting, not on a mission like this. "You're welcome," he replied then indicated the grassy ground with the muzzle of his rifle. "I know your blood's probably up, but try and get some rest. We've got a long trek tomorrow."

And with luck, very little else.

CHAPTER FIVE

"*What the hell… What the bloody hell…*"

Cal's eyes blinked open. He was pretty sure that someone was shouting.

"*Fricking son of a…*"

Someone was definitely shouting. A rush of adrenaline brought him quickly to his feet, rifle in hand.

The night was dark. *Too* dark. The shield was emanating nothing but a weird buzzing noise.

"*Shit… shit…*"

The shouting continued. Someone really wasn't happy; that much was clear. Cal hit the light on his weapon and set it to wide beam. Seconds later, six other lights flicked on and were all directed at the source of the commotion; Franco was dancing around like a lunatic, grabbing desperately at the crotch of his pants.

"What the hell, Corporal?" Becker shouted.

Cal couldn't have said it better himself.

"Something's got me. Some little bastard's bloody got

me." Franco barked the words as he clumsily shoved his hands into his pants. After a good deal of wincing, he pulled out a thin, wriggling form. "It's a goddamned snake!"

"Did it bite you?" Forester asked.

"Yes, it goddamned bit me, right on the… Yes, it bit me." Franco held the wriggling creature at arm's length and stared at it like it was his lifelong mortal enemy.

"Looks like you've made a close friend to me," Becker said. "Maybe you should just shove it back in there."

The suggestion set off Orisho's big laugh.

Despite himself, Franco managed something close to a grin. "Hey, there's only room for one snake in these pants, baby."

Becker shrugged. "Looks more like a worm if you ask me."

"It's a snake, goddamn it," Franco said, moving toward her and holding it to the light.

"I wasn't talking about the thing in your hands."

"Don't let it go, Corporal," Forester said. "I'll need to check it's not venomous."

"*What*! But it bit me right on the…"

"Perhaps Wilson should use his sword to stop the poison spreading?" Becker suggested.

This made Orisho laugh even louder.

Catching movement in his peripheral vision, Cal directed his light to the ground on his left. Another tiny snake was slithering across the ground. What the hell was wrong with the shield? Tracking his light further to his left, he saw two more snakes before he reached the shield's perimeter, then the number jumped up alarmingly. *Holy…* Sweeping his light from side to side, he saw what looked like hundreds of pale snakes writhing around the perimeter of the shield—something that made little sense as the shield had obviously stopped functioning and should no longer be keeping them at bay. Some of the snakes were quite large, close to the size of an Earth python, but for some reason, only the very smallest were crossing the non-existent barrier.

"Corporal Franco," Cal shouted. "Hand that snake to Forester, and get the shield up and running. And do it quickly." As he knew it would, his tone triggered action. As Franco hurried—albeit awkwardly—to the shield's central device, the rest of the team directed their light beams toward the perimeter.

"Why aren't they moving in?" Poots asked as she took up a protective position over Franco.

"Some of them are," Couter answered. "The small ones at least."

"That one isn't so small," Wilson pointed out as he directed his light toward a snake that was a good three times thicker and longer than Franco's little attacker. The beast had spilled past the perimeter and was slithering around Max's big left foot.

"Max, back up toward us; there's a good chap," Cal said as he kicked away another of the smaller snakes that was doing its best to become acquainted with his leg. "Okay, let's all try and remain bite-free. I doubt their teeth can get through combat boots or webbing, so kick them away, and refrain from shooting any for now." Cal heard Orisho and Wilson unsheathe their swords. Turning on the spot, he swept his beam around the entire circumference of the now imaginary shield. It was a strange sight. The snakes were ghostly pale and almost seemed one entity: a writhing mass of intertwining forms maintaining an imaginary circular perimeter.

"I don't think they're venomous."

Cal turned to Forester, who had forced open the mouth of Franco's little attacker and practically had his light beam shoved down its throat.

"I don't see any glands."

"Thank fuck for that," Franco said without looking up from his work on the shield.

"Of course, they're probably harboring bacteria that could cause a nasty infection."

"What kind of infection?"

"Franco, stop worrying about your prick, and get that shield up," Cal said as he booted away another small snake. The strange, contorting perimeter was starting to lose its structure now. Some of the larger creatures were overcoming whatever fear or dislike they had of the circle and were breaking through.

"Think I've found the issue," Franco announced. "God knows how, but the power supply's malfunctioned. Couter, grab me a fresh power pack. And some surge tubing."

Couter was quick to respond.

Cal sucked in a sharp breath as a large snake darted straight for him. He had faced off against some pretty nasty aliens in his time, some that appeared straight from hell with teeth as long as he was tall, but there was something about snakes that put him on edge—not a phobia, just a strong dislike. To top it off, these beasts seemed particularly aggressive, and the larger ones were a fair bit faster than their smaller kin. He booted his attacker away and then swore audibly as it coiled up and came straight back at him. He wasn't the only one being attacked. Many of the beasts were moving in now, and the sound of swishing swords, kicking feet, and swearing filled the air. Cal stamped on his attacker, which to his amazement didn't kill it. It had slowed it down, but its aggressive tendencies weren't affected in the least. Opening its mouth wide, it managed to latch onto his boot. *Seriously tough,* he thought as he activated the blade at the end of his rifle and put it to use.

Cal looked over at Franco. The corporal appeared composed and was working fast while Couter and Poots stood on either side of him, kicking away snakes. Max was standing nearby, doing nothing whatsoever. "Max, you wanna help us out here?" Cal shouted. The big battle robot slowly twisted its domed head toward him and seemed to contemplate for a few seconds—which for an AI such as he was far too long—and then began bringing its big, solid feet down on the slithering attackers. Cal shook his head. *What the hell is wrong with him?* he thought as he turned from the robot and thrust his rifle's blade at another advancing snake. He made sure the creature was dead before looking up. The strange, circular barrier had pretty much lost all of its structure now, and the snakes were advancing in swarms. "Okay, fire at will," he shouted.

The pulse blasts were short and controlled, and by the time Franco had the shield operational, the ground was littered with mangled, pale flesh, which oozed dark blue blood.

Cal assessed the new, softly glowing barrier. Already, more snakes were pressing up against its perimeter. Where the hell were they coming from? Had they unwittingly camped within a nest? But the site had seemed so clear in the light of day. He looked around at the team. "Anyone hurt?"

"Unclear," Franco answered. He was pulling at his pants and doing his best to shine a light down them.

"Get your bloody armor back on," Cal said. "Forester, see to his injury, will you?"

Not looking overly happy about it, Forester nodded and went to aid his comrade.

"Couter."

"Yes, sir."

"Gather any tools and spare components we have for the shield, and set yourself up next to the central device. If it fails again, I want it fixed fast."

With a nod, Couter went about his duty.

Cal looked toward Orisho and Wilson; they were already cleaning the strange, blue blood off their swords.

Both looked entirely calm, their expressions suggesting they'd seen it all before—which they probably had. Taking a leaf out of their book, Cal took a seat and set about cleaning the blade on his rifle. The blood was particularly sticky and would probably be difficult to remove once dry.

"So, snakes, eh," Becker said as she came to sit next to him. "Your favorite."

Cal shot her a half grin. "Not quite a hellhole, but it's fast losing its paradise rating."

"I've never known a shield to fail like that. You?"

Cal shook his head. "Shouldn't happen, not without prior warning. This is definitely not a tech-friendly planet."

"You think Sinclair and Malloy will be okay?"

"Sinclair knows what she's doing," Cal replied confidently. "Plus, they have the safety of the ship. If that shield continues to fail, we'll be exposed. Bottom line, I don't think we'll be getting a great deal of sleep tonight." Cal looked toward the shield. There was already a twenty-inch-deep, writhing mass pressed against its entire circumference. "Assuming our admirers have gone by the morning, we'll head directly for the research base. If we don't hit any major obstacles, we should make it before the first sun goes down. God knows what we'll find, but I'd rather not spend a second night out in the open."

"Agreed." Becker nudged the mouth of a nearby carcass and after a moment said, "Teeth aren't big, but there's plenty of them."

Cal stared at it. The snake was almost completely

white, its scales partially translucent like smoky glass, giving it a distinctly alien look. It had black, lifeless eyes, and the teeth that Becker referred to were cone-shaped like those of an orca whale but set in rows like those of a shark. Every snake appeared the same, the only variation being the size difference.

"Seems we're not the only ones intrigued," Becker said, pulling Cal's attention from the carcass with a nod in Max's direction.

Cal looked up to see the big robot standing a few meters away. One of his long arms was stretched out in front of him, and he was grasping the tip of a snake's tail. The robot's domed head rocked from side to side ever so slightly as it watched the dead snake swing gently in his grasp like a pendulum.

"I have a nasty feeling that our mechanized comrade might be losing the plot a little," Becker suggested.

Cal rubbed at his jaw and shook his head. "So what do you suppose a combat robot built for death and destruction would look like if he lost the plot *a lot*?"

Becker gave him a friendly pat on the leg. "You're the boss," she said, lying back and turning on her side. "You figure it out while I get some sleep."

"Sweet bloody dreams," Cal replied. Sometimes, he really missed being a sergeant.

CHAPTER SIX

Thankfully, the snakes had dispersed shortly before the dawn of the first sun. Cal had wasted no time getting his team on the move. If they were going to make it to the research base before sundown, they'd have to make the most out of every minute. So far, that daylight was proving every bit as pleasant as the previous day. The skies were clear, and the temperature remained warm without ever becoming overly hot. The terrain had also remained unchallenging with only gentle inclines and thick, soft grass underfoot. Small flocks of birds occasionally passed overhead, swift and elegant in their flight as they painted ever changing patterns in the vibrant sky. Far in the distance, herds of deer-like animals could be seen lazily crossing the meadows, their pace suggesting a collective calm, blessedly free from peril. Cal took comfort in that. He was also encouraged that he'd not yet seen any snakes, but to be on the safe side, he'd done his best to avoid the worst of the shrubland.

"*Lieutenant...*"

Cal turned to see Couter jogging to catch up with him. "Private Couter, how you holding up?"

"Just fine, sir," he said, falling alongside Cal and matching his pace.

"Something on your mind?"

"Actually, sir, there is. I've been pondering the snakes that attacked last night, and I think I might have a theory. I thought I should let you know."

"Theories can be helpful."

Couter looked serious, but there was a level of enthusiasm in his eyes that was rarely seen in anyone but the young. "It occurred to me this morning, after the snakes dispersed, that perhaps they don't like the heat."

Cal nodded. The very same thought had occurred to him. "Oh yes?" he said, encouraging the private to continue.

"It's been fairly warm during the day, and the snakes didn't arrive until a while into the night...once the ground had cooled. They had no trouble pressing up against the outside of our shield because it's designed not to give off an external heat signature. But once it went down, there was that weird perimeter thing. I think the shield's internal temperature control had warmed the ground... Once it malfunctioned, the snakes were waiting for the ground to cool before they moved in."

"Sounds entirely feasible."

"Another thing, sir, is the local wildlife." Couter rested his rifle in the nook of his left arm and pointed toward one of the distant herds of deer-like creatures. "As far as I've observed, those herbivores never go near the woodland or the thicker shrubland. If the snakes can't handle heat, it would make sense for them to reside in the shade during the day. Perhaps the deer avoid those areas due to fear of the snakes. I've seen them drinking at the lakes, but they seem jittery, so I'm not sure what the deal is there."

Cal smiled.

"What do you think, sir?"

"I think, Couter, that you're going to do very well in our team."

The young man seemed to straighten up at that. "Thank you, sir. I'm proud to be a part of it. I'm just sorry I didn't perform better in Orisho's test. I should have defused the situation without losing my temper."

"Trust me; you did just fine. The idea of the test is for Orisho not to listen to reason, no matter what's said. Some enemies crave conflict, and you'll never persuade them otherwise. Others simply have a darkness in them. You just have to hope that when you come up against such people, you end up being that bit stronger or at least that bit quicker."

Couter nodded and remained silent for a time, seeming to muse over what had been said. Cal was pleased that his new recruit wasn't just brawn. He was possibly a touch sensitive for the line of work, but if it didn't break you in the process, the lifestyle had a way of hammering out excess sensitivity. Cal was confident that Couter wouldn't break; he'd seen real steel in the young man during his faceoff with Orisho. In truth, he wouldn't have expected any less from the son of Captain Maria Coutes. But there were always occasions when the apple fell far from the tree—Captain Decker being a case in point.

"Did you ever go through a test like that?" Couter asked him after a moment.

"As a matter of fact, I did…same as you when I first joined the team. Orisho picked the fight as always."

"So what happened?"

Cal hesitated, unsure of whether or not he should elaborate on his experience. "It went… Well, it went a little differently for me."

"In what way?" Couter persisted. "Did he pull the sword on you?"

Cal shook his head then shrugged. "I actually had a rather substantial advantage."

"How so?"

"I had a strong suspicion it was coming," Cal replied with a grin. "I'd heard rumors of the test during my time in the Academy. A friend of mine overheard a conversation between a couple of drill sergeants. We had no idea if the rumors were actually true, but when I joined the team, I was on the lookout and thought I better be prepared."

"Prepared how?" Couter was staring at him, clearly intrigued.

"I decided to keep it simple," Cal replied. "Orisho picked a fight with me in a similar way he did with you. Because of the rumor, I cottoned on fairly quick but continued to play my part."

"So what happened? Did you call his bluff?"

Cal shook his head. "No, not exactly. Once Orisho got into his flow, I made sure that things became very heated. I did my best seem in a rage… made out that I'd completely lost it, shouting, cursing, throwing my arms about. I really laid it on thick to the point that they were sure I'd cracked."

"What then? You attacked him?"

"No. It's not wise to attack Orisho, prank or no prank."

"So what then?"

Cal grinned. "I pulled out a live point grenade and dropped it at my feet."

"*You did what?*"

Cal laughed at his young recruit's expression. "It was a dud of course, but Orisho and the rest of the team didn't know that. They all ran and dived for cover. It took a while before they realized I'd turned the tables on them. They were pretty pissed to say the least."

Couter's grin was wide. "Christ," he said, shaking his head. "That's brilliant. I wish I'd had a heads up. That must've been a blast."

"It was," Cal admitted. "In truth, I don't think I've ever laughed so much in my life. I wasn't too popular for a time. Took them a couple of weeks to see the funny side."

After the chuckling died down, the two of them walked on in silence for a while. The terrain was still blessedly unchallenging, and they were making good time.

Nevertheless, Cal kept the pace up. If there were any problems concerning pirates or scavengers, he'd rather have the matter dealt with before their pickup arrived. Malloy's last message to the Starship detailing the engine malfunctions would have activated a rescue protocol. As long as Captain Decker didn't screw things up again, help would arrive by dawn. He wanted the civilians gathered and for them all to be on that ship and out of the planet's strange atmosphere without delay. Capsun 23 could be someone else's puzzle, someone who was part of a team with an out of orbit research facility—the sort of facility that should have been sent in the first place.

As they continued on, Cal caught Couter glancing his way a couple of times in his peripheral vision. He had the distinct feeling the young man wanted to ask him something. "Anything else on your mind, Couter?"

"Actually, well yes... Orisho and Wilson, what's their story? They been in the team long?"

Cal smiled at that. "Longer than I've been *alive*. They went through the Krail wars together when they weren't much older than you...even survived the first wave during the battle of Chalice Zite. They've been like brothers ever since."

"Really? Chalice Zite? I was under the impression that no one had survived the first wave."

"Only a handful," Cal replied. "Orisho and Wilson were among them, and trust me, it wasn't just luck. I don't usually believe in the concept of born survivors, but those two might just be the exception to the rule."

"I'd love to hear more about the battle," Couter said eagerly.

"You will. When you get to know them better, they'll start telling you stories that will blow your mind and not just about the Krail wars. The two of them have survived missions and witnessed events that you could scarcely believe. Once you get them talking, you'll start to realize just how strange our little slice of the universe can be, especially some of the worlds in the Krill strip."

Cal almost laughed at the at the look on Couter's face; he was a young man eager to hear these stories of adventure but even more eager to chalk up some of his own. Cal remembered the feeling well. In fact, just being around the young man was starting to rekindle a good deal of his own enthusiasm. They walked on a little further, and eventually, Couter's expression changed back to one of curiosity.

"And Beck—Sergeant Becker? How long has she been on the team?"

Cal looked at him with a creased brow and hoped this conversation wasn't about to head the way he thought it was. Couter had asked the question in a breezy manner but had completely overcooked it. "She joined as a private just over five years ago. Why do you ask?"

"I was just curious about her."

Ah crap, here we go. Cal had already dealt with Franco's crush on Sergeant Becker a few years back. Fortunately, after realizing that the corporal also had a crush on Poots and Sinclair, it had become apparent that the man simply had a crush on women in general. But Cal suspected that Couter wasn't the *general crush* type of person. "Curious about her in what way?" He put a purposeful edge to his voice.

"Oh, sorry, sir, I didn't mean… Well, Sergeant Becker is very attractive, no one could deny that, but I would never disrespect a team member like that. Never, sir, I promise."

Satisfied by the young man's sincerity, Cal nodded with a little sigh of relief. "Good. So what are you curious about?"

Couter was beginning to look as though he wished he'd kept his mouth shut, but he continued anyway. "For her to be on a team like this… She just seems so… Well, she looks strong, but she's… Well, she's incredibly pretty—"

"Hold up, Private," Cal said, his tone hard enough to stop the young man in his tracks. "Your reports from the Academy are exemplary, and they prove you have skills to be admired. You've also gone some way to proving that you have metal in you. But your real education starts now. Situations are going to get very real, very fast, and you're going to find yourself facing dangers that you never even knew were coming at you."

Couter suddenly looked downtrodden and frustrated that his mouth had betrayed him, but he looked Cal in the eye and nodded his understanding.

"Good. Now, I think that it's best I do you a big favor and teach you a couple of lessons right here." Cal paused to make sure his recruit was actually listening and not just silently berating himself. "Firstly, never show Sergeant Becker any less respect than you would the toughest of soldiers because, and trust me when I say this, she *is* the toughest of soldiers. Second, and I can't stress this enough, under no circumstances should you ever call her pretty. She really doesn't like it and rightly so." Cal looked at the young man with an expression that left no room to doubt the sincerity of his words. "Understand that I'm telling you this now because I don't want my new recruit's career cut short by an injury that you might not recover from."

"I understand, sir."

"Good."

They continued on. Couter busied himself by surveying the surrounding hills. Occasionally, he would turn to look back at the rest of the team. His attempts to mask the fact he was looking specifically at Becker as she observed a ravine a little distance behind were unsuccessful.

"You know, Sergeant Becker also underwent Orisho's test," Cal said after a while in a ploy to recapture the recruit's attention. "Just like you. Soon after she joined the team."

"Really?" Couter asked, his eyebrows raised a little. "What happened?"

"She knocked him flat on his back."

Couter laughed. Then abruptly stopped upon seeing that Cal's expression lacked anything resembling sarcasm. Then his eyebrows shot all the way up. "You're messing with me?"

"I speak the truth," Cal replied sincerely. "It was one hell of a surprise to all of us, not least Orisho. I don't think he ever quite got over it."

Couter turned again and this time took no pains in trying to hide the fact that he was staring at Becker. Only after almost tripping on a thick shrub did he turn back around. "Holy shit."

Cal nodded in agreement. "Just remember; don't call her pretty."

Their trek eventually brought them to another lake, which was every bit as serene as the first. Cal instructed Franco to lead them around its banks. The lake wasn't particularly large, but Cal had the distinct impression that it was deep. The breeze was practically nonexistent now, and the surface of the water was as smooth as glass.

"You think there's something in there, sir?"

Cal glanced up to see that Franco had slowed his pace a short distance ahead and was looking back at him.

"Undoubtedly," Cal replied as he caught up with him. "The dry land's certainly abundant with life, so I don't see that the water should be any different." Despite believing this, he hadn't actually spotted one fish in the crystal clear shallows or any other forms of life for that matter. And it wasn't for lack of looking. "I'll admit it's not readily presenting itself, but I've a hunch there's plenty of life in there. Why do you ask?"

Franco shrugged. "I don't know, just the way you keep glancing at it as if something's going to leap out and try to bite one of us in half. If I'm honest, sir, you're not looking your usual calm self. More than a little tense for a man who—"

Cal slapped his hand hard on the Franco's shoulder, breaking him off midsentence. "You mention those bravery awards, Corporal, and I'll be testing the buoyancy of your armor in the center of the lake."

Franco raised a hand and shot him a placating grin. "Sorry, Lieutenant. Guess I'm just a little jealous of those shiny medals."

"You're welcome to them," Cal mumbled in reply as the two of them walked on.

"All joking aside," Franco continued after a moment. "You really don't seem to have a lot of trust in this planet. I'll admit that those snakes last night were a little strange. Had quite a bite on them too," he said, shifting awkwardly. "But they weren't exactly man eaters."

"Perhaps not, but they were highly aggressive," Cal replied. "And don't forget that the eight of us are well-armed and have a big combat robot backing us up."

"You're concerned for the civilians?"

Cal nodded. "With good reason, I think."

"Maybe," Franco replied. "But it could just be that they're experiencing a technical fault…simply a hitch with their communications."

"Perhaps," Cal admitted as he glanced out over the lake. "I hope you're right. But there seems to be a hell of a lot of technical hitches going on. Far too many, and that's what's concerning me… And if a research team of scientists can't rectify the malfunctions…"

"I see your point," Franco conceded.

The two men continued to skirt the bank of the lake for a time in silent thought. Eventually, the silence was disturbed by Poots, who was mumbling a growing number of curses behind them.

"Poots is getting tetchy. I guess it's lunchtime," Franco said as he glanced back at the private.

In agreement with his corporal, Cal ordered a pit stop and had Forester hand out their nutri-packs. Snacking on one of the high energy packs often made Poots complain even more—usually about the taste—but once the calories got into her system, she always calmed down.

Along with most of the others, Cal took a moment to sit back and relax against the ridge that lined the entirety of the lake like a solid, grassy wave. Max stood further back on higher ground, diligently keeping watch over their surroundings. Other than Max, the only one to remain on his feet was Forester, who had leisurely approached the water's edge. Looking lost in thought as he chewed on his nutri-pack, the medic casually kicked a loose tuft of grass into the lake, causing its smooth surface to ripple. Cal watched as the bright, warm rays from twin suns seemed to surf the disturbed water, the ripples expanding out in neat, golden circles.

"Mind if I collect some plants and flowers, sir?" Forester asked. The medic had knelt down and was examining some of the myriad of plant life that was dotted around the water's edge. "My wife would never forgive me if I returned from a planet like this without something to show for it."

Cal nodded with a quick smile. The flower collecting wasn't a romantic gesture but an act of scientific research. Forester's wife was a well-respected botanist who worked within the ecology department on their Starship. She was a lovely woman, but Cal could attest to the fact that she'd be furious if her husband failed to collect samples from an abundant planet such as this. "Just a few small cuttings," Cal ordered. "I don't want you doubling the weight of your pack like you did on that Taylon drop. We need to keep the pace up."

Forester unsheathed a small pair of clippers from his pack and raised them in a gesture of thanks.

"And make sure they go through the proper quarantine procedures," Cal added. "I don't want to be responsible for some weird pest causing mayhem in the starship's eco-deck."

"Of course, sir," Forester replied as he pulled up a small plant to expose the roots. "Mary wouldn't have it any other way," he assured him. Clipping off a single root, the medic tossed the rest of the plant into the shallows, sending out another set of ever expanding ripples.

Satisfied, Cal relaxed back. Taking a bite of his nutri-pack, he once again gazed out over the water. Reflected on the lake's mirror-like surface, the huge neighboring planet sat low in the blue sky and made for a stunning view. As he chewed on the semi-appetizing food, he couldn't deny that the calm vista was dissolving a good deal of his tension. Lying back under the planet's lazy warmth with just the soft buzzing of insects and the occasional call from an overhead bird reminded him of some of his quieter moments as a boy on Mars. Of course, that landscape had been mostly jungle, but it had been beautiful and peaceful in its own way.

Unfortunately, the moment of calm didn't last. Max's loud, synthesized voice suddenly barked out a warning, which split the peace like an unexpected thunderclap. Something was moving—something in the lake. The whole team surged to their feet, pulse rifles quickly raised.

"*Head gear up*," Cal shouted while activating his own. The head-gear's multiple layers speedily ejected from the neck of his armor, covering his head in an instant. Then, his visor shot down to shield his eyes from the glare of the suns. Peering toward the center of the lake, he pinpointed the movement that Max had warned against: a smooth swell of water that gave the impression that something was moving beneath the surface—something fast and most definitely large.

"Forester, back up," Cal ordered. "*Quickly.*"

The medic didn't hesitate. Spitting out a mouthful of food, he snatched up his pack and rifle.

Cal moved a couple of steps forward. "Set pulse rifles to maximum; I want a staggered defensive position."

As the team arranged their defense, Cal continued to track the movement of the swell. It had shifted slightly, angling toward them, and he had the distinct feeling that it was speeding up.

"It's coming straight at us," Forester confirmed after a moment.

"Yep," Franco agreed. The corporal was kneeling in a forward position, his rifle pressed hard into his shoulder. "And whatever it is, it's big."

"No frickin' shit, Sherlock," Poots said in quick reply.

The swell continued to move toward them, escalating in speed and size the closer in got. Cal felt a strange excitement. His heart began thudding increasingly harder, each beat seeming to vibrate through his armor and right down to the muzzle of his rifle. In his peripheral vision, he could see Max standing slightly apart from the rest of the team, ready to move forward in a kinetic burst of cybernetic power should it be needed.

"Christ, it's *really* big," Franco said, keeping his voice low.

"You said that already," Poots growled.

"Ok, can it," Cal ordered. "Stay calm, and be ready to fire on my command."

The swell surged closer.

Twenty-five meters…twenty meters…

It's not slowing, Cal thought as he involuntarily gripped his weapon a little tighter.

Fifteen meters…

Cal swallowed a curse. He could make out a dark shape now, and Franco was right; it was worryingly large. "On my mark…" he said, ensuring that he had the head of the dark shape tracked in his sights.

Ten meters…

"*Fire.*" Cal bellowed the order, and an instant later, the din of repeating pulse rifle rounds filled the air. The blasts pounded into the swell of water like a hail of flaming meteorites. But whatever was approaching still didn't slow or deviate. Instead, it continued its relentless charge, covering the last few meters in a mere second before erupting out of the water in a huge, confusing, dark blur that was starkly contrasted by a mass of bright spray that dazzled in the sunlight. At the front of the group, both Franco and Forester fell backwards, hitting the ground hard but not easing their fire for a second. Max started to run forward but came to an abrupt halt way short of the threat. Cal eased off his trigger, aware that Max's superior eyesight had detected something that the rest of them couldn't yet make sense of.

Cal lowered the muzzle of his rifle an inch. Something strange was happening. Through the flashes of the other weapons and the dazzling spray, he could see the dark attacker coming apart—not torn apart by pulse blasts but separating into countless tiny shapes, each seeming to have a life of its own.

"*Hold your fire,*" he shouted. "*I said hold your fire.* That means you too, Franco."

As the din quieted and the last of the spray hit the ground, a mass of tiny creatures—which seemed an odd melding of a fish and a frog—continued their speedy journey. Now that they'd left the water, their tightly packed, coordinated swimming had turned into a chaotic display of clumsy mass hopping. Most of the tiny creatures were effectively managing to negotiate their way around the team, but some were colliding with armor, pinging off it harmlessly before changing direction and finding a way around. A little stunned, the whole team—including Max—turned and watched the strange, hopping parade as it swiftly moved past them and disappeared over the grassy ridge.

For a moment, all that could be heard was the fading sound of the creatures combined with the sizzling water that had been subjected to a barrage of plasma rounds.

"Well done, Corporal," Becker said, eventually breaking the silence. She turned back to direct an amused grin at Franco, who was still lying on the ground. "I think you might have managed to kill quite a few of the vicious little bastards."

This set off a few laughs.

"Yeah, well, it was them or me," Franco retorted, sounding a little disgruntled.

Grinning, Cal stepped forward and helped him to his feet. "I have to say, Corporal, you're not looking your usual, calm self."

Franco managed a wry smile. "Yeah well… I guess I'm just going to have to toughen up a bit before I go winning any medals."

CHAPTER SEVEN

A wrecked ship lay crippled on the top edge of a high ridge, an ugly score carved out of the pristine ground from its less than graceful landing. Even from this distance—and despite its mangled state—Cal could identify it as a scavenger ship. An unregistered, black market build. Its hull was a patchwork of poorly executed repairs, most likely carried out on a fringe space colony by a less than reputable ship yarder. Concealed behind the lip of an opposite ridge, Cal peered at the wreck though his scope. He could tell by studying the scarred earth that the crash was fairly recent; no more than a couple of days, he guessed. Perhaps fresh enough for any survivors to still be in the area. At least it wasn't pirates—not keen on their rides falling apart in between atmospheres, pirates always took good care of their ships.

"Scavengers?" Becker asked. She was lying by his side.

Cal passed her the scope. "Yep."

"You think they were after the drones?" Couter asked.

Staying low, Cal looked back at him. Both he and Poots were kneeling a few meters down the ridge, keeping a watchful eye. "Undoubtedly," Cal replied.

"I guess this planet liked their ship even less than ours. Looks like it was a pretty bad crash," Poots said.

"Or they simply had a piss-poor pilot," Becker suggested.

"Yeah, Sergeant, that's probably it," Couter agreed, shooting an odd sort of half smile in Becker's direction.

Cal glanced at his young recruit with a shake of the head. He hoped the young man's sudden awkwardness in Becker's presence was only obvious to him.

"You think they're still around?" Poots asked.

Cal stared down at his comm. "We'll know more soon." He had sent Orisho and Wilson scouting to the east while Franco and Forester skirted west. He wanted to make sure that none of the scavengers were milling about before they moved in. Normally, he'd have Max perform a thorough scan, but right now, he wasn't feeling overly confident in his mechanized comrade's abilities—the terrain had become notably steeper of late, and the robot had remained at the foot of this particular ridge seeming worryingly put off by its gradient.

As they continued their wait, Cal felt himself growing impatient; they weren't exactly lavished with endless daylight. *Why couldn't these inconsiderate bastards have crashed on the other side of the planet?* he thought as he took his scope back off Becker and scanned the surrounding landscape. In truth, he doubted the scavengers were still in the area—assuming any of them had even survived—but he had to be sure, and the wreck needed to be investigated.

Fortunately, it wasn't long before his growing impatience was put to rest by Franco and Wilson sounding the all clear over the comm.

"Poots, do me a favor will you and lead Max the long way around this ridge?"

Poots mumbled an acknowledgement, her tone as solemn as always, but her movements as she descended the ridge were impressively swift.

"Okay," Cal said, turning to Becker and Couter. "Let's go take a peek."

Up close, the ship appeared in even worse shape than the crash markings had suggested. The entire front end was torn apart, exposing the cockpit. Whoever had been piloting had definitely not fared well.

"Signs of life, Corporal?"

Franco was moving alongside the wreck, a holographic display emanating from the data pad on his wrist. "My pad's playing up a bit, but the ship appears empty. Completely lifeless in fact. And I doubt the owners of a ship like this would have the tech to deflect even a basic scanner let alone a military one."

Cal had to agree. In fact, he was surprised this heap of junk had even made it through space to arrive at the planet let alone function within its atmosphere.

"It's a damn ghost ship," Franco announced a moment later.

"Getting a little over dramatic, Corporal," Becker said as she directed her pulse rifle through a large, ragged tear in the side of the ship's hull.

"I don't think so," Franco replied. "A crash like this should have killed, or at least injured, some of the crew. I'm finding no bodies and only minimal signs of blood."

"Perhaps they managed to abandon ship when they knew it was going down," Poots suggested.

"Possibly," Cal replied.

"Or perhaps the local wildlife did a thorough cleanup job," Forester said.

"Whatever happened, we've no time to play detectives," Cal said. "I want a quick visual check of the ship's interior, and then, we're moving on. Corporal, see if you can identify any tracks. If there were survivors, I want to know which direction they headed."

Franco nodded and directed his display toward the ground to begin his sweep.

"Shall I load the drone onto the ship?"

Cal turned to see Max looming over him. He stared up at the round eyes. "Which drone would that be, Max?"

The robot remained silent for a time—enough time for Cal to wonder whether he'd even taken the question on board. "What drone, Max?"

"I made an error," Max said simply.

Cal shook his head. It was a little distressing seeing Max confused. The big combat robot had been a part of the team for as long as he had. He was a formidable fighter and had saved their backsides on countless occasions, often tipping the balance of a failing mission back in their favor. Cal wasn't afraid to admit that he was fond of the big guy, plain and simple. Despite the laconic nature of the robot's communication, there was definitely a personality lurking in there. But, over and above that, Max was a member of his team, and Cal didn't like to see any of them struggling. "You seem confused, Max. I think the atmosphere on this planet is messing with your systems."

"Yes. My systems are compromised. Should I shut myself down?"

"No," Cal replied without hesitation. "Stick to your duties…as best you can."

Max continued to look down at him as if contemplating his words. Cal wished he knew what was happening in that domed head of his. He was really starting to regret not having Malloy with him. The science officer could probably diagnose the problem in seconds. As the situation currently stood, however, all he had was his data pad, which gave him a host of confusing, continuously updating information regarding Max's systems. Even if he could decipher it all, however, he suspected there was a fair bit going on in that metal head that even his data pad wasn't privy to.

Eventually, Max answered with a simple, "Yes," then turned and headed toward the front of the wreck.

Cal watched him go and spent a few moments considering possible ways in which he could improve or at least slow the progression of the robot's failing mind and body. But of course there were none, at least not until they returned to the starship. Cal turned back to the wrecked craft and swung his rifle over his back where his armor's smart clips took hold of it and fixed it in position. He looked up at the side of the wreck, made a quick assessment, then began to scale it. Having crashed on a high ridge, the roof of the ship would make a good vantage point.

The ascent was an easy one, and it wasn't long before he reached the top. The skies were still clear, and the view almost took his breath away. The land ahead was becoming distinctly more alien. Grassy ridges rippled into the distance, each one peppered with specks of red moss and patches of vegetation literally bursting with color. A river cut a silvery line through the landscape, narrowing in parts to create a faster flow but still retained a lazy quality as it snaked its way toward the horizon. The huge neighboring planet had become increasingly dominant in the sky and was beginning to reflect the light from the two suns in such a way that it colored the entire landscape with a yellow hue. It was a strange light that only seemed to enhance the vista's vibrancy.

As he bathed in the warm rays and breathed in the fresh air, Cal again found himself impressed with the planet's beauty. Assuming you weren't overly fond of technology and had no strong feelings toward snakes, he had to admit, Capsun 23 would make one hell of a place to live.

CHAPTER EIGHT

"You look a little on edge, boss."

Cal looked at Becker, who was wading through the thick vegetation next to him. He was getting a little fed up of people telling him that although in this particular instance, it was entirely accurate. He shrugged. "I guess I just miss the neat, grassy fields."

Since leaving the wreck, they'd stuck to the river bank, which had led them most of the way to their destination. But two klicks back, they'd had to leave the river behind and were now faced with a valley brimming with knee-high shrubland.

"Worried those scavengers might be lying in wait…try an ambush?" Becker asked.

Cal shook his head. A decent ambush required a certain amount of intelligence, and Cal suspected that anyone who traveled through space in a ship that barely looked fit for a junkyard possessed very little. Franco's investigations had suggested that at least five people had left the wreck and set off on foot in the direction of the research base—one more reason to feel concern for the civilians. Cal had deliberated whether this was merely coincidence or a deliberate action on their part. It was a tough one to call. If the scavengers had done the same as him and climbed on top of their ship, there was a good chance they'd have chosen this direction due to the increased plant life offering a greater chance of sustenance. And it made sense to stick to the river, which would have narrowed their choice of direction down to two. But there was also a chance they'd identified the research base before their ship went down.

"Worried something might try and snack on us then?" Becker asked. "Something that might actually be up to the job this time?"

"You never know."

"Nothing very big could hide in here." Becker kicked at the low vegetation surrounding her.

"Size isn't everything, Sergeant. Besides, I've seen plants that like to eat soldiers, armor and all." Cal looked up at the suns. They were sinking low in the sky, but it didn't concern him; they were close enough to their destination that they'd easily make it before dark. He tapped his data pad, activating Sinclair's map, and studied it for a moment. "We should get a clear view of the base from that far ridge." He deactivated the map and pointed dead ahead, where a long crest on the opposite side of the valley cut across the horizon. He was pleased to see that the plant life ran dry near the top of the ridge, the terrain reverting back to grassland.

"So what are we waiting for?"

Cal rubbed at his chin and continued to survey the landscape. "I didn't get to be the boss without a certain amount of caution," he replied as he scanned the valley's line; it ran in both directions as far as the eye could see.

"I think caution is overrated."

"Oh?"

Becker nodded. "And I don't think there'll be any walking around this valley unless we want to spend another night under the stars...not unless your map says otherwise?"

Cal shook his head.

"And there's certainly no turning back, so why are we wasting time with caution?"

Cal shot her an annoyed look, which only made her smile.

"It's my job to point that out," she said with a shrug.

Cal did his best to retain his frown. "Keep the chatter down, Sergeant." He turned to the rest of the team. "We're heading for that ridge. Stay sharp, and fingers on triggers."

It wasn't long before they were at the valley bottom. The pleasant breeze that they'd enjoyed on higher ground wasn't finding its way this low. Instead, Cal and his team were treated to a constant, high-pitched buzzing created by an army of minuscule flying insects that swarmed in the still air. Cal didn't bother trying to swat them; they were too small and numerous for his swishing hand to do any good. The insects weren't the only annoyance; the vegetation was covered in a sort of sticky sap and damp dew that was fast finding its way into the joints of their armor. And with the shrubland being waist deep, it was becoming difficult to negotiate with any sort of speed.

The buzzing was setting Cal's nerves on edge. Twice, he'd been sure that something had rubbed against his leg, but doing his best to part the vegetation and peer through the leaves and insects, nothing was revealed but roots and mud.

"I think I stepped on something."

Cal glanced over at Forester. The medic had wandered into a particularly deep patch of shrubland and was having to hold his pulse rifle up to his shoulder level while he tried to part the foliage surrounding him.

"It's just roots," Becker informed him.

"No, it crunched."

"Then it's dry roots."

Forester continued to push aside the thick leaves and leaned forward in an attempt to improve his view.

Cal was about to tell him to forget it and move on when the medic straightened up and turned to him, his face a pale. "I think it could be bones."

Cal gritted his teeth. "How big?"

Forester shook his head, looking as though he'd just been given a life sentence. "Big enough," he said quietly. "Possibly human."

Cal felt his heart quicken. "Okay, get moving." He

jerked his head, indicating for him to move back toward the others.

But Forester didn't get the chance to obey. The medic let out a shocked cry as he disappeared beneath the thick foliage. Cal started forward but paused as the cry was abruptly cut short. He'd heard soldiers silenced like that before and knew only too well what it meant.

"Forester's down," Franco shouted, alerting those of the team who were further away.

Cal shot out a hand and grabbed Becker as she tried to move past him in Forester's direction. "Hold up."

Becker didn't need to be ordered twice, but still, she felt like a coiled spring in his grip.

"Everyone stay still," Cal ordered. Releasing his grip on Becker, he tapped his data pad. "Vitals, Medic J. Forester." There was a brief moment where all that could be heard was the incessant buzzing of the insects. Then, the data pad emanated a simple, impassive reply. *Deceased.* Cal continued to grit his teeth, feeling his pulse thump harder in his neck. Holding up a hand, he signaled for everyone to stay put. Carefully, he crouched down until he was enveloped by the large leaves surrounding him and peered through the thicket of stalks. Forester's body couldn't be seen. There was something though. Something moving, disturbing the foliage, large and pale. Straightening up, Cal pressed one arm across Becker's chest and backed them both away from the point of the attack. Once they were closer to the others, he used hand signals to move them on, slow and quiet.

Barely had they started to move when Poots yelled out in pain up ahead. Being in closest proximity, Franco lunged forward and managed to grab her before she too disappeared. Cal waded toward the pair as fast as he could. The private's cries continued, loud enough that she almost drowned out Franco's stream of expletives. With Becker's help, Cal kicked aside some of the leaves and roots surrounding Poots. The snake's pale head looked almost demonic amid the dark foliage. It was big. Bigger than any snake he'd ever seen on Earth or even Mars. Its jaws were completely wrapped around Poots' armored thigh, and blood was already seeping out from the connective webbing above her knee joint. Cal thrust his weapon at the creature and tugged on the trigger.

Nothing happened.

He tugged again…and again.

Nothing.

"*Shit.*" The curse came from Becker, her weapon seeming about as responsive as his own.

The snake began to writhe and succeeded in moving back, causing Franco's curses to double in volume as he strained to keep Poots in his grasp.

Activating his rifle's blade, Cal drove it down into the back of the snake's neck. Instantly, the beast relinquished its hold and retreated into the shadows, almost taking the rifle with it.

"Ignore that last order," Cal shouted as he grabbed hold of the now unconscious Poots and heaved her over his shoulders. "Rifle blades out, and everyone fucking run."

As it turned out, Cal wasn't finding running an easy thing to achieve. If it had been difficult moving through the vegetation before; moving through it now on an incline with someone on your back was painfully slow. Becker had remained a few paces to his right, deliberately reducing her pace to match his own. They had only fallen a little way behind before Poots miraculously floated off his shoulders. Max had veered in from the left to pluck the woman off him as if she were a mere toddler. With his powerful, cybernetic limbs, he accelerated away and thundered on ahead. Cal didn't waste time watching the robot. He knew Max would deposit Poots at the relative safety of the bare ridge above before assessing where his assistance was most needed next.

Cal surged on, much faster now that he was only carrying his own weight. His rifle was tight in his grip, blade still extended. Looking ahead, he did his best to judge the terrain. Finding that some of the vegetation had been flattened in Max's wake, he started to follow its line, shouting to Becker to join him.

But Becker didn't answer. He looked to his side and then behind him only to find her gone. Without missing a beat, he came to an abrupt halt and doubled back. "Becker... *Becker*..."

"Here." The reply was strained but clear.

Cal ran a few more paces before he spotted her. She was on the ground amid some flattened shrubs. Her legs were clamped in a figure of four hold around the neck of another giant snake, this one bigger even than Poots' attacker. Becker's arms were locked straight, muscles bulging as her hands gripped the underside of the beast's massive jaw. Her shoulders were pressed into the ground, her own weight and most of the snake's bearing down as she arched her back in an attempt not to be tipped. Cal burst forward, thrusting the blade of his weapon out before him. As the point found its mark and partially buried its way into the creature's side, he became aware of movement to his left. Pulling his rifle free, he twisted around just in time to meet the jaws of a second snake that exploded from the foliage. As the creature's massive jaws closed around the muzzle of his weapon, Cal found himself knocked back by the ferocity of the attack. Hitting the ground hard, it seemed only a second or two before the snake was coiling itself around him. Considering the size of the creature, the force it was exerting shouldn't have come as a surprise, but still it did.

Taking a leaf out of Becker's book, Cal attempted to lock his legs around his attacker, but it had landed heavily upon him, its weight already pinning him down. He did his best to quash his panic as he grappled with the beast—not an easy thing to do as its brute strength was fast overwhelming him. Unable to turn his rifle in such a way that he could utilize the blade on its end, Cal let it go, freeing up his right hand. He had another knife within the armor on his left thigh but, try as he might, it was no longer within his reach. Everything was happening too damn fast. He felt himself being turned as the attacker continued to coil itself around his torso.

Desperately, he jabbed at the snake's head with his thumb. Perhaps if he could injure its eyes, it would reconsider its prey. But the one eye that he could reach felt hard as stone, as if protected by a toughened lid. Cal could hear and feel grinding as his armor was shifted by the creature's constricting body. The armor was Corrian built, crafted from the highest grade alloys. The creature would never have the power to come even close to crushing it, but this came as little consolation as it wasn't one solid piece but a series of interlocking pieces connected by flexible, smart webbing. The webbing allowed for unrestricted movement and would repel any number of projectiles, but it had little rigidity. Before long, the armor would be parted enough that nothing would resist the killing squeeze. Cal felt the snake pinning his right arm then slide under his left, forcing it up until it was pressed against his face. Panic well and truly took hold then. The constriction increased and set about stealing the last of his breath. Cal suddenly had an overwhelming need to see sky, just a glimpse of that blue expanse. But as he turned his eyes upward, all he could see was shadowy leaves…then pale, scaly flesh.

All went dark. Only his cold panic remained—that and the muffled sounds of armor creaking and his heart thudding. He tried one last-ditch effort to move, but it was futile, as if he'd been paralyzed from head to toe. A little spike of anger pierced through his fear. *What a way to die.*

But it seemed his time hadn't come just yet.

A sudden, merciful breath rushed into his throat, filling his lungs and extinguishing at least some of the panic. The pressure and the undulating movement of the snake had ceased. Not only that but the deathly coil was beginning to unravel.

Then, his eyes found the sky, blessedly bright above him. His mind whirled for a moment in confusion as he tried to blink away his blurred vision.

"Let's get moving."

The sound of Oshiro's deep voice cleanly cut through the confusion like a guiding light. The big veteran stood over him, thick, blue blood dripping from his sword. Cal rubbed at his eyes and indulged in a couple more breaths before a coughing fit took over.

Without waiting for him to fully recover, Orisho pulled him to his feet. "Come on; no time to hang about."

Still feeling as though he was hacking up a lung, Cal turned to see Wilson kicking the corpse of the other snake off Becker. She too was coughing and looked mightily pissed off.

Finally gaining control of his breath, Cal stooped down and snatched up his rifle. "Agreed," he said, his voice more of a wheeze. "Let's get the hell out of here."

Cal collapsed, exhausted, onto the grassy ridge and once again fought to catch his breath. He wasn't the only one. The whole team, bar Max, were on the ground, doing their best to remain poised for battle while their chests heaved and their fatigued limbs battled gravity. Not for the first time, it occurred to Cal how even the fittest of people could be reduced to gasping wrecks after running from something that was planning to eat them. He looked back to the line where the thick vegetation petered out to become short, mossy grass. For now, it seemed they weren't going to be pursued into the open. Only one other snake had attacked during their run out of the valley—a smaller specimen that Orisho had sliced in two with swift efficiency.

His pulse finally slowing, Cal propped himself up on his elbows and stared down to the valley bottom where the attacks had taken place. It seemed the snakes preferred to lurk where the vegetation was taller, denser, and damp—where it was cooler. The fact gave validity to Couter's theories. He continued to stare, breaths now coming slow and easy. He had many close calls in his time, but this encounter perhaps topped the list. He'd been a heartbeat from passing through the veil that concealed the mysteries of any possible afterlife. Cal squeezed his eyes shut and pushed the thought aside. He thought instead about Forester. A good man cut down far too early by a cruel fate. The vitals on the data pad had confirmed that the medic had gone quickly. That was something at least—not to have suffered the slow, crushing death that he'd almost experienced.

The first to die under my command. The realization hit Cal like a lance in his side. When you were a tight-knit group, enduring such extreme experiences together, becoming friends was almost a certainty. And Forester had been young, and he had a wife. Mary's face flashed into Cal's mind. *Christ, how the hell am I going to break this to her?* The weight of his new rank suddenly felt that much heavier. And to make matters worse, he knew it could have been avoided. If he'd just trusted his instincts and ignored Captain Decker's order from the start. He should have forgotten about the damn drone and headed straight for the base; then, none of this would have happened. Forester would be alive and well.

Climbing stiffly to his feet, Cal looked down into the valley one last time and tried to suppress the anger he felt in himself. Wallowing in regret and guilt wouldn't do him any good and certainly wouldn't help the rest of his team. *I'm sorry, my friend.* He turned away and forced himself to bring his mind back into focus and orient it on those who still lived. Moving over to Orisho, he set a hand on his armored shoulder. "I owe you one, Orisho."

The veteran turned his broad face up to him. "If we're keeping score, I'm pretty sure I still owe *you* one…possibly two."

Cal shrugged, his expression devoid of any humor. "Well, keep that sword unsheathed. It's likely you might get to fulfill them soon."

The rest of the team were recovering quickly and checking their weapons. Couter had already stripped the armor from Poots' leg and was seeing to her injury. Cal walked over to them. "How's the leg?"

Having regained consciousness, Poots looked up with a

barely contained grimace. "Still attached. Might slow me down some, but I'll live. Young Couter here seems to know his stuff."

Cal almost shook his head in bewilderment. It wasn't the first time that Poots had suddenly gained a positive mindset after the shit had hit the fan. When things were good, she was cranky and cynical, but the worse things got, the more optimistic she seemed to become.

"Anyone possess a working rifle?" Cal asked the team in general.

"I managed to get one shot off," Wilson said. "But it was faulty and had about as much impact as badly thrown punch." He pointed the rifle to the sky and tugged on the trigger a few times. "Now, nothing at all."

As the others began climbing to their feet, Cal unclipped a point grenade and tried to activate it.

Nothing.

Damn it. What the hell is it with this planet? It seemed knives and swords were going to be the way forward from now on. At least they were close to the base.

Leaving Max, Orisho, and Wilson to keep an eye on the valley's edge, Cal climbed to the peak of the ridge with Becker and Franco in tow.

"There she is," Franco said, the normal playful edge devoid from his tone. The three of them peered into the distance where the research base was glittering like a little bundle of silver shells beneath the two suns.

Cal breathed a sigh of relief. He'd half expected to be faced with another shrub-filled valley. Fortunately, the remaining vegetation between them and the base was scattered about the landscape sparsely with plenty of bare ground in between. In fact, the terrain was suddenly far less vibrant. A large lake could be seen in the distance to the north, but the grassy landscape was worn thin to reveal large expanses of grayish brown mud. In places the ground was pierced by clusters of sharp, towering rocks that sprouted skyward like giant thorns.

"Looks like the clearest path is around to the south," Becker suggested after some time.

"Agreed," Franco said.

Cal brought his scope up to his eye. *Damn.* All he could see was a juddering blur. *Screw this bloody place,* he thought angrily as he held the scope out in front of him. If he'd had the power to crush the little malfunctioning lump of tech in his frustrated grip, he would have. "Anyone in the market for a paperweight?"

"A paper what?" Franco asked.

"A paperweight. They used them back in…never mind. My scope is screwed."

Franco smiled grimly. "Figures," he said without breaking his gaze from the distant base. "You know, I'm half hoping there's a fight waiting for us down there."

Both Cal and Becker looked at him quizzically.

"Against something that's upright and doesn't slither," he elaborated. "I could do with letting off some steam."

Cal nodded. "I think we could all do with that."

CHAPTER NINE

"You're going to have to cover those arms, Sergeant," Cal said as he and Becker stripped off their armor. "I need you looking as pathetic as possible," he said, throwing her a long-sleeved top.

Becker snatched it out of the air. "Pathetic? You sure Franco wouldn't be better for this job?"

"I've already sent him scouting," Cal replied quickly. He grinned at her, but Forester's final cry was still echoing in his mind, and the thought of his friend's demise soon wiped the smile away.

"Wouldn't work anyway, Sarge," Poots said. "The idea is only to *appear* pathetic; to *be so* might ruin the plan."

Cal looked over at the private. She was propped against a tall, twisted rock. As well as her newfound optimism, it seemed the multiple pain patches on her injured leg had given her a sense of humor. Max was standing tall next to her. Since their run out of the valley, the combat robot's limp had become decidedly worse, and his attention span was nearing that of a bored child.

"I'm not quite sure I get the plan," Couter admitted as he crouched down for the tenth time to check the healing wrap on Poots' injury. The young man seemed keen to excel no matter what task he was assigned. "I know our rifles are screwed, but we've still got our blades. Why go in unarmed? Isn't that against protocol?"

Becker put her last piece of armor aside and climbed to her feet. "*Protocol*. Oh man, you really are green."

"Deception is sometimes the best weapon," Cal said plainly. He detached his data pad from his wrist. Half of its screen had gone blank; the other half was twitching in a weird, electronic spasm. Bored of getting frustrated with failing tech, he shook his head and tossed it to the ground. A reprimand from the starship quartermaster was the least of his worries. Again, he surveyed the base. They were close enough now that good, old-fashioned, unadorned eyes were sufficient for the job.

Before arriving on Capsun 23's surface, the base had been a large ship, bulbous and ugly in its design but capable of traveling vast distances. Once it touched down, however, the bulky mass had opened up and unfurled like a colossal, metallic flower to reveal an altogether more attractive interior. Once fully spread out, the base consisted of multiple silver pods interconnected to one large, central dome out of which a tall communications tower soared. Multiple decks circled the tower like giant, horizontal wheels, their linking structures like spokes. Cal continued to survey the scene with growing unease. To say that the base was now bashed up would be a gross understatement. Most of its outer hull looked as though it had fallen foul to a hail of plasma charges then crudely patched back together by backworld scrappers. Many of the pods were barely recognizable, and two of them had been virtually crushed flat. Whatever the hell had happened here, it hadn't been a joyous experience for those involved. A cold feeling descended on Cal as he thought about the civilians and what they might have been through.

They would have to be careful. Whoever was left in the base would either be immensely relieved to see them or shell-shocked enough to attack in error. But it was the scavengers from the wrecked ship that Cal knew could pose more of a problem, and he had a feeling they were in there—only a gut feeling, but he was suddenly in the mood to trust his instincts.

As if pulling the thoughts from his head, Couter stood and asked, "You think the survivors from that wreck are in there, sir?"

"I do," Cal said. "And the way our tech is failing, there's no guarantee we'll get into the base without an invite. If the scavengers have taken control and their tech is in the same state, they've probably manually activated the pneumatic locks."

"So we'll have to lure them out," Becker explained. "Make them think they're the top dogs with something to gain from letting us in."

Couter nodded, seeming satisfied by the explanation.

Cal pulled off his last piece of armor. With his blade, he made a small cut on his left hand and, squeezing out some of the blood, rubbed it into his hair and smeared it down the side of his face. "Okay, Sergeant, let's get this show on the road." Both he and Becker were now entirely free from armor and smart webbing, leaving only their black under suits.

"I look sweet and innocent enough for you, boss?"

Cal shrugged. "I guess we'll find out."

Cal banged on the main door to the base's central dome for the tenth time and, with one arm around Becker's shoulders, hobbled over to take yet another look through the viewing panel. He felt like an idiot keeping up this charade when it seemed there was no one around to fool. But he wasn't quite ready to give it up yet.

"Perhaps there's no one left alive in there," Becker suggested. "Or they're too afraid to show themselves."

"Or we just don't look worth the effort," Cal suggested as he continued to peer through the viewing panel. The cold feeling concerning the civilians' fate was growing harsher by the second. There wasn't much to see through the panel; the suns were getting very low in the sky, which made for a dim view of an already gloomy interior. From what he could see, the inside looked just as bashed up as the exterior—damaged work stations, equipment strewn across the floor.

"Maybe it's time to try and force entry, boss. I'm not sure any of us are keen to spend another night out in the open after the crap we experienced earlier."

Cal sighed. Becker was right. If they were to stand any chance of getting into the compound before dark, they were going to have to start the attempt soon. Unfortunately, he didn't fancy their chances. The cutting lasers on their rifles were screwed. None of them had had any luck activating grenades or explosives. They could try and override the technical elements of some of the explosives, but that definitely wouldn't be a quick job. Their best, and possibly only, chance was Max. Unfortunately, Max was fast becoming a hindrance rather than a help. Just before he and Becker had made their approach to the base, the big robot's left arm had developed a twitch that looked far from encouraging.

"You could be right," Cal admitted as he continued to stare through the panel.

"Won't be easy," Becker said. "These bases are tough, made to withstand nasty environments. Even this glass is—"

"Hold up," Cal interrupted quietly. "There's movement."

Someone was emerging from the gloom, and another figure followed close behind. Cal was pretty sure they were both male. He couldn't make out their features, but one thing that was clear was the shape of their rifles: old bolt rifles that Cal had no reason to doubt would be fully operational due to their exclusively mechanical workings.

"Two of them, both armed," he mumbled to Becker. Then, he did his best to appear like a desperate idiot by waving at them erratically.

Soon, a face was practically pressed against the window, and it wasn't a pretty one. The man was probably in his late fifties and had large, protruding eyes that jerked up and down as he assessed them through the glass. Cal mouthed a plea of help, but the man was barely paying him any attention, his gaze having become fixed on Becker. Despite this being what he'd hoped would happen, Cal was finding it hard not to slam his fist against the glass as the man continued to leer at his sergeant.

Despite the obvious lust in the man's twitchy eyes, it still took him a long while before he decided to move to the door.

"Here we go," Becker said as she helped Cal hobble over to the entrance.

Cal almost made his move straight away as the imbecile opening the door stuck the muzzle of his rifle through the gap before it was fully open. He could have easily disarmed him, but the second man was still out of view, and it was entirely possible he was a little less of a moron.

"Thank God," Cal said once the door was fully open. "We need refuge." It quickly became clear that he'd been right not to make his move; the second man had stayed well back, his bolt rifle raised and as steady as his gaze. This second man was a good ten years younger with long, jet-black hair; a pale complexion; and cold, calculating eyes. If looks could be relied upon to judge character, this younger man was a prize prick although perhaps one with at least an ounce of intelligence. But sure as hell, neither one of them was a scientist.

"Who the hell are you?" the older, bug-eyed man asked. His rifle was directed at Cal, but his attention was still dominated by Becker.

"I'm Callum Harper, a chief engineer from SanCorp. This is our pilot, Carley Becker. We were sent to fix the drones and check in here at the base, but our ship crashed three klicks back."

The older man sniffed loudly and inched forward, raising his rifle toward Cal's face. "Your ship still flyable? How many of you?"

"Please, there's no need for guns," Cal said, turning his head from the weapon. "Our ship's a ruin. And it's just us…at least it is now. We pose no threat; we're just looking to receive aid…and give it if we can."

"Where's the rest of yuh?"

"Three died in the crash. Three more disappeared on our way here. We don't know what happened to—"

"Please, just help us," Becker interrupted in the most pitiful tone Cal had ever heard her utter. "It's getting dark. Please don't leave us in the dark. I think there's something out there," she said with a quick, anxious glance back. "Something horrible… Please protect us."

Maybe next time, I should just let her do all the talking, Cal thought, doing his best not to smile. Becker had always been the better actor.

The man stared at her for a moment. Then, he sniffed a few times before his mouth split into a wide, gray-toothed grin. "Don't worry, girly, we won't be leavin' *you* out here. We got some use for you."

Cal noticed that the younger, black-haired man broke his steady gaze for a quick smirk.

"As for you," the older man said, turning his attention back to Cal. "Chief engineer, eh. Good at fixin' stuff, are ya?"

Cal nodded. "I am."

"He can fix anything," Becker blurted enthusiastically. "I've seen him do it…a miracle worker."

This time, the man had the sense to back up before he turned to his comrade. "What you reckon, Durron? Both of 'um?"

The man named Durron stared at Cal for a time, his gaze still unflinching. Then, without saying a word, he nodded.

"Okay, looks like you're in luck, fella. At least for now." The older man turned and headed for the door. "Come on then before we change our minds and unload a couple of slugs into the both of ya."

With Becker's aid, Cal hobbled toward the entrance. Durron watched him carefully, his pale face an unreadable mask. Then, he used his rifle to indicate for them to lead the way through the door. Cal hoped the man's demeanor was simply a façade. He had known men like that before—able to appear shrewd and calculating, but in actuality, they were witless and incapable of any real skill other than acting.

Either way, Cal was looking forward to smashing his face.

CHAPTER TEN

The older, bug-eyed scavenger led the way through various rooms and corridors, kicking aside equipment as he went. There were a handful of lights that still had power, but most of those were faded and flickering. Cal could hear Durron behind him closing and locking doors after each room, the pneumatic locks hissing eerily in the dusty gloom. Eventually, they came to a closed entrance. There was a small, round window in its center through which a bright, steady light shone. The older scavenger banged on the door with the butt of his rifle, and within seconds, a man's face appeared at the window.

"Hurry up, Billy, you bloody idiot. It's us."

Billy looked to be in his early twenties, and once he'd opened the door, Cal could see that he was a tall, rangy fellow who stood awkwardly as if uncomfortable with his own physique.

"Nice. Nice one. What you found? Nice." Billy's voice was jittery. Just like the other two scavengers, his lustful eyes immediately settled on Becker.

"Like that, do ya, Billy?" the older man said. "She's a pilot."

"Nice, real nice." Billy scratched skittishly at his face.

"God damn it, Billy, you been sucking on that dreamwitch pipe again? That stuff'll pop your brain."

"Just a little," Billy replied, glancing nervously at Durron, who stood a few paces back. Then, his eyes locked on Cal. "What the hell d'you let the square jaw in for?" His expression turned to something between aggression and disgust.

"He's a fixer," the older man replied. "We might need him. Now, get your lanky ass outa the way, and let us in," he said, practically barging Billy into the room.

After a nudge in the back from Durron's bolt rifle, Cal followed, hobbling with Becker still under his arm. It was a large space, well-lit by numerous, chemically reactive glow-tubes that were strewn across tables and workstations. Other than Billy, there were three people in the room. One older man, possibly in his late seventies, and two women: one young, maybe seventeen or eighteen, and the other in her forties. Cal could see immediately from their attire that they were part of the research team. The older man was chained to the desk at which he sat, the side of his face black and blue and his lip bloody. The two women sat huddled together, the younger of the two clearly traumatized. From the state of their torn clothing, it didn't take a genius to piece together what had happened here.

"I didn't tell you to stop working," Billy shouted, striding over to the old man at the desk. "I catch you slacking again, you old bastard, an' I swear I'll wrap those bloody chains 'round your scrawny neck."

With Becker helping him hobble to a nearby table, Cal watched as the old man reluctantly turned his attentions back to the equipment before him.

"What the hell!" the older scavenger suddenly exclaimed. "Christ, Billy, only one chem-bomb made? Me 'n Durron's been scavenging the base for hours. What the hell you been doin'?"

"Don't blame me; the old man's slow as hell."

"I'll blame you all right. Got ya brain all popped up on dreamwitch." the older scavenger thrust his finger toward the two women in the corner. "Probably been having a little fun too before it's your bloody turn."

"I ain't touched them, not since you left."

Cal braced himself against the table. Becker had moved away from him and now seemed frozen on the spot, transfixed by the two women.

"Okay, both of you shut the hell up." The order came from Durron, who had remained near the entrance.

Cal turned to the man, surprised that he'd finally opened his mouth.

"Couple of witless imbeciles."

Cal's surprise bumped up a notch; this Durron sounded like an educated man. *Or perhaps just more acting.*

Despite his obvious irritation at his men, Durron appeared calm and collected. His rifle was still raised.

"Pryce, get our irksome bomb maker back on track."

The older scavenger acknowledged the order with a nod.

"And use force if required. I'll trust you to deem whether it's necessary."

Definitely just an act, Cal decided. The man was seriously overcooking it.

"Billy, acquaint the new woman with the others."

Billy looked toward Becker, his bewildered, drug-addled expression suggesting that he'd already forgotten she was there. "Right, yeah, nice."

"And Billy, if you indulge in any more dreamwitch before sunup, I might just set you guarding outside for the remainder of the night."

Billy paled, twitched a few times, then scratched at his face. Then, he waved a beckoning hand at Becker.

Becker didn't move.

"Go on, doll face," the older scavenger barked. "Don't make him drag you."

Cal gripped the edge of the table hard. "It's okay, Carley," he said calmly.

Becker turned to him, her expression as hard as stone.

Cal stared back and gave her a little nod. "Best do what they say and move over there."

Despite her eyes only growing harder, she eventually nodded and moved toward Billy.

"I'm not sure I approve of what's going on here," Cal said, straightening up off the table. As he knew it would, this simple statement put the attention of all three scavengers on him. "If you want me to fix things, I'm afraid I can't allow you to take advantage of these people the way you are." This well and truly got their attention. The older scavenger named Pryce fixed his bug eyes on him and took a noticeably tighter grip on his rifle while his younger companion just loomed next to Becker and chuckled albeit nervously.

Durron, on the other hand, walked forward, each step as cocky and assured as the last. Taking up position directly in front of Cal, he raised his rifle. "You seem to be under the impression that you have the luxury of choices."

Cal smiled at that and limped forward a little. "Oh, we all have choices, Durron. What's life but one long, chaotic stream of choices?"

"Careful, Durron. This one seems reckless. A ballsy one," Pryce warned. "And you're too close," he added, shifting in an attempt to get a decent line of fire around his comrade.

Durron scoffed. "Shut up, Pryce. You don't fucking presume to tell me—"

Pryce was right; Durron *was* too close, and the little lapse in concentration that Cal had been hoping for presented itself in that moment: a simple little glance over the shoulder that allowed him to spring forward and force the man's rifle upward hard and fast. The scavenger's face stopped the weapon's momentum with an impressive crunch—one that Cal repeated just for good measure. Twisting the weapon out of the stunned man's hands, Cal took a calm step back and looked over to Becker. It came as no surprise to see that the older of the two scavengers was already sprawled unconscious on the floor, his bolt rifle lying a few feet away. Young Billy, on the other hand, was on his backside, his nose bloody and his long limbs flapping erratically as Becker secured her arm around his neck and squeezed. Despite being in Becker's company for many years, Cal was still astounded at her speed and efficiency when it came to beating the crap out of people.

Cal turned his attention back to Durron. Seeming confused, the man was stumbling about in the middle of the room, his nose badly broken.

"What… What…" was about all he managed to say.

Allowing his anger to finally reign free, Cal raised the bolt rifle and leveled it at him. "Give me one good reason I shouldn't put a bullet in you."

"No… No…" The question seemed to act as an abrupt remedy for the man's dazed state. He looked up and thrust out a hand. "No…" he repeated lamely, seeming to have entirely and spectacularly lost his love of words.

"*No* is not a good enough reason," Cal said as he noisily activated the rifle.

Durron let out a kind of hiss and continued to hold up his hand. "Okay, okay…okay."

"*Okay* won't do it either." Cal shook his head, not sure that his patience could endure another single-word answer. "Where are the rest of you?"

"We crashed," Durron replied, his voice a frustrated rasp. "Only the three of us survived."

Cal directed the muzzle of the rifle lower. "Lie to me

again, and I'll put a hole in your left kneecap."

"Okay, okay, three others made it out of the crash, but they died on the way here. Something attacked them. I don't know what it was."

This, Cal could believe. Still, he gripped the rifle harder. Even when the scavenger told the truth, his rasping voice seemed to elevate his anger. "What brought you here?"

"To scrap the bloody drones. Why else would we fucking be here?"

For the sake of saving time, Cal let that one slide. "And other than terrorizing these people, what are you doing here at this base?"

Durron only offered a sneer in reply.

"They were waiting for a rescue ship." This came from the old man who was chained to the table. "I overheard them yesterday. Their plan was to wait here for our rescue to arrive, and then they'd use us as hostages to commandeer the ship."

Durron sneered again with a brief glance in the man's direction. "You heard wrong, old man. We were going to ensure that we all made it off the planet safe and—"

Seemingly having heard enough, Becker denied the scavenger the end of his sentence. Having rendered Billy unconscious, she rushed at Durron and, without missing a beat, thrust her knuckles into his throat. The man's mouth gaped open, and his eyes bulged as he stumbled back in search of some breath. Swiftly following him, Becker grabbed his wrist and twisted it in such a way that the man seemed to become weightless and flew into a nearby workstation. As he rebounded off it, she drove a punch into his gut and met his falling face with her knee. The scavenger hit the floor hard.

Surprised that Durron had remained conscious, Cal watched as Becker took hold of his collar and dragged him across the floor toward the two women in the corner. She said nothing, but it seemed she wanted them to have a clear view of what she was about to do. The younger of the two women seemed to stare straight through the violence, as if transfixed by something a whole world away. The older woman, however, watched without so much as a blink, her expression a strange mix of fear, anger, and fascination as Becker began to pound the man with her fist.

Feeling his anger wane, Cal moved swiftly over to them. "Sergeant."

Becker continued to rain down punches, oblivious and consumed.

"Sergeant, that's enough."

Still, she ignored him.

"*Becker.*" Cal grabbed her wrist, preventing the next punch.

Becker whipped her head up and glared at him, her eyes fierce and hungry for violence. Cal had never seen her so out of control; she was usually incredibly composed even in the heat of battle. "*That's enough.*" He shouted the order in the hope that it would penetrate her rage.

Becker continued to glare at him, breathing heavily.

Cal did his best to soften his expression. "I'd rather you didn't break your hand on this worthless prick."

Becker seemed to calm ever so slightly at that, and Cal felt the tension leave her arm.

"We'll deal with them," he assured her. "But not like this."

Becker didn't answer, but her breathing slowed, and the fervent heat in her eyes began to diminish.

"Bitch."

The word was barely audible. Cal looked down at Durron's face and wondered if the man was even aware that he'd said it out loud.

Durron sniggered through his blood-caked mouth and glanced at the two women. "They both bloody deserved it," he said. Then, he attempted a grin.

Feeling his blood boil, Cal let go of Becker's wrist and let her fist fly one last time.

CHAPTER ELEVEN

Doctor Heinrich Ebner had pleaded for the robot to be left outside. Cal hadn't had long to consider his decision; darkness had been closing in, and ominous shapes were beginning to move in the gloom. In the end, he'd conceded to the doctor's reasoning and had ordered Max to remain outside. It hadn't been an easy choice. The big combat robot had been with him for years and was well and truly a part of his team. Cal felt his gut twist as he made the order and had almost changed his mind as they shut the door on those round, glowing eyes and sealed it shut. He couldn't explain how he'd become so emotionally attached to a machine, but he couldn't deny it either.

But in the end, Dr. Ebner had the right of it. This planet was far from tech friendly, and Max had already shown signs that he was malfunctioning. A human soldier losing it on a mission was one thing, but Cal didn't like to think of the resulting chaos if Max's AI systems continued to take a turn for the worse.

Having completed a quick sweep of the base, Cal had decided to move everyone up to observation level 3, a circular deck set high above the main dome and consisted of a series of rooms, each connected to the next by a wide corridor. Every room had a large, smart-glass window that faced the outside world. It was unfortunate that none of the smart-glass had remained operational; without it, little could be seen in the darkness of night, but Cal was keen to retain at least some idea of what was happening outside. The choosing of the observation level was also influenced by the fact that it showed far less signs of damage, the lower portion of the base having taken the brunt of whatever chaos had taken place.

Once he'd confirmed that there were no other scavengers milling about, Cal had ordered for Durron, Billy, and Pryce to be tied up and dumped in the corner of the room. Durron was still unconscious from Becker's beating, and Cal had to wonder whether the man would ever wake again. The other two had come around. The younger one, Billy, had been gagged in order to put an end to his constant jabbering. He seemed to be experiencing quite the nasty come down from whatever drug he'd been indulging. In contrast, the older man, Pryce, remained mostly still and silent, his protruding bug eyes alert but wary.

On the other side of the room, Dr. Campbell, the older of the two female researchers, was examining Poots' injury. Campbell wasn't a medical doctor but had assured them that she had plenty of experience in the area. Her young colleague sat close by and stared at nothing in particular. Cal had seen that fixed gaze before; she was badly traumatized, and her mind had shut down to the point that she would barely function. He couldn't say why, but he had a nasty feeling that the young woman's trauma had peaked before the scavengers had even arrived.

Cal shifted in his chair and turned his attention back to Dr. Ebner. For the last few minutes, the whole team had listened intently as the man recounted their arrival on the planet.

"There were twenty-eight of us to begin with," Ebner explained. "Seventeen men and eleven women. All of us capable and dedicated." The old man stared down at his trembling hands as he talked. He looked as though he'd been dragged to the center of hell and left there for a good while. Private Couter had applied a healing salve to the man's face as well as the cuts that had been caused by his bound wrists. Despite his trauma and age, however, Ebner was composed enough and seemed to have a good amount of steel in him.

"We first noticed the technical problems only a few hours after touching down," Ebner continued. "The base had fully unfurled and assembled itself by that point, but we were beginning to experience issues with some of our sensor equipment. Pretty soon, none of it was any good to us. Communications died shortly thereafter, and that's when we really knew we were in trouble. Eventually, we tried reassembling the base for flight but were far from successful. Some of the technology has proven to be more resilient, but eventually, it all fails. We're fortunate we have an ample supply of these chemiluminescence glow-tubes to give us light."

"You believe it's the moisture on the planet that's causing these problems?" Cal asked. Earlier, when Ebner had pleaded for Max to be left outside, he'd suggested that the robot activate his water proofing capabilities to help reduce any further malfunctioning. Cal hadn't hesitated or questioned it and had ordered Max to activate his deep sea settings—the seals within his joints would reduce his movements, but not a drop of water would make it in.

"How the hell can moisture be causing it?" Franco asked. "Our tech's designed to handle water."

"It's not the actual water," Ebner said. "It's what's *in* the water—strange and minute particles that hold a rather unusual charge. I can't fully explain the nature of the charge, but it seems detrimental to anything electrical. Once enough of the particles remain in close proximity for long enough, this charge has a neutralizing effect."

"Well, that's a damn shame," Franco said.

"How sure are you of this?" Cal asked.

"I managed to run a few tests before all of my equipment died," Ebner replied. "But some of my conclusions were simple deductions. There's moisture throughout the atmosphere, but it's more concentrated in some areas than others. Did your ship pass through clouds when you entered the atmosphere?"

Cal nodded. "As a matter of fact, it did."

"As did ours," Ebner said. "That was the start—the

effects on the engines. Communications also died quickly due to much of their workings being located externally. What else have you had problems with?"

"Our shield last night," Couter answered.

Ebner looked at him. "Was its central hub sat directly on the ground?"

Couter nodded.

"There you go," Ebner said with a somewhat eccentric sweep of his hand. "It absorbed moisture directly from the ground."

"And our rifles," Franco said, "All of our weaponry screwed up after we passed through that damned valley. The vegetation was covered in dew." He looked at Cal. "He might be right; it may well have been the moisture."

"The particles within the moisture," Ebner corrected, his tone a touch impatient and seeming a little affronted that his theory was in question.

"Right, the particles," Franco said, his expression slowly turning to one of fascination. "So this charge—"

Cal raised his hand. "Hold up a minute, Corporal." Despite this line of questioning being important, at this moment, Cal had other concerns. "Dr. Ebner, would you be so kind as to tell us what the hell happened here? What happened to the rest of your team? And this base. All the damage."

Ebner stared at him for a moment then looked back down at his hands. "I'm afraid these strange particles aren't the only inhospitable element of this planet…not by some margin."

"You're referring to the snakes," Cal said. "We've already encountered them."

"No, I'm afraid you haven't," Ebner replied. He turned and nodded toward Poots. "The bite radius on your friend's leg there tells me that you've only encountered the smaller specimens."

"Oh, you gotta be shitting me." Franco stood up and moved toward the back of the room, rubbing his face as he went. And he wasn't the only one to react; curses were mumbled throughout the team.

Cal kept his curses silent, but it wasn't easy. "How big?"

Ebner looked at him. "Two of them were big and powerful enough to breach the outer hull of this base. And these compounds are built tough, designed for the harshest environments. Up until a week ago, we'd experienced problems every night with some of the much smaller snakes. They would get into the base through the air ducts. Fortunately, they were small enough that we could deal with them. Some of us were injured, but none were killed. We even managed to keep a few specimens trapped and alive for study. Then, we set about patching up the air ducts so even the smallest specimens couldn't get in. For a time, we were safe. We thought we'd just sit tight and wait for aid."

"So what changed?" Cal asked.

"The rain came."

At the back of the room, Franco began to laugh. "Don't tell me there's some sort of acid in it too!"

Ebner shook his head. "No, nothing like that. For a time, I managed to study a few of the smaller snakes that we'd captured. We were limited by our lack of functioning equipment, but we did make some discoveries. The snakes are similar in many ways to Earth specimens albeit far more aggressive. They show the typical characteristics of squamates: amniote vertebrates with overlapping scales. They are also ectotherms."

Couter sat up at that last statement. "They can't regulate their own body temperature."

Ebner pointed at him. "Very good, young man," he said enthusiastically. "But unlike the species of snakes that we're familiar with, they need to stay cool rather than warm. That's why they only emerge from the shade once the suns have set."

"I was right; I knew it." Couter looked to Cal. "The shield last night. That's why they didn't cross the perimeter even after the shield had deactivated. They were waiting for the ground to cool."

Ebner nodded. "They're extremely sensitive to heat. They'll do near anything to avoid it…unless they're in a killing frenzy."

"Anyone keen for a campfire?" Franco suggested.

Ebner shot him a brief smile. "Our thoughts exactly. Unfortunately, we encountered two problems. With the faulty air conditioning and the fact we had to patch up the air ducts, it meant we would smoke ourselves out in no time. But, more problematic than that, the vegetation on this planet really doesn't like to burn."

Franco laughed again. "I'm really starting to dislike this rock."

Cal rubbed the back of his head. For once, he was in total agreement with his corporal. "What about in the base itself? Surely there's—"

"Everything on this base is purposely designed *not* to burn, Lieutenant, even down to our clothes. It minimizes risk. We managed to collect some dead branches from the edge of the nearest wooded area that burned sufficiently. Unfortunately, the two members of our team who went collecting the next day never returned. We searched for them of course, but none of us were brave enough to venture too close to the forest."

"So what happened a week ago?" Cal asked the question even though he had a good idea what the answer was.

"Rain came down for the first time since our arrival, and it came down hard." The older man shifted uncomfortably in his seat and shot a brief glance at his two colleagues. "Our studies suggested that the smaller the stature of the snake, the less susceptible they are to heat. After the rains, I became certain of the fact. The moisture cooled the ground to the point where larger specimens started to reveal themselves. But it wasn't until two snakes arrived from the north that the trouble started. They were far larger than the others. We briefly observed them circling the base, but none of us were brave enough to stay by the windows for long. Then, the base began to shudder. At first, we indulged in the hope that a ship had arrived and was landing too close.

But of course, it was the snakes. They were incredibly aggressive, far more so than any other species I've encountered. I suspect the motivation must be territorial rather than seeking sustenance. Once the outer hull was breached, we didn't stand a chance. The two snakes that caused the damage were too large to enter the base themselves, but they allowed for all the others to pour in."

"*Too large to enter the base?*" Franco repeated. "Bloody damn it to hell."

Ebner offered the corporal an almost apologetic smile as if all this was somehow his fault; then, he glanced again toward his colleagues. Having finished working on Poots' injury, Dr. Campbell was now sitting next to her young colleague, a comforting arm laid around her slender shoulders. Still catatonic, the younger woman barely seemed aware of her presence.

Ebner looked back at Cal. "The three of us managed to hide just long enough to survive. The rest of the team all fell victim to the snakes. I have no doubt that if the night had lasted but an hour longer, we too wouldn't be here to tell the tale. Fortunately, the beasts didn't seem keen on remaining in the base once daylight approached."

Christ, all those people, Cal thought soberly. *What a horrific way to go.* To be hunted down like that with no weapons, no way to defend themselves. He couldn't imagine the terror they must have felt. If only he and his team had arrived sooner, *much* sooner. "I'm sorry," he said sincerely. "That's a hell of a lot for the three of you to endure." In any normal situation, he would have attempted to comfort them further, but the harsh fact was their ordeal hadn't yet resolved itself. "Has it rained since?"

Ebner shook his head. "Not a drop."

"So you've not encountered the larger snakes again?"

"No, certainly none big enough to breach the base. We've spent our days trying to patch up the outer hull with weld-glue. It's a poor substitute for a plasma torch, but it's all we had."

"Have you tried—"

"Excuse me, Lieutenant."

Cal turned to see that Dr. Campbell had stood up.

"You've asked many questions," she said, a stern edge to her voice. "I feel it's time we were permitted to ask a few."

Cal raised an eyebrow and nodded. "Of course."

"Where is your ship?"

"Unfortunately, our ship succumbed to the planet's environmental issues before we could make it to you. It took us a day and a half to get here on foot. Two of my team remained on the ship and are attempting to rectify the malfunctions."

"Well, I think we can all agree that their attempts will likely be futile."

Cal wasn't keen on the tone the doctor was adopting, but considering what she'd been through, he could understand it. "Nevertheless, they'll do their absolute best."

"And assuming their best isn't good enough,"

Campbell said, "where does that leave us? We appreciate you saving us from these thugs, but unless we get off this planet, it will all be for naught."

Cal glanced at the scavengers. Durron was still unconscious, Billy looked as though he wished he were unconscious, and Pryce's wary gaze was gradually turning to one of anger.

"My flight officer successfully sent a message to our starship detailing our situation," Cal explained in an attempt to encourage the woman. "At that point, our communications were still intact. Protocol dictates that a rescue mission will dispatch immediately."

"And what's to say their rescue will be any more successful than yours?"

"A second rescue will ensure that at least two ships are sent," Cal explained. "Considering the location of our starship, they should arrive within the next nine hours. One of the ships will remain out of the planet's atmosphere whilst the other heads directly for our ship. This base will then be their next port of call, so we need to be ready and waiting." Cal kept eye contact with Campbell until she acknowledged his words with a small nod. He doubted that the young, catatonic researcher next to her had any awareness of what had been said, but it was important that Ebner and Campbell had confidence in him. If it became necessary, he needed them to trust him enough to do what he said when he said it.

It was a shame, then, that none of what he'd just told them was strictly true. It should have been if that idiot

Captain Decker wasn't the one relied upon for the rescue protocol to be carried out. But who knew what whims the captain might have been inflicted with when the message had gone through? Cal was fairly sure that he would have dispatched at least one ship, but sending two might just have proved too much for the man. When that ship arrived, they couldn't afford to linger while the atmosphere did its damage. They would have to get on it fast no matter what.

Cal stood up and turned to his team. "There are more discussions to be had, but for now, I want the doors to these corridors sealed shut." He indicated the wide doors behind him and the others at the far end of the room that led to more viewing rooms. "Leave the entrance to the stairwell open for now." He turned back to Ebner and Campbell. "I promise you that help is on its way. But until then, we need to make sure we're prepared for any eventuality. To do that, we'll have to cooperate and work together, agreed?"

"Agreed," Ebner said without hesitation.

Campbell nodded. "I'll be holding you to that promise, Lieutenant."

"They're en route as we speak," Cal replied, wishing to God that he felt as confident as he sounded.

CHAPTER TWELVE

Cal stood at the viewing panel and stared out at the night sky. Capsun 23's moons were small and distant but still offered some illumination. The landscape that he could discern appeared placid and entirely non-threatening, but Cal had learned that lesson. Occasionally, clouds would pass by, but he tried not to be overly worried; Ebner had assured him that they developed every night, and only once had they produced rain. From time to time, a snake could be spotted, ghostly pale in the moonlight, seeming to swim through the darkness. None of the snakes appeared particularly large, but then, he was a good sixty feet up.

Turning from the viewing panel, Cal approached the room's central table. "What's the detonation count on these?" he asked Ebner as he picked up one of his homemade chem-bombs. They had nine of the bombs in total, all laid out before them, as well as the three scavenger bolt rifles and one pistol, none of which depended on vulnerable, electrical tech for their operation.

"Quite long, I'm afraid," Ebner replied. "Crafting homemade explosives isn't exactly my area of expertise. And I was under a fair amount of pressure when making most of them," he said, shooting a glance toward the scavengers. Durron had finally regained consciousness and, despite his swollen, bruised face, his expression of seething hatred couldn't be mistaken.

Ebner looked back to Cal. "Once the pin is pulled, the chemicals will mix, and you'll have fifty-five seconds before it detonates."

Cal sucked on his teeth. That was quite a bit longer than he'd hoped; it wasn't easy to judge where to throw an explosive with that much detonation time. "How sure are you of that timing?"

"Extremely," Ebner replied without hesitation. "I've been precise with the chemical quantities." He nodded with certainty and repeated, "Fifty-five seconds."

Cal was encouraged by the man's confidence, but he still felt troubled by the long detonation time. He weighed the little explosive in his hand and studied it closely.

Seemingly offended by the look on Cal's face, Ebner continued, "Also, be assured that until the pin is pulled, there's absolutely no chance of accidental detonation. These glass containers are as tough as they come." The old man took the bomb from his hand and gave it a good shake. Cal could see the bright liquids sloshing about within their separate compartments. If he hadn't been told otherwise, he would have thought it nothing more than an elaborate Christmas decoration. Ebner then struck it hard against the edge of the table, making Cal take an involuntary step back. "See, solid as a rock."

Having taken an interest, Franco moved around the table to join Cal in getting a closer look. "What's the burn radius and duration?"

Ebner considered for a moment before answering. "I would say, on average, a four-meter radius and an extremely hot burn of about thirty seconds."

"Only thirty?" Franco asked.

"Trust me; it's long enough," Ebner replied. "I managed to set a few of these off during the attack. It's the only reason the three of us survived. Bought us time to run and hide. The big snakes are incredibly sensitive to the heat. To the point they'll practically attack each other in order to retreat from it. Then, it takes time for the area to cool... Some of the more vicious snakes endure the residual heat, but most avoid it for a good while."

Cal thought for a time then asked, "What do you think attracts these snakes? Could lights be drawing them in?"

Ebner nodded. "Lights, movement, taste, smell, vibrations. If they're anything like the snakes we know, just about all of these could be a factor."

Franco mumbled a curse then leaned over to stare at the liquids within one of the bombs. "Well, I'm glad we've at least got something decent to fight with if it comes to it. I don't fancy relying on the arts and crafts those Boy Scouts are whipping up over there." The corporal nodded toward the far side of the room, where Couter, Wilson, and Orisho were fashioning spears by attaching their blades to whatever suitable lengths of metal they could detach from the base. The spears would act as a lighter-weight weapon rather than keeping the blades on their bulky, inert pulse rifles. The makeshift weapons would also allow them a far longer reach. Cal didn't imagine they'd actually be needed. It was likely their rescue would arrive within hours. But he didn't like to take chances. What if the ship didn't come directly and encountered the same problem as their own? Or perhaps more likely, what if that idiot Captain Decker conjured up some nonsensical reason to delay the rescue? Whatever the case may be, Cal always liked to keep his team busy under such circumstances—the death of a comrade always hit hard as soon as the *doing* stopped. Accepting such loss was part of being a soldier, but it never got any easier. When the time came, they would all deal with it in their own way. Some hit the sparring ring, some indulged in the battle-sim arena, but most hit the rec-club and got blind drunk.

"This really is quite the vacation you've dragged us on, Lieutenant."

Corporal Franco, on the other hand, dealt with just about everything with attempts at humor.

"I'm still waiting for those Amazon women you promised."

Cal raised an eyebrow at him. "Save your fantasies for the pleasure pods back on the starship, Corporal."

"No can do. I broke one of the pods on my last visit. I'm banned from the entire entertainment deck. You frickin' believe that? Probably be paying that damn thing off well into my retirement."

"Sorry to hear that," Cal said, and he meant it. The pleasure pods were damn good fun. They could fool the body and brain and immerse the user into just about any virtual world or situation imaginable.

"Yeah, not half as sorry as I am," Franco mumbled, seeming genuinely distraught.

Cal wasn't keen to know how the pod was broken and was glad for the lack of elaboration.

Franco shrugged then held a glow-tube over the chem-bombs. "You know, these little baubles are quite ingenious." He glanced over at Ebner, who was now organizing materials on the other side of the lab. "The old guy's got some real skill."

"Just as well," Cal replied. "It seems no one would have been left alive otherwise."

Franco nodded. "If only we'd gotten here earlier."

"If only *a lot more* of us had gotten here earlier," Cal said. "Maybe an out-of-orbit carrier ship to boot. If only the captain of our starship wasn't an ignorant moron."

Franco put the glow-tube down and smiled grimly. "You're thinking of paying him an unfriendly visit when we get back, aren't you?"

"The thought had crossed my mind."

"Well, just don't go getting yourself slung. I like this little team of ours."

Cal shrugged. "I'll try my best."

"Speaking of our little team," Franco said after a

moment, "you think Becker's okay?"

Cal turned to see Becker perched on the edge of a storage crate, her elbows resting on her knees. She was staring intently at Dr. Campbell and her young colleague. "Becker's always okay," he replied. But he didn't entirely believe his own words. For as long as he'd known her, Becker had been steadfast. As calm and collected as anyone he'd ever worked with. But that was before he saw her almost end a man in a bare-knuckled rage. It was a reaction he could understand—all three of those men had done despicable things—but dealing with contemptible individuals was part of the job, and it was best done in a measured way. *But then, I didn't exactly rush to stop the beating*, Cal thought as he continued to watch Becker.

"I'm not so sure," Franco said. "Something's got her riled or spooked… I'm not sure which."

Cal sucked in a slow breath. *Maybe if she hadn't been there, I'd have thrown the punches myself.* "I think it's best we get these handed out, Corporal," he said, turning his attentions back to the explosives on the table.

"To the civvies as well?"

"Only Ebner and Campbell," Cal replied. The state the girl was in, he doubted whether she could even hold one let alone use it effectively. She still showed no signs of escaping her catatonia, but perhaps that was the safest place for her mind right now. "Arming them might help keep their confidence up," Cal reasoned. "I doubt we'll actually have to fight, but…"

"Always got to keep in mind the *but*," Franco agreed.

"Don't worry; I'll get them dished out."

Cal nodded his appreciation then headed over to Becker.

"All okay, Sergeant?"

"Of course, boss," Becker replied without looking up.

Cal took a seat on the crate next to her. "It's just you seem a little…*distant.*"

Becker didn't reply, just sat staring at the young, catatonic researcher.

"She's called Christie," Becker said, finally breaking the silence. "Reminds me of my sister."

"Your sister?" Cal had known that Becker's parents had been killed when she was young by raiders, but nothing had ever been mentioned about a sister.

"She was older than me," Becker said, nodding toward Christie, "about the same age as her when she was killed. She died from her injuries a few weeks after the raiders." Becker's gaze remained fixed on the girl, as if to look away might result in more tragedy. "She looks like her too."

"I didn't know. I'm sorry, Becker, I truly am." Cal thought his words lame and completely inadequate, but they were sincere.

"She looks like a doll, don't you think?" Becker's voice was quiet and laced with sadness, her expression distant, a world away in a lifetime long past. "…a china doll. So fragile you couldn't touch her for fear she'd shatter into a million pieces."

Cal nodded. She was right. Christie was as pale as a ghost and far too frail to be amid such a storm.

Sometimes, life could be incredibly harsh to those who deserved it the least.

"I couldn't protect my sister," Becker said, an edge of bitterness clutching at her throat. "I was small then…and weak." Finally, her gaze broke from Christie, and she turned to look at him. There were tears in her eyes, but they didn't spill, and her expression was hard. It was as if she'd forged an invisible shell to contain the tears and any emotion that came with them. "I'm not helpless anymore."

"No, you're far from that," Cal replied. "But you know it's not always possible to protect everyone no matter how strong you are."

Becker's hard countenance was broken for a moment by a brief, tight-lipped smile. "You're a fine one to talk, boss. I've seen the way you look at young Couter. Like you want to cut him from the team and send him off to some peaceful, first-world colony. Maybe persuade him to study art or something."

Cal shrugged. "Less chance of getting eaten as an artist."

Becker's smile took on a genuine edge but soon faded. The two of them sat again in silence for a while, as if in a tranquil bubble, indiscernible by the rest of the team as they continued on with their tasks.

But Cal knew that tranquility could never last, not in this line of work and certainly not in a situation such as this. Durron began shouting across the room, demanding for someone to hear him out. Cal's jaw clenched almost as hard as his fists. The scavenger's timing was even worse than his manners.

Becker's head snapped around, fierceness instantly returning to her eyes.

Cal stood. "Stay put for now."

Becker hardly seemed to hear him, her eyes locked on Durron.

"*Sergeant*," Cal said, raising his voice and waiting for Becker to respond. "That's an order."

Reluctantly, Becker looked up at him and nodded.

"Just so you know, my sergeant is about two of your shouts away from marching over here and ripping your tongue out." Cal crouched down and looked into Durron's bruised, battered face. All three scavengers were slumped together in the corner of the room, their feet and hands bound tight. The back wall was bending Durron's neck into a particularly awkward angle, but with his hands tied, there wasn't much he could do about it. Cal certainly wasn't going to help him. "And if for some reason she decides you're not worth the effort, I might just do it for her."

"Inconse…inconsequen…empty threats."

Durron was having trouble talking, the execution of some words obviously proving too much for him. He sounded like a man who'd been punched in the face twenty times. Cal hoped that the obvious pain caused from moving his mangled mouth might just keep conversation to a minimum. Or at the very least lessen the man's vocabulary.

"You keep that…blond bitch on a leash. Else you might come to regret it."

"You're right; I might regret it," Cal replied, doing his best to keep his temper locked down. "But I doubt for the reasons you're thinking."

"You're a soldier," Durron replied. "Bound by laws."

"My memory gets a little hazy when it comes to those laws," Cal replied evenly. "When we're so far from civilization, I occasionally begin to feel a bit like judge, jury, and executioner."

Durron laughed at that, a little blood bubbling from his swollen nose. "You're lying. You're a *by the book* man…can smell it a mile away."

"I doubt you can smell much of anything through that broken snout."

Durron snarled and awkwardly snorted out a large clump of dried blood from the snout in question. Unfortunately, the action went a long way to restoring the clarity of his voice. "A by the book man," he repeated.

Pryce shifted by his side. "Aye, you're nothin' but grunts," he growled, having seemingly come out of his silent stupor. "Ain't no bloody evidence on us. You grunts didn't see nothin'. Can't prove nothin'."

"Shut it," Durron hissed at him. He tried to smile at Cal, but he looked more like a deformed pig chewing on a truffle. "I've been in this game a while, Lieutenant. I know Fed laws inside out. What that bitch did to me… I could get her a hefty sentence. They don't like soldiers losing it like that…makes them look bad. Us on the other hand… You've nothing on us that will stand in a Fed court, no cam evidence. We'll be free to go about our business in no time. But I'll admit it would be a hassle to go through the rigma…rigmar…to go through the trouble. So here's the deal; you keep your mouth shut, and I'll let the blond bitch off scot-free."

Cal raised an eyebrow and looked at Pryce. "Has your friend always been so delusional, or has my sergeant caused some serious brain damage?"

Pryce simply looked at him blankly. Cal shook his head and stood up. He stretched his back for a moment and took a couple of deep breaths. Then, he looked down at the three men as a person might look upon some inconveniently located excrement. Still gagged, Billy wasn't paying the slightest attention to the conversation. The young man's eyes were darting about as if watching some activity that the rest of them weren't privy to. All three men were nefarious thugs, but Durron seemed the only one with an ounce of intelligence, and that somehow made him all the worse.

Cal pulled out his knife. He began tapping its edge on his armored leg and took some time to decide just how *by the book* he was feeling.

Durron looked up with that deformed approximation of a smile. It seemed the deluded man was convinced he'd achieved some sort of victory on account of his gumption and wit. Cal wasn't about to kill or even hurt a bound prisoner, no matter how despicable, but there was a moment there when the man's *gumption* almost caused him to reconsider those ethics. It was fast becoming another one of those occasions when he wished he hadn't become quite so dedicated to his position, so steadfast to the rules of his profession. *Perhaps he's right; maybe I am a by the book man.*

"The truth is, Durron, when the time comes for my sergeant and I to make our report, I'd imagine our memories of the events may differ substantially from yours and those of your little criminal sidekicks here. Of course, there were other witnesses in the room at the time," Cal said, glancing back toward the civilians. Both Ebner and Campbell appeared to be intently listening to what was being said. "I find myself wondering whether your victims' memories will fall in line with ours or with yours."

Durron's approximated smile began to lose its rigidity. Cal stared down at him for a few more moments. "Now, keep your mouth shut," he said before turning away.

"Actually, there was one more thing I wanted to discuss if I may, Lieutenant?"

Feeling his patience wearing very thin, Cal looked stiffly back to the scavenger.

"I was just curious," Durron said, the tone of his voice suddenly elevated as if to ensure it could be heard by all. "Why exactly did it take you so long to come to the rescue of these poor, vulnerable civilians?"

Cal paused mid turn.

"You see, my comrade, Pryce here," Durron continued, "he's been filling me in on the older gentleman's theories of the disrupting water particles on this planet…the reason for all this failing tech. Correct me if I'm wrong, but the way I understand it, a substantial amount of time must have passed before your ship was affected and ultimately rendered inert."

Cal felt his jaw involuntarily tighten as well as his fist. *Damn.* It seemed he'd underestimated this bastard.

"Why then did you not arrive here at the base before that happened?" Durron asked loudly. "Surely, you would have known its exact location, and your first priority would have been to ensure the wellbeing and safety of these unfortunate innocents?"

Cal could feel the gaze of the researchers burning into his back, particularly Campbell. He should have come clean with them from the start, but ironically, he was trying to build their trust—not an easy thing to achieve when the first thing you tell them is that a hulking lump of tech took priority over their lives.

Durron's smile was beginning to return now, and it had a shrewd edge to it. "My colleagues and I are scavengers, plain and simple. We've never tried to hide the fact…never tried to pretend that we're something that we're not."

Cal had an overwhelming urge to knock the man unconscious, but an act of violence wasn't exactly going to help his cause in this situation.

"I'll admit it," Durron continued. "Our objective when we arrived here on this planet was to try and eke out a living by unlawfully acquiring a few bits here and there to put food on our table and make basic repairs to our ship. That was why we headed for one of these drones that we'd been informed of... It was possibly a perfect business opportunity for us—valuable parts and nobody around that could potentially get hurt in the process of acquiring them. As it turned out, we spent a fair bit of time at that drone, which, unfortunately for us, was near impossible to breach. Even with its shields down, it was incredibly well-protected. I'd imagine that the Federation and the military must place an awful lot of worth on those pieces of tech...to go to all that trouble of protecting them so thoroughly. Am I right in this, Lieutenant? Are they incredibly valuable?"

Cal didn't answer. The scavenger was baiting him as well as revealing a truth that he simply couldn't argue against. If he forcibly shut the man up, it would show him as guilty...which of course he was.

Durron snorted out a little more dried blood before continuing. "Anyway, like I was saying, we spent a good deal of time attempting to crack this drone before moving on, enough time for our ship to gradually succumb to these strange disrupting particles that the old man speaks of. After we crashed, we came here, driven by a simple instinct to survive... It's unfortunate that the fear resulting from the loss of our fellow crew members and the dire situation drove us to do things we're not proud of. But once the fear settles and we have time to reflect on our actions, the three of us will have to start living with the consequential guilt." Durron shifted uncomfortably, but his stare never left Cal. "So that's our story, as honest and transparent as I can make it." The scavenger's smile lessened, and his bruised, bloodshot eyes darkened. "What's your *honest* story, Lieutenant? Why is it that your ship didn't make it here on time? If it had, these good people would be on their way to your starship by now, wouldn't they?"

Cal wanted to strangle the man. He was clearly attempting to turn the civilians against him, but for what purpose? Surely not to try and get them on his side—after what he and his men had done to them, there was no chance of that. No, it seemed he wanted to create discord and conflict just for the hell of it—perhaps unsurprising considering the man's character.

"You need to shut your damn mouth," Becker said. She was on her feet and moving toward Durron.

Cal stopped her with an outstretched arm. "Ease up, Sergeant."

"Is this true, Lieutenant?" Campbell asked. Her tone was sharp, and the question cut into Cal like a knife. "Forgive me if I'm wrong, but the suggestion is that you put your drones in priority over our lives."

Making sure he retained a hold on Becker, Cal turned to face Campbell. He was aware that this could turn ugly very fast. But there was no avoiding the truth now. "I'm afraid it is. My orders were clear. I was to secure the drones before coming to your aid."

"*My God.*" Campbell's expression quickly became one of incredulous anger. "I've never heard anything so bloody...*amoral*." She shook her head, disbelieving. "To put a lump of technology before human lives. Do you have no conscience? You expect us to trust you now? To put our faith in you?"

"Ease up," Franco said, stepping forward into Campbell and Ebner's line of sight. "The lieutenant wasn't the one making the orders. And he risked harsh consequences breaking them after the first drone. There's no one you should trust more. If anyone else was in charge, the ship would have crashed on the other side of the planet. The only reason we're here is because he was willing to defy his superiors."

"And a damn lot of good it's done us, you being here?" Campbell replied, her face now red with anger. She seemed not in the least placated or convinced by Franco's words.

"*Jesus, lady*," Franco said, struggling to keep his own temper in check. "Have you already forgotten the situation he saved you from when he arrived?"

This turned Campbell from angry to seething. "Let me assure you, Corporal, that neither myself nor my colleagues will ever forget that situation, not for as long as we live. But I'm wondering how much better that situation would have been had your Lieutenant found his conscience as soon as he'd entered the planet's atmosphere? How much sooner would you have arrived if you hadn't been seeing to your precious drone and then had to *walk here?*"

Shaking his head in disbelief, Franco was about bark a

reply when Cal stopped him. "It's okay, Corporal. I appreciate your support, but she's right. I made a huge mistake, and the consequences are on me."

Franco shot him a look that made it clear he disagreed, but he backed down nonetheless.

"Finally, some honesty from the fearless leader," Durron said in a clear attempt to poke the fire.

Cal ignored him and kept his attention on the civilians. His admission of guilt didn't seem to have dampened Campbell's anger a great deal, and Ebner just looked worn to the bone.

"I realize that trusting me is a big ask," Cal said. "I should have been honest with you from the start. I wish I could turn back the clock, but the situation is what it is. I'm afraid that putting your faith in me and in my team is—"

Cal's words caught in his throat as a deep boom rippled through the air, causing the floor to quite literally shake beneath his feet. There was a stunned silence as if no one could quite believe what they'd heard. Then Cal turned and ran to the viewing panel, his heart thudding against his chest. He was quickly joined by the others. Peering through the glass, his eyes were immediately drawn to distant flames that were tearing a hole in the featureless darkness. Amid the blaze was a downed craft.

"*Christ*, that's our ship," Franco said. "Sinclair and Malloy."

"You're not wrong," Wilson answered. "And it looks like a nasty crash."

Cal swallowed the dread that was trying to rise up from his gut and quickly scanned the surrounding landscape for signs of snakes. He spotted a few in the gloom but nowhere near enough to discourage him. Turning away from the window, he quickly picked up a bolt rifle for himself and threw the other to Franco. The corporal deftly snatched it out of the air. "Franco, Becker, you're with me. Orisho, Wilson, I need you by the entrance. Poots, Couter, mind the civilians."

"Request civi duty, sir," Becker said quickly.

Cal looked at her while Franco passed him one of the chem-bombs. He suspected Becker's motivations were personal. She wanted to stay near Christie, to ensure her safety. With no time to delay, he turned to Couter. Perhaps it was time to allow his new young recruit into the fray. "Okay, private, grab that last bolt rifle. You're with me."

CHAPTER THIRTEEN

Cal led Franco and Couter silently through the darkness, the distant flames from the crash acting as a guiding beacon. Their head protectors—which should have ejected from the neck of their armor with the touch of a button—had fallen foul of Capsun 23's tech curse. This meant their night vision visors were also unavailable, making negotiation of the terrain tricky to say the least. Cal had brought a few of the glow-tubes but, not keen to attract unwanted attention, had decided not to activate them until it became absolutely necessary. As it stood, the light from the distant moons was giving them a small amount of illumination. Unfortunately, the clouds were thickening fast, bringing an almost complete darkness. The three men moved as swiftly as possible, relying mostly on the sound of each other's the footfalls to stay close.

Cal tried not to think of what he might find in the ship. It had been a bad crash; that much was clear. He hoped to God that Sinclair and Malloy had been strapped in. His heart thudded almost painfully against his chest as his adrenaline surged him forward. His near-death experience with the snake a few hours earlier had set him on edge, and the fact he could barely see what surrounded him certainly wasn't helping. The old-fashioned bolt rifle nestled tight in his grip didn't fill him with confidence either. The weapon was fine for long-distance shooting, but it had very little stopping power when compared to a pulse rifle—better for shooting tins in a sunny field than aggressive man-eaters in the dead of night. The temptation to swap it with the spear-like weapon strapped to his back gnawed at him, but the familiar comfort of a trigger against his finger kept bullying the thought away.

As they neared the ship, Cal felt his heart slow a little; if Ebner was right, the heat from the flames should keep any snakes at bay. But those fires wouldn't last. Quickly, he scanned the burning debris that lay throughout the gouged ground. It seemed the ship had come down hard and fast without functional landing gear or even emergency thrusters. *What the hell were you thinking, Sinclair?* Cal did his best to peer through the black, acrid smoke. *Why risk it?* His eyes began to sting from the assaulting fumes. Fortunately, their armor shielded them from the worst of the intense heat. All three of them called out, but no answer came. Seeing no obvious bodies, Cal picked up the pace. If Sinclair and Malloy had survived, it was likely they'd need urgent medical attention.

Nearing the rear of the ship, Cal put up a hand, ordering a quiet halt. There was something up ahead.

Something tall and wide silhouetted against the flames. He knew that shape well. Max's eyes were still glowing softly, but he stood as still as a rock and did nothing to acknowledge their presence. The robot must have been drawn in by the crash, but he was showing no signs as to his intentions. Cal paused for a moment, his mind conflicted. He suspected their malfunctioning teammate could just as likely hinder them as much as help. *Shit, we really don't have time for this.* Unwilling to risk any issues with the big combat robot, he decided to lead Franco and Couter in a wide arc around. As they moved, he noticed Max's domed head slowly turning, those lambent eyes tracking their progress like an inscrutable cat. He continued to observe them for some time but still made no move in their direction.

Satisfied that Max wasn't going to be a problem, Cal searched for a way into the ship. It didn't take long; a huge tear had been opened up in the belly of the fuselage, and the craft had come to rest at an angle, allowing relatively easy access. The interior was a twisted mess. Some of the lights were still active, but most were dim and flickering. Cal shouted again for Sinclair and Malloy. Still, no answer came. He waited for a moment to be sure then led the way as swiftly as he could through the bowels of the ship. It wasn't a particularly large vessel, but its mangled state and the fact that everything was at the wrong angle made the going hard.

"I'll try and get us to the cockpit," Cal said as he pushed aside a storage crate with his boot. "Strike up one of those glow-tubes, Corporal? That damn flickering's giving me a headache."

"With pleasure," Franco replied.

Under the steady light of the glow-tube, the three of them crawled up through a lift shaft and pulled themselves into the main docking bay. Cal took a moment to call out again, but still, no answer came, and the near silence only served to feed their foreboding. His expression grim, he shook his head at his two teammates then began to negotiate a path toward the storage lockers.

"Hold up," Couter said after only a few steps. "You hear that?"

At first Cal, heard nothing except the faint crackling of the outside fires and the occasional creaking of expanding metal.

Then, a dull clunking reached his ears. Once…twice…and a third time.

"There." Couter moved back a couple of paces and pointed through a gap in a twisted door to his left. "There's movement."

Cal stepped up to the gap and peered through into a dark corridor. A single light had been dislodged and was hanging awkwardly. Like most of the others, it flickered in a mild, strobe-like manner. His eyes struggling to adjust, Cal just about discerned a person slumped facedown midway along the corridor. There was a metal bar in the prone figure's hand, which was rising and falling against the grated floor. Grasping the edges of the door, the three of them tried to force it open. There was a short, sharp screech as the door shifted an inch and then stuck fast. Handing his rifle to Couter, Cal quickly removed the top half of his armor and forced his body through the gap. Taking his rifle back, he made his way over to the figure.

"It's Malloy," he said as he gently turned him over. Despite the poor lighting, Cal could see blood caked in the science officer's hair and smeared across his face. His eyes were half open, his T-tech-enhanced corneas shining gold in the disturbed light. Malloy looked confused, a sheen of sweat mingling with the blood on his forehead. Cal laid a hand on his neck. "He's conscious," he shouted. "Pulse strong. I need a glow-tube."

"I'll bring it in," Couter said as he began deactivating his armor.

Cal held up a hand. "No. Throw it. I'll see to Malloy. You two head towards the cockpit; find Sinclair."

Couter threw the glow-tube and wished him luck before following Franco. Their footfalls quickly faded.

"It's okay, Malloy," Cal said calmly as he squeezed the tube until its chemicals shone their brightest. "I'll just check you over; then, we'll get you out of here, okay?" The science officer didn't answer, but Cal continued to assure him while systematically searching for injuries. After a few minutes, he found nothing but superficial cuts and bruises—a small miracle. It was entirely possible that the man had sustained less obvious injuries, but a more thorough check would have to wait until they were back at the base. "Okay, I think we're good to get moving," Cal said with as much optimism as he could muster.

Still, Malloy said nothing. He seemed unable to focus, head lolling aimlessly.

Probably just a concussion, Cal thought as he held the man's head still and looked into his eyes. There wasn't the slightest recognition. "Can you hear me, Malloy? It's me, Callum. Try to speak to me."

No answer.

"Okay…" Cal looked about, thinking through his next move. "Okay, don't worry about speaking. How about standing; think you can manage that?"

Seeming to snap out of his stupor, Malloy abruptly stared directly at him, eyes wide, the intensity of his golden gaze unnerving in the dim light. "You can't sell me," he said, his voice a harsh rasp.

Cal shook his head again, this time in confusion. "*Sell you?* I think you might have taken a bit of a knock to the head, my friend." He forced a smile. "But if it makes you feel better, I promise not to hand you over to the highest bidder."

Malloy pulled his lips back in a feral sort of sneer—a vicious look that instantly made Cal's smile falter.

"*Spicer, I see you, spicer.*" Malloy hissed the words and, with a swipe of his arm, knocked the glow-tube from Cal's grip. It skittered across the hard floor, where it fell through a gap in the grating. Once again, the dim, flickering beam overhead became the dominant light source.

"Calm down, Malloy. You're just in shock," Cal said as gently as he could. *Or just plain fucking delusional,* he thought as he turned to see if the glow-tube was retrievable. "Damn it," he mumbled. It must have fallen some distance or perhaps rolled under something. He couldn't even see its glow. Leaning further forward, he tried to look from a different angle. *Were the hell did it—*

Suddenly, there was movement.

Already on edge, Cal reacted quickly and dodged to his left. It was a move that probably saved his life. Instead of caving in the back of his skull, the metal bar struck his shoulder, causing pain to sear down his arm. Ignoring it, he sprang up, twisting around as he did so. Malloy was on his feet, metal bar in hand and teeth bared in a fierce, almost demonic grimace. *What the—* Cal barely had time to finish his thought before the crazed man charged toward him in a rabid attack, his crude weapon swinging wildly. Dodging right, Cal managed to swerve out of reach. But Malloy came at him again, his augmented, golden eyes flashing in the flickering light.

Cal blocked a swipe, almost breaking his arm in the process—in the heat of the moment, he'd forgotten about his lack of armor. Swiftly stepping in close, he head-butted Malloy just hard enough to stun him then shoved him hard with his palms. The science officer stumbled but managed to retain his footing.

"Malloy, it's me, dammit," Cal shouted. He stepped forward and turned his face toward the flickering light. "Lieutenant Callum Harper. Look at my face. I think your T-tech augment is compromised."

Malloy shook his head.

"The augment's messing with your brain," Cal

explained. "Try to think past it."

Malloy shook his head again. He was breathing hard. "You're a spicer," he sneered. "I've dealt with spicers before. You won't spice my brain…not my brain. I won't let you."

Cal gritted his teeth. *Christ, he's pretty far gone.*

"Put down the bar, Malloy. I really don't want to hurt you." Malloy was a good fighter, but Cal was confident in his abilities to take him down should it come to it.

Malloy ignored the warning and lunged again.

This time, Cal didn't let him get close. A surge of anger fueled a front kick that he planted in the center of the man's chest. Malloy flew back and went down hard. But to Cal's dismay, he scrambled back onto his feet in seconds as if barely registering that he'd been hit. Cal glanced at his rifle; it was a good few paces from him. He could make a grab for it, but to what end? He wasn't about to shoot Malloy no matter how screwed up he'd become. And he doubted that pointing the weapon at the man would dissuade him from launching further attacks; he seemed too far gone for that.

Jerking his head erratically, Malloy began making weird guttural noises and fixed Cal with a deathly stare. If he'd seemed mad before, the kick to the chest seemed to have triggered a look of insanity the likes of which Cal had never seen, and he'd met more than his fair share of messed up folk. He looked nothing short of possessed to the point that Cal was finding it tough to look at him. They weren't exactly close friends, but they'd both been on the team for years. *I'm going to have to knock him out cold,* he thought as he braced himself for the next attack. They'd just have to cart him back to the base unconscious and deal with him there.

Malloy began to shuffle forward like some kind of demented, golden-eyed zombie. After a couple of steps, however, he stopped, his gaze drifting up to the flickering light, which hung awkwardly above him. Then, his lips peeled back to create something akin to a smile. Cal had no time to question the expression before Malloy swung his metal bar at the light, sending the room into a near complete darkness.

Fuck.

Cal couldn't see a damn thing—something that possibly wouldn't be a problem for Malloy. If his optic implants were still functioning, they would make the inky black corridor as clear as day. He heard a rush of movement and brought his arms up a fraction of a second before the metal bar pounded against his wrist. His adrenaline pumping, Cal barely registered the pain. Leaping back, he did his best to blindly defend himself while his mind sifted furiously through his options. He briefly considered making a dash for the gap through which he came, but it had been a tight fit, and it would take him time to get back through—moments that would leave him even more vulnerable to Malloy's attacks.

Maybe the rifle would have been a good idea. The redundant thought was obliterated by the sound of Malloy rushing toward him again. Once more, Cal brought up his arms, but this time, the metal bar found its way through, its edge connecting with the side of his head. Cal felt a flash of pain that sent his dark vision into a popping matrix of color. He retreated again, but this time, it was more of a dazed stumble. He tried to stay on his feet, but the combination of the darkness and dizziness made it near impossible. Realizing that the fight would likely be over in a matter of seconds, he took a chance. Relying heavily on luck, he launched himself forward and felt a small amount of relief as he collided with his opponent. Wrapping his arms around him, he clumsily succeeded in dragging him to the ground and held on with everything he had. Unfortunately, the blow to the head had left his limbs feeling weak and unresponsive. Malloy, on the other hand, seemed fueled by madness, an unnatural strength coursing through him.

Twisting his torso, the crazed man managed to get the upper hand, forcing himself on top of Cal to press an arm against his throat. "*Kill you, kill you, kill you…*" The hissed words were brimming with corrupted zeal.

Cal did his best to break the hold, but Malloy was leaning heavily on him. He fought for breath and tried to harness some strength from his growing anger.

"*Kill you, kill you, kill you…*"

"Fuck you, Malloy," Cal growled back as he shifted his grip and partially managed to push the man away.

"*Kill you, spicer, kill you, kill you, kill you…*"

Despite his spinning head, Cal's anger started to boil over. The words being hissed in his face were really starting to grate. Shifting his grip again, he managed to get a hold of the fingers on Malloy's left hand. With a slow, strained effort, he maneuvered them sideways into a position where the man's own weight put stress on them. The harder Malloy bore down, the greater pressure he put on his own twisted fingers. Against any sane person, this move would have been enough to make them reconsider their actions. Unfortunately, Malloy was pretty far from sane.

Seconds later, three of the fingers snapped, and Malloy's arm thumped back against Cal's neck.

"*Kill you, kill you, kill you, kill you…*"

A barrage of curses exploded in Cal's head. If he'd been able to get them past his throat, he would have gladly unleashed them into Malloy's face. He'd had some tough fights in his time but never against someone suffering this level of rage. And the fact that Malloy didn't seem to feel pain really wasn't helping.

"*Kill you, kill you, spicer, kill you…*"

Cal tried for another counter move, one that he hoped to God would work before the pressure on his neck took its final toll. Without breaking his hold, he angled his right arm up and pressed his elbow against Malloy's chest.

"*Kill you, kill you, kill you…*"

Cal pushed his elbow against the man with all the strength he had left.

"*Kill you, kill you, kill—*"

His neck burning and shoulders straining, a dull thud reached Cal's ears. Almost immediately—and somewhat ironically—Malloy's menacing death chant suddenly died in his throat.

Cal sucked in a breath as the attack abruptly ceased, and Malloy slumped forward on top of him. He could see a haze of blue light disturbing the darkness, once again giving his eyes purpose. As he heaved Malloy's dead weight off him, the light grew infinitely brighter. He gave his battered head a gentle shake and blinked a few times. Once his vision had finally adjusted, he saw that there was a figure standing over him.

Sinclair looked as if she'd taken a slow walk through a long war. She held a lump of nondescript metal in her hand and was staring down at Malloy with pallid anguish. "I think I've killed him," she said, her voice as worn as her countenance.

Cal managed to prop himself up on one unsteady elbow and, for the second time in what seemed like hours—but was certainly only a few minutes—he placed a hand on Malloy's neck.

This time, there was no pulse.

CHAPTER FOURTEEN

Cal sat on a buckled storage crate, manually clipping his armor back into place while Couter patched up his head. The young private had already given him a stim to rekindle his wits and eliminate the last of the dizziness. The stims were incredibly effective, and already, he was feeling close to normal. Even the throbbing pain in his arm had been masked. He could worry about the lasting damage and the nasty aftereffects of the drug later, which with any luck would be during their safe passage back to the starship.

He wasn't the only one injured. As well as a myriad of cuts and bruises, Sinclair had a makeshift bandage wrapped around her middle, and he could see a red patch off blood seeping through.

"Malloy stabbed me earlier in the day," Sinclair said as she saw Cal observing the wound. "I managed to fight him off and barricaded myself in the cockpit. I passed out for a while but luckily came around in time to patch it up before I bled out."

"What the hell happened to him?" Franco asked. The corporal remained on his feet, bolt rifle in hand. He looked as though he expected Malloy's corpse to rise up at any moment and burst out of the dark corridor to attack them. "The guy was always so quiet and mild-mannered."

"His T-tech implant became compromised," Sinclair replied. She shook her head. "What a screwed up planet we found, eh!"

"Paradise with a dark heart," Couter mumbled in agreement.

Sinclair smiled briefly at that. "Well said." She turned back to Cal. "Malloy started showing signs of losing it shortly after you left. Small blunders at first. Then, he became argumentative. Then aggressive. Fortunately, we'd already isolated the ship's functional systems before he really started to lose it. We got it into a state where it might just about fly. I mentioned the idea of trying to get closer to the base, but honestly, I had no real intention of trying it. Far too risky." Sinclair looked down at her bandage and winced as she dabbed at the red patch. "Unfortunately, the throwaway comment seemed to tip him over the edge. To say he went berserk would be an understatement."

"Can I give you a stim?" Couter asked. "Just enough to give you a boost?"

Sinclair shook her head. "Thanks, but no. I've had my fair share of stims already." She dabbed at the bandage again then gave it a gentle tug to reposition it. She looked deathly pale, and Cal could tell that she was putting a brave face on the pain. Unfortunately, there was little they could do until they made it back to the base.

"At least let me put a fresh bandage on," Couter persisted.

Again, Sinclair shook her head. "Might as well do it later." She looked up at them with a tight smile. "He stabbed me with a goddamned pick tool. You believe that? He even grinned at me as he shoved it in." She shrugged nonchalantly. "You think you know a guy…"

Cal wasn't fooled by the bravado; Sinclair had always been tough, but she'd obviously been through one hell of an ordeal, and she wasn't as young as she once was. There were cracks appearing in her resilient cast, and the physical toll was fast prizing them open. But there was also pain in her eyes that had nothing to do with her wounds.

"You know you had to kill him, don't you?" Cal said.

She looked at him as if he'd just thrown her a lifeline.

"If you hadn't, he would have killed me," Cal continued. "There's no doubt in my mind. And after that, God knows who else he might have attacked?"

Sinclair took some time before answering. "Possibly you're right. But I should've just knocked him out… I *meant* to just knock him out. I guess my blood was up."

"I think the Malloy we all knew would have thanked you for it," Cal said. "I doubt there would have been any returning from insanity like that. T-tech augs are too deeply ingrained. Once they go wrong… Malloy deserved better than to live an eternal nightmare."

Sinclair nodded and seemed to appreciate the words.

"Any contact with the powers that be?" Franco asked after a moment.

"There was no answer to our signal," Sinclair replied. "But that doesn't mean anything. The comm tech seemed extremely vulnerable to whatever it is this planet is dishing out."

Cal nodded, deciding that now wasn't the time to explain Ebner's findings on the tech issues. "The research team found the same. Sensor and communication tech went first, then the rest gradually followed suit. I'm actually astonished you managed to get the ship here."

"So am I," Sinclair admitted.

"I particularly liked the landing," Franco said.

"The landing gear was screwed. I thought I could rely on the belly thrusters to touch down, but they packed in shortly after I took off. I guided the ship here by varying the power of the rear thrusters and tweaking the stabilizers."

Franco chuckled. "Jesus, Sinclair. Pretty soon, you won't need a ship. You'll just start flapping those arms of yours."

"Trust me, it was mostly blind luck that I managed to crash so close to the base."

Cal managed a brief smile at that. *Luck built on a solid foundation of skill and ability,* he mused. Sinclair had always been modest. He looked up at Couter. "Okay, Private, that'll have to do," he said, putting an end to the young man's medic attempts. He stood up and was relieved to find that the stim's effects endured. "So let's try and rekindle some of that luck and get ourselves back to the base in one piece."

"Had no trouble getting here, sir," Couter pointed out.

"True, but best not get cocky."

"You want me to retrieve Malloy's body?" Franco asked. "Carry him back with us?"

Cal turned and looked toward the gap and the dark corridor beyond. "No," he said after some thought.

"You sure?"

"I'm sure, Corporal," Cal said without taking his eyes from the corridor. "Malloy is long gone from this place."

CHAPTER FIFTEEN

It had started to rain.

Only light drops but enough to bump Cal's adrenaline up a notch and make all four of them run that bit faster through the night. The fires from the crash had all but died out, and the clouds had thickened to the point that almost no moonlight penetrated. Cal had been forced to use glow-tubes but had only activated the chemicals to their dimmest setting. The decision was born out of necessity, but he still wasn't happy about it. The rain was sure to attract larger snakes out into the open. He didn't know how long it would take, but he wasn't about to hang around in a static, blue glow to find out.

The four of them moved as swiftly as possible. The muted, distant light emanating from the base made for a poor beacon compared to the earlier flames from the crash, but it was enough to stop them running in circles. Cal's head was throbbing a little, but the stim drug was proving lasting in its effect. They ran in a line, ten feet between each of them—close enough to offer aid if a problem occurred but not so close as to be falling over each other. His bolt rifle thrust before him, Franco led the way, Sinclair next, then Couter. Cal stayed at the rear, keen to keep an eye on Sinclair. He suspected that her wound was worse than she was letting on, but so far, she was managing to keep up.

They made it almost halfway before their luck ran dry.

A loud thump up ahead was quickly followed by a sharp curse. Cal squeezed his glow-tube a little harder, increasing its luminosity, and after a few paces found Franco flat on his back. Thankfully, the corporal was still moving and looked reassuringly pissed off. Cal swept the muzzle of the old bolt rifle around, his trigger finger poised as he searched for the attacker. Couter did likewise. For a time, nothing could be seen; then, a familiar noise sounded a short distance ahead. Max's cybernetic joints whirred softly as he emerged out of the darkness. The limp in his left leg had become worse, and his eyes seemed dimmer. He came to a halt a few paces in front of them and remained still and silent.

"You okay, Corporal?" Cal asked as he reached down to pull Franco to his feet.

"Yeah, armor took the worst of it. Hit me damn bloody hard though," Franco said as he retrieved his bolt rifle and directed it at Max.

"Hold up," Cal said as he pushed the muzzle downward. Max was clearly out of sorts, and he didn't want the big robot taking offense. Besides, pointing such a weapon at him was a futile exercise; it might as well have been a child's pea-shooter. "Max," he said tentatively. "You okay?"

Silence.

"Are you fully functional, Max?"

Silence.

The rain was becoming heavier, large drops that made plunking sounds as they struck Max's domed head and wide, armored shoulders. From what he could see in the dull light, Cal was sure the combat robot still had his water proofing seals activated. But, as Ebner had pointed out, that would probably do little more than slow the progress of his already malfunctioning systems.

Max gazed down at them blankly. Cal had always found those glowing eyes somehow endearing; now, they seemed a little intimidating. "Stand aside, Max. We're returning to the base."

As if frozen in time, Max made no move and said nothing.

"I need you to scout the area for me, Max," Cal said in an attempt to change tack.

It didn't work. Instead, the robot took two abrupt steps forward—the sound of his footfalls seeming horribly amplified in the darkness—and moved one of his great fists back to adopt a combat stance.

Recognizing the posture, all four of them took a step back.

"Okay, everyone stay calm," Cal said, doing his best to take his own advice. He briefly wondered what sort of effect the chem-bombs would have on Max. He suspected very little. He had personally witnessed the robot fight on when completely engulfed in flames, and there'd been almost no resulting damage. If Max decided to attack, they'd be like a group of children facing a raging bear.

Franco cursed again, quietly this time. "The gods must really be pissed at us today," he mumbled.

Cal wholeheartedly agreed. *First Malloy, now this.* And to top it off, he spotted his first snake: a small one that slithered past his foot. He ignored it and kept his attention on Max. "You don't want to hurt us, Max. We're your team…your friends. We look out for one another… We protect each other." Cal wasn't entirely sure that talking of friendship to a robot was going to be all that effective. Max's AI system was fairly advanced, but there were laws limiting AI capabilities, particularly when it came to emotional intelligence. Right at this moment, however, he could think of nothing else that might help. "Are you going to protect us, Max?"

The robot just stared at them, still unmoving except for his left hand, which had begun to twitch, the fingers fluttering in some sort of malfunctioning spasm. Another snake slithered past, a good deal larger this time. Max didn't shift an inch, the soft, blue light from the glow-tubes highlighting the multitude of rain drops trailing down his smooth chassis.

"Max, I—"

Cal's words were cut short as Max made another abrupt move forward. Now, he well and truly loomed over them, his stance still poised for destruction. Cal did his best not to appear fearful—not an easy thing when it was clear he'd been picked as the first target.

"*Sir.*" Couter shifted slightly beside him.

Cal slowly held up a hand. "It's okay, Private. Stand down. Max won't hurt me…will you, Max?" The next few seconds seemed to stretch into hours that were counted down by his thudding heart. Again, the robot remained completely still, but Cal suspected there was a great deal of confusion and conflict going on behind those round eyes.

"We're your team, Max."

More long seconds ticked by.

Then, Max stepped back.

Swiftly twisting to his left, the big robot brought his fist down and pounded it into the ground with shocking force. Then, he lifted it and repeated the action, harder this time. Then again, and again.

Cal breathed a slow, quiet sigh of relief. "Okay, go," he whispered.

Max didn't react as Couter, Franco, and Sinclair slowly stepped away. Instead, he continued to smash his great fist into the dirt as if a part of him was desperate not to hurt them—the loyal, dutiful side attempting to distract the savage, killer side.

Once the others had safely made it past, Cal followed. But only once he was a dozen steps away did he give the order to run. The rain had started to come down hard, and he suspected that very soon, Max would be the least of their problems.

CHAPTER SIXTEEN

Without slowing his pace, Cal brought the old bolt rifle up and shot the snake just behind the head. The shot wasn't fatal, but it stunned the beast enough for him to leap over its gaping jaws and continue his run. Ahead of him, Sinclair was struggling through the heavy rain. It was obvious now that her injury was rapidly eating away her strength. Cal caught up and forced her reluctant arm over his shoulders. She whispered something in his ear, her voice seeming as exhausted as her body. Cal couldn't decipher what she'd said, but he imagined it was along the lines of saving himself. He ignored the words and surged on, half hauling her as he went. More than anything, he wanted to scoop her up and carry her the rest of the way to the base, but to do so would compromise his ability to shoot. He couldn't risk it. More and more snakes of varying sizes were emerging from the darkness, the scales on their long, pale forms shimmering almost supernaturally as they met the bubble of blue light that emanated from the glow-tubes. Cal glimpsed one beast with a head as wide as his torso, armor and all. Franco and Couter were doing a good job keeping the majority at bay, dispensing round after round from their bolt rifles. But occasionally, a snake would slip past unscathed, and Cal was finding his reactions tested to the limit.

Sinclair suddenly slipped, and Cal almost went down himself in an attempt to right her. The deluge of rain was softening the mud beneath their feet. Yet again, he found himself cursing the malfunctioning tech. Normally, the soles of his Corrian armored boots would detect the slick terrain and activate hundreds of tiny smart-spikes that would thrust in and out, their lengths adjusting accordingly within a fraction of a second. With this function inert, the soles remained close to flat, and Cal suspected they'd have been better off with even the cheapest civi boots.

As he and Sinclair stumbled and slid in a battle to regain their pace, a snake burst out of the darkness to their left. Cal twisted and swung his rifle around with a curse. It wasn't the biggest he'd seen, but on this planet, that wasn't saying much. Trying to retain his footing, he unloaded three quick, clumsy shots that, more by luck than anything else, found their mark. The snake recoiled, swiftly disappearing into the black void. Gritting his teeth, Cal pulled Sinclair up and tried to gain a better positioning. She was leaning heavily on him, her feet starting to drag. Cal felt a cold anxiety creep into his gut; he knew better than anyone how tough Sinclair was and what it would take for her efforts to fail. Fortunately, they were almost at the base. There were lights up ahead, and as he peered through the gloom, he could see Orisho dispatching snakes with fierce precision, his sword little more than a blur. The entrance behind the veteran was closed, but Cal knew that Wilson would be on its other side, preventing snakes entering and waiting until they were closer before opening up.

They were almost at the entrance when Cal felt Sinclair go completely limp in his grip. Her dead weight slowed him to a halt. His chest heaving and limbs burning, he tried to lift her onto his shoulders but didn't even get close before he slipped again. He shouted out as he went down onto his knees, the sharp angles of his armor sinking deep into the soft mud. Couter was by his side in a second, almost going down himself as he skidded on the slick ground. Grasping Sinclair's other arm, he helped haul her up as best he could.

Suddenly, a large snake burst out of the shadows to their right, jaws wide, rows of lethal teeth ready to fulfill their one and only purpose. Cal barely had time to acknowledge the beast's presence before it jerked in midair and dropped in two lifeless halves to the ground. Orisho shouted something in Japanese that sounded like encouragement before lunging to meet another attacker. With an effort, Cal managed to get his feet back under him, and together, he and Couter bore Sinclair across the final strait to the base. Wilson had the door open, and they wasted no time crashing through it.

"Get us sealed in," Cal shouted over his shoulder as he and Couter left the others in their wake and headed for the stairwell.

"What the hell happened?" Becker asked as they entered the observation room.

"Get the med kit," Cal replied as he and Couter carried Sinclair into the room and placed her on the central table. He laid his hand on her neck and found her pulse; it was weak, but at least it was there. "Get her wounds checked and patched up, Private," he said to Couter as he looked about. Nothing had changed; the scavengers were still bound and slumped in the corner, and the three civilians were together on the other side of the room. Cal felt a small knot of tension leave him that he didn't even realize had been there—somewhere at the back of his mind, he'd half expected that his decision to leave Becker alone with the scavengers would have resulted in them dead at her feet. Or at the very least Durron. Fortunately, it seemed Becker had managed to control her burning hatred for the man.

"I can help with her," Campbell said as she broke from her group and approached Sinclair.

Cal nodded his appreciation. "Ebner, how does this rain compare to the last time?" he asked as he quickly moved over to the observation window.

"It's on a par," Ebner said as he reluctantly joined him. His pallid flesh looked paper thin, his expression drawn, and the tremble in his hands had grown worse. "Actually, it's possibly a touch heavier." He looked out of the window hesitantly, as if afraid of what he might see.

Understandable, Cal thought. At the moment, there was little to see when he peered directly out into the night; the clouds were still thick, and a torrent of rain fell in the featureless dark. But when he looked directly down, the remaining dim light of the base illuminated a multitude of snakes far below, appearing like distant wraiths swimming in an inky lake. There were so many he was astounded they'd made back alive.

"It won't be long now before the larger snakes come out," Ebner said. "Then, our fate will run on a knife's edge." He looked at Cal with eyes that seemed desperate to drive home the severity of their situation.

Cal held his gaze for a moment before turning back into the room. "Sergeant, deactivate some of these glowtubes; I don't want us lit up any more than we have to be."

Becker nodded and set about the task as Cal moved back to the center of the room to check on Sinclair. She was still unconscious. Campbell had stripped away the clothing around her wound as well as the bloodstained bandaging. Cal couldn't help but wince at the sight. Sinclair must've been running on adrenaline and pure force of will to have made it as far as she had. But she'd lost a lot of blood, and nobody was infallible.

Campbell looked at him. "I have no way of knowing the severity of her condition. But I can clean this wound and plug it up with a patch-gel. It should work as a temporary measure until we get her to a proper medical facility."

"Do it," Cal replied without hesitation. "And get a strong stim ready; I want her awake and ready to move if need be."

Campbell looked about to object, but the look on Cal's face changed her mind.

It wasn't long before Wilson, Orisho, and Franco joined them in the observation room. All three were breathing hard and covered with splatters of dark blue blood.

"Are we sealed in?" Cal asked.

Franco nodded.

"As far as we can tell, none of the bastards made it inside," Wilson said.

Cal nodded his approval. "Catch your breath, then I want you back down there to snuff out the last of the faulty lighting. I want the base in complete darkness bar this room." He looked at Couter. "Private, bring the shielding down to cover two thirds of that observation window. Open that panel on the far right; you should find a manual hand crank. Then, I want you keeping watch through the gap. You see anything moving out there is wider than me, feel free to make some noise." Cal turned to the rest of the team. "I want all of you triple-checking the rigidity of your weapons. We can't afford them failing us at a crucial time. Franco, get the weld-glue, and seal up any removable ceiling or floor panels. I want this room secure. If the base is breached, we make our stand here." He waited for any objections.

There were none.

CHAPTER SEVENTEEN

Cal joined Couter and Ebner in staring through the remaining gap of the observation window. Still the rain was coming down hard, and now that the base's remaining lighting had been extinguished, there was even less to see. The others were dotted around the room, relatively idle. Everything that could be done had been done, and now, there was nothing but waiting. Wilson dozed while Orisho sat nearby. Rarely did Cal see them both asleep at once. Becker remained on her feet, never moving far from the girl, Christie. Every now and then, the sergeant's eyes would flick in the direction of the bound scavengers as if concerned they might break their bonds—or perhaps hoping they would so she had another reason to do them damage. Franco was sitting upon a large crate, carving something in its top with his knife. Cal was encouraged by the stillness; every uneventful minute that ticked by was a minute closer to their rescue.

Climbing to his feet, Cal took a turn around the room.

Campbell had done a good job patching up Sinclair and had pulled a chair up to the table so she could remain by her side. Sinclair had yet to regain consciousness, but Cal had insisted that a stim was prepared and ready to go. Twice, he'd tried to talk to Campbell about the business regarding the drones, but she'd told him to forget it and that what was done was done. The tone of her voice, however, had fallen short of forgiving, and for that, Cal didn't blame her one bit. The results of his poor decision were continuing to mount up. He thought about trying to broach the subject again but decided against it and instead strolled to the other side of the room.

"You know you can't predict every outcome, Lieutenant."

Cal looked up to see that Orisho was now on his feet and was staring at him with those deep set eyes of his. The veteran had timed the statement as if he had the ability to read minds. *Or perhaps my thoughts were just plainly written on my face.*

"You don't say," Cal said a little more sarcastically than he'd intended.

"It's something you'll have to come to terms with," Orisho continued, ignoring the tone of the reply. "Something that can't be avoided if you're going to continue to lead a team."

"I'm fast learning that," Cal said. "But that's not what I'm struggling with."

Orisho raised a questioning eyebrow.

"The problem isn't that I failed to predict the

outcomes but that I ignored my conscience and continued to follow orders even though I knew them to be morally wrong. Not only that but my instincts were clearly telling me that the lives of the civilians were at serious risk."

Orisho stood silent for a time, seeming to mull over the words. Again, it occurred to Cal just how similar the two veterans were—although Orisho was a touch more approachable than Wilson and certainly quicker to laugh. Eventually, the big Japanese man nodded. "Perhaps you're right."

This answer surprised Cal, and the look on his face seemed to amuse the veteran.

"Nevertheless, you have to decide whether you want this role of leader, Cal," Orisho said. "And to shoulder all the inevitable crap that comes with it. There are going to be occasions when you might have to let your conscience slip away for a time. It's unfortunate, but it's inevitable…especially when you're under a piss-poor Captain."

Again, Cal found himself surprised.

"That's right; I said it," Orisho mumbled. "The man's a bloody idiot. You could of course refuse to deviate from your morals, but you can only bend or break orders so many times before you find yourself court martialed or worse—slung in a military prison."

Cal nodded. "I guess that's what it boils down to, isn't it?"

"I'm afraid it does," Orisho replied quietly.

Cal found himself wondering what compromises the

veteran had made himself over the years, particularly during the war.

"If it makes you feel any better," Orisho said after a moment, "Wilson and I would have opposed you had you tried to break orders before the first drone. And if that happened, the situation could have ended up a hell of a lot worse."

Cal was about to thank him for his honesty, but before he had the chance, the big man wandered off without another word.

"Everyone okay, sir?" Couter asked as Cal rejoined him and Ebner at the window.

"They're fine," Cal replied as he took a seat. The rain hadn't eased, and still, no moonlight penetrated the thick clouds.

"I was thinking that perhaps they won't come again," Couter said after a moment. "The big snakes I mean. Perhaps they're satisfied. They've already warned of their presence once; maybe they consider the job done."

"They'll come," Ebner replied quietly. "It took them a while to emerge before."

"And if they come," Cal said, "how long do you estimate it will take them to breach the base?"

"It took them no more than an hour last time. But that was when the base was intact. Most of our repairs are crude at best."

"Why do you think they attack the base?" Couter asked. "Why such aggression?"

Ebner considered for a moment before answering. "Perhaps we can't blame them. Think of this base as a foreign body suddenly appearing within their ecosystem. Maybe that's all the motivation they need. They're acting like an immune response on a huge, planetary scale." Ebner shot them a humorless smile. "Uncannily apt, don't you think? Even *we've* likened ourselves to a destructive cancer on occasion…eating away at a planet's resources and giving nothing back in return." Ebner stared silently out of the window for a time before continuing. "You know, part of me suspects that the rain somehow stimulates the snakes. We know that the moisture helps to keep them cool, but possibly, there's more to it than that. It's feasible that these tech-disrupting particles are created up in the atmosphere, within the clouds. I'm no meteorologist, but the theory seems possible… Perhaps this charge also has an effect on the snakes' physiology, particularly when it rains."

"How would that work?" Couter asked.

"I really don't know," Ebner admitted. "But we know that negative and positive ions can have an effect on human physiology—the uptake of oxygen and influences on our serotonin levels for example—so it's not inconceivable that these snakes are being affected in a similar way or possibly in a far stronger way."

"You mean making them more aggressive?" Couter suggested.

Ebner nodded. "Perhaps with purpose. I might go as far to speculate that the snake's evolution was greatly influenced by this relationship; the increased aggression resulting from the rain fall is a necessary reaction to encourage them to hunt and feed during the limited time that the ground is cooled sufficiently. I've no shred of evidence, you understand, and none of this is provable in our current situation." Ebner turned to them with a brief smile. "Not that proving it would help in any case. After all, we can't stop it raining! But it can be interesting to theorize, don't you think? It diverts the mind from all the...well, it simply diverts it."

Cal felt for the old man. A drawn-out wait for a horror that you were sure was coming was worse in many ways than staring it in the face. "How long since you had any sleep?"

The doctor looked up and offered him another brief smile. "You know, I have no idea. But I don't think I could. Not now."

Cal nodded his understanding; he wasn't about to order someone to try and sleep. "How about you, Couter, how you holding up?"

"Just fine, sir," Couter replied, keeping his eyes fixed on the outside darkness. "I've been pondering whether they'll ever manage to colonize this planet...with the technology problems I mean."

Cal shrugged. "I kind of hope they don't. It would be nice if not every corner of our little area of space is colonized. I've always liked the idea that there's still wild, untamed planets left. Makes for a more interesting universe."

"I guess so."

Cal stared out the hammering rain, lost in thought. "You know, I wasn't happy when I received the brief for this mission," he said quietly. "But I can't deny that there was a touch of excitement…anticipation."

"I can understand that," Couter said with a smile.

"Of course you can. You're new to the game; everything's exciting! But for me, coming somewhere like this, somewhere new and untouched, makes me feel like an explorer. Like an adventurer of old."

Couter chuckled.

"Laugh it up, Private. You might feel the same way some day. Once the thrill of soldiering wears a little thin. You might just get fed up of shooting things and dealing with idiots like those scavengers over there."

"Someone's got to do it."

"That's true," Cal replied. "Don't get me wrong; I'm glad for the opportunities I get to help people, but sometimes, that selfish side pokes through, that inner kid who just wants pure adventure without protocols and agendas." *And bullshit orders.*

"I doubt my mother would approve of that."

"You never know," Cal said. "Obviously, you know her far better than me, but there can be a lot going on inside a person's head that perhaps even family aren't privy to. For all you know, the great Captain Maria Coots might have a secret desire to be a sculptor or a pro spike ball player."

"Perhaps you're right," Couter conceded with another soft chuckle. "I wonder what she'll think of her son's first mission."

"Well, you can tell her that your commanding officer's

decided to keep you."

"Why thank you, sir," Couter replied, still without turning from the window. "I appreciate that. In return, I'll be sure to get you a signed holo poster of her."

"See that you do."

Couter grinned.

"I mean it," Cal said. "And not one of those cheap factory knock-offs. An original, and I want it signed personally."

"It seems I've been sleeping on the job," Sinclair said as she looked up at Cal. She tried to sit up, but Campbell quickly laid a hand on her arm, putting a stop to the effort.

"You mustn't move," Campbell said. "You've lost a lot of blood from the stab wound."

"How're you feeling?" Cal asked.

"To be honest, everything feels pretty numb," Sinclair replied.

"Well, your chest is black and blue," Campbell informed her. "I suspect you hit it hard during the crash. I've no way of knowing what internal damage is done, so I strongly suggest you don't move."

"Sure, I'll try to be a good girl," Sinclair said with a wry smile. "I appreciate the patch up."

Her expression as stern as ever, Campbell nodded and walked away to rejoin her young colleague.

"Sorry, Cal," Sinclair said quietly. "It seems I've made a bit of a mess of myself."

"Considering what you've just been through, I'd say you're looking damn good."

"Sorry you had to drag me in here."

Cal shook his head, eyebrows raised. "And how many times did you have to drag me around back in the Academy? I'm not sure I'd have made it through that first year if it wasn't for you."

Sinclair tried to laugh, but her broken body quickly put an end to it. "Bullshit," she said once she was able. "You were the best in my class…the best in the year. And not just when it came to piloting. That mentor on Mars already had you well-primed before—" Sinclair's words turned into a wince and then a cough.

"Okay, that's enough speaking for you," Cal said, setting his hand on her shoulder. "Our rescue will be here in a matter of hours, and I need you well-rested. I want you on that ship without having to be dragged."

Sinclair smiled. There was no fear in it, but it was laced with sadness. "I'm not sure a bit of a rest is going to do it this time."

"Now who's talking bullshit."

Sinclair put her hand on his. "It's okay, Cal. I never did fancy dying of old age in a comfortable bed."

Cal felt the words twisting his heart, but he did his best to keep his expression optimistic and light. "Well, I'm quite keen on the idea," he replied quickly. "So I need you to rest and recover. That's an order."

Sinclair smiled again. "You always were a stubborn one."

Having finally persuaded Sinclair to rest, Cal continued to walk around the room, a strange feeling that his movements could somehow miraculously speed up the passing minutes. He paused at the observation window for a time. The rain had started to ease, and some of the clouds were thinning, allowing little bursts of moonlight to shine through. He could see snakes, *a lot* of snakes, but none appeared monstrous enough to tear apart metal. As he stared down at them, he allowed himself the thought that they might just make it through the night without trouble. Perhaps a dangerous thought, but he couldn't help himself. He glanced at Ebner. Unfortunately, the look on the older man's face suggested he didn't share in his optimism.

"I'm going to get some sleep, Private," Cal said, resting a hand on Couter's shoulder. "Wake me in half an hour; then, I'll take over the watch."

Couter nodded and checked his data pad. Then, he shook his head at the blank screen. "I keep forgetting it's screwed."

Cal shot him a small smile. "*Roughly* half an hour will do."

Moving back to the central table, Cal pulled up a chair and made himself comfortable. Despite Ebner's expression lingering at the forefront of his mind, he tried his best to hold onto his optimism. No matter how grim the situation, it was always a good mindset for an effective leader. *People follow warriors, not worriers.* That had been a favorite quote of Sinclair's, which she'd fired relentlessly at her new piloting recruits. *Optimism is the forger of steel... It keeps ships in the air.* That had been another. Ever the eager young man, Cal had soaked up every word she'd uttered and had done his best to stick to them ever since. They'd already paid enough of a price on this mission; it was time for a bit of luck to come their way.

Resting his head on the table, he closed his eyes. Sleep came quickly, but it also came with visions of gaping maws, teeth, and shimmering scales, ghostly white in the darkness. Then came the feeling of being crushed. He slept on and, as he did when awake, did his best to fight the fear.

"I see something moving...something big."

The words seeped into Cal's brain slowly, like butter melting into warm bread. He knew the voice to be Couter's, but despite the urgency of the tone, he struggled for a moment to rouse himself. Those stim drugs could work wonders, but the lingering side effects could be a bitch.

"Something's definitely out there."

Cal forced his eyes open.

"And it's really damn big."

Rising from his chair as swiftly as he could manage, Cal ran to the observation window. Leaning forward, he peered through the glass. He could hear weapons being snatched up as the rest of his team came to join him. The rain had all but stopped now, and bright moonlight was pouring through gaps in the patchy clouds. Couter was right; the new light had revealed something slowly moving in the distance. It was impossible to judge the creature's exact size, but one thing was clear; it was a monster in the true sense of the word.

CHAPTER EIGHTEEN

"There's another to the east," Couter said. "Smaller, but still huge."

Cal spotted it: a ghostly apparition coiling out of the distant forest like a giant serpent of myth.

"And there," Orisho pointed, "another one."

"Christ, Ebner," Franco said, briefly turning to the old man. "You really weren't exaggerating when you said they were big."

"Wait," Ebner said quietly.

Cal turned to look at him; he was staring out of the window, his eyes dark but his face as white as marble.

"That lake in the distance."

All of them stared through the thick glass, fixing their gaze on the lake in question. The moonlight was reflecting brightly off its rippling surface. For a moment, nothing happened. Then, like leviathans straight out of a sea captain's nightmare, two huge, pale shapes began to emerge from its depths. Cal knew that they too were snakes, but at the same time, he couldn't quite believe it.

"*My God*," Orisho whispered.

Cal glanced at the veteran. Hearing a soldier of his experience react in such a way really seemed to drive home the nightmare they were facing.

"They're turning towards us," Franco said after a time. "They're heading this way?"

Cal nodded, feeling his jaw tighten. The corporal was right. The beasts were slow in their movements, but it seemed a pace set by the certainty of dominance rather than a lack of ability. Cal again did his best to judge their size. It wasn't easy from this distance, but he guessed the two largest creatures were close to fifteen feet wide and over a hundred feet in length. He'd faced more than his fair share of predators of similar proportions but never without some form of pulse rifle or energy weapon. He cursed and didn't bother to keep it quiet. "Okay, they could be on us in a few minutes. Couter, get the shielding fully closed." He turned back into the room to see that Ebner had rejoined his colleagues. The three of them looked terrified. He didn't blame them one bit. They knew better than anyone what was drawing near, and he suspected that being on the cusp of a rescue was making this deathly approach all the worse. Ebner looked as though he was caught between disbelief and denial. The girl, Christie, rocked back and forth, hands clenched tight. Of the three, it was Campbell who, although clearly afraid, seemed to be retaining a semblance of composure.

"Campbell, I want Sinclair awake. Use as much stim as

it takes."

Campbell shot him a hard look, clearly angry and disapproving of his insistence.

Good, he thought, *let her be angry.* It was better than fear. Cal stared her down. "Do it. I want her conscious and mobile."

Reluctantly, the woman lowered her gaze and moved toward Sinclair.

"Ebner… *Ebner.*" Cal had to shout the man's name to snap him out of his growing state of terror. "Where did the last breach happen?" Cal already knew the answer, but he wanted the older man thinking and alert.

"The east…the ground level of the east wing," Ebner replied, his voice distant.

Cal walked up to him and grasped him by the shoulders. "And if they breach the base at the same spot now that it's weakened, at which point do you think the snakes will come at this room?"

Ebner shook his head and stared distractedly past him toward Couter, who was cranking the last portion of the shield down over the window. "It won't do any good. They'll hear us. They'll taste us in the air." He looked back to Cal, shaking his head. "They'll sense our movements, even the vibrations of our hearts. I can't do it again. I can't go through it again."

Cal firmly squeezed his shoulders. "You can, and you *will.*" He snatched up the older man's chem-bomb that he'd left on the table and pushed it into his trembling hand. "We're going to survive this. Help is on its way, but you need to fight for as long as it takes." He nodded toward Christie, who was sitting beside them. The young woman was still deathly pale, her wide eyes staring at nothing. "Your colleague needs you, Ebner. It's your duty to protect her."

Ebner glanced down at Christie before managing a small nod. "Yes…" he said eventually. "Yes… I'll do my best."

Cal smiled. "That's good. That's all I'm asking." He turned to see that Campbell was standing in the center of the room, idly watching them. "The stim, Doctor." He tried not to shout the words, but he was fast losing patience. "Quickly, we're running out of time."

Campbell shook her head.

Christ, don't tell me she's losing it too. "Do it. I need Sinclair up on her feet. No matter what it takes."

Campbell shook her head again. "I can't."

Cal walked toward her, feeling his temper rising. "Why not?"

"Because, Lieutenant," Campbell replied, her tone firm, "the stim drugs are effective, but I'm afraid they're not capable of resurrecting the dead."

Cal stopped in his tracks, his anger instantly draining out of him.

Campbell's eyes lost their hard edge as he moved past her to lay his hand on Sinclair's neck. It wasn't that he didn't believe the woman but more that he didn't *want* to. There was no pulse, and the skin on Sinclair's neck already felt cold, entirely lifeless. Cal's legs weakened, and he had to grasp the edge of the table to right himself. He felt as though someone had seized his heart and was crushing it. As he stared at Sinclair's pale face, it took everything he had not to try resuscitating her. Even if he succeeded, what hope would she have surviving what was soon to come? He looked over her broken form, his jaw locked tight as if in spasm. He'd always reacted to loss with anger—the sorrow came later, finding a way in once the rage had passed.

Gripping the table hard, he took a deep breath and tried to calm himself. Sinclair had guided him through much of his young life, protected him at times when no one else would—perhaps the closest thing he'd had to a mother. But she'd also spent years teaching him to be strong, to keep a cool head and find focus amid pain and chaos. He wouldn't let her down, not now. Taking another slow breath, he leaned forward, kissed her once on the forehead, then straightened up and did his best to steel himself. There was a room full of people, some of whom trusted him implicitly and looked to him as their leader and others who needed nothing more than a protector.

"Wilson, Orisho," he said, glancing at the two men, "lay Sinclair in one of the crates. I want her body protected for a later retrieval." He took one last look at his mentor before stepping back and allowing the two veterans to get to work. With a glance to confirm that Couter had the shield fully closed, he turned to the others in the room. "Okay, I want everyone as silent and—"

"*Lieutenant… Lieutenant Harper.* I wish to converse

with you."

The words traveled across the room like acid in the wind. As he turned to look at Durron, Cal felt his anger instantly boil up again, but this time, it was an entirely different kind—one without pain, one that he could use. Pushing aside the urge to unleash Becker on the man, Cal swiftly approached him. The expression on Durron's face caused a surge of darkness, but he refrained from knocking him out cold with his boot. "Your mouth is going to get us all killed," he said quietly and with as much calm as he could muster. "If you don't shut it, I'll have no choice but to snap your neck." He wanted so much to give into the rage, to snuff the man out of existence; the universe would be all the better for it. But as always, the faces of those who'd trained him, who'd shaped him into the man he was, shined a light on the darkness.

"I understand your concern, Lieutenant," Durron hissed back. He struggled to sit up and failed miserably. "But I insist you cut my bonds. If those creatures get in, you know as well as I do that I won't stand a chance. It would be as good as murder."

"What about *us*, you bastard," Pryce growled next to him. "Me and Billy."

"I meant all of us, you fool," Durron spat.

Cal stood over them, letting the anger burn inside him, allowing it to fuel him but not control him. His choice was simple: to give these poor excuses for human beings a fighting chance or allow them to die. It pained him to admit it, but as despicable as they were, he didn't want their deaths on his hands. "Sergeant."

As if waiting for her cue, Becker appeared by his side, spear in hand.

"I'm going to cut you free," Cal said in hushed tones, his eyes shifting between the three men. "Any one of you does anything remotely out of the ordinary, either myself or my sergeant will end you. As you've already witnessed, she's not one to hesitate, particularly over the likes of you." Kneeling down, he pulled out his knife and began cutting the bonds.

A sly smile appeared on Durron's swollen face.

Having cut the bonds, Cal put the knife away before he lost his cool. He stood and turned to Becker. "I won't lose any sleep if you kill them by accident," he told her, saying it loud enough for all three scavengers to hear.

Durron's smile faltered a little.

"Are you sure, boss? You know how clumsy I've been of late," Becker said, her eyes cold as she looked down at Durron.

"Completely sure," Cal replied.

Durron scoffed, but his smile had disappeared completely.

CHAPTER NINETEEN

There was a horrendous boom.

Then another. Worse this time. Forceful enough to make the floor of the observation deck shudder beneath them and reverberate up their spines. All, bar the girl Christie, were on their feet. Even Poots was now upright—with help, she'd managed to refit her armor over her injured leg, but she still couldn't put any real weight on it. Holding his bolt rifle in his right hand, Cal held out his left in a gesture of calm, hoping it would encourage everyone to stay still and quiet. In truth, he doubted they needed it—there was something about having predators the size of hovertrains knocking on your door that encouraged silence all on its own.

Another sickening boom quickly followed by a couple of smaller ones. Then a grinding vibration that seemed to go on for minutes but was likely just seconds. Cal tried to pinpoint where the giant beasts were attempting to breach the base, but it was proving a near impossible task. The noise seemed to come from everywhere but nowhere, as if the gods were hammering on the roof while the devil simultaneously tunneled up from beneath.

There was silence for a time, but it was far from comforting. Cal looked at his team spread out in the dim, blue light around him. Unlike the civilians, they all appeared calm and composed, but he suspected their hearts were thundering against their ribs just as intensely as his own. No amount of training could prevent that nor should it. On this particular occasion, however, Cal had to wonder whether their pounding pulses might actually be giving them away. There'd been little doubt in Ebner's tone when he'd said the creatures could sense even those vibrations.

Another boom.

Then more silence.

Strangely, the quiet seemed more disturbing than the noise. It was one thing not being able to see a monster seeking you out, but to not hear it either…

But the grinding vibration soon started again, longer and louder this time as if drawing close. Cal continued to look at the others in the room. The glow-tubes offered just enough light to reveal that all eyes were on him: his team watching diligently for orders while Ebner and Campbell stared at him as if he might be able to simply beam them up if it all got a bit too desperate. Even Christie seemed to be looking in his direction as she rocked back and forth. The light, however, wasn't good enough to judge whether she was actually aware of him and seeking some sort of reassurance or simply staring straight through him in her catatonic stupor.

Another boom was quickly followed by a low rumble. The noise seemed to ebb and flow, fraying their nerves like ropes being rubbed against sharp rocks. Cal breathed steadily and turned his attentions to the scavengers. They too were on their feet. Pryce and Billy looked ready to run, but the fact there was nowhere to run to was causing a great deal of anxiety. Durron showed no such emotion. It was as if the snakes didn't exist to him. Instead, all his focus was on the man who had ruined his plans and disturbed his neat little band of morons over which he'd ruled supreme. He stared through the dim, blue light at Cal with spite practically dripping from his eyes. This time, Cal suspected it wasn't an act. Perhaps he should have let Becker finish the job or done it himself.

The booming noises restarted. Becoming louder like depth charges closing in on their mark. Then, an almighty crash was followed by a deafening screech—the sound of huge, metal struts being twisted and churned against each other. The din continued for some time. Then, part of the base ruptured like a tendon snapping in a leg. Cal felt the floor shudder for the briefest of moments before dropping out from beneath them. It didn't go far, but it was enough to send them all stumbling. As they struggled to regain their footing, the cacophony once again simmered.

But there was no silence.

The approaching mayhem had finally pushed Christie over the edge. The girl had spilled from her chair and was balled up on the floor, crying and muttering softly. Her words were indecipherable, but their meaning was clear. She wanted it to stop. She wanted to be swept away from the horror. She wanted to be anywhere but here even if it meant death.

Cal moved swiftly toward her, but Becker got there first. Slinging her makeshift spear over her back, the sergeant wrapped one arm around the girl's waist, pulled her from the floor, and placed a gentle but firm hand over her mouth. Much to the relief of all those in the room, Becker's actions instantly reverted the girl back into her mute state. She didn't struggle or even attempt a muffled cry. Instead, she became still in the embrace as if suddenly blessed by an immunity from all that could do her harm—a small miracle that Cal hoped to God lasted. With impressive stealth, Couter took up a protective position next to Becker. Cal smiled inwardly, the thought repeating in his mind that the young man would do well on his team.

The minutes of silence that followed seemed to stretch on as if warped by some cruel anomaly created to test their resolve. Then, Cal felt a subtle shift of the floor accompanied by a sinister creaking. It was slow and muted at first then steadily grew in intensity. It was as if the metal bubble in which they were cocooned was slipping into a deep abyss, the escalating noise like a gauge counting down the moments until the building pressure crushed them in the blink of an eye.

Cal looked up. For the first time, he managed to

pinpoint the source of at least some of the sound. The wide struts directly above them were bending inwards and groaning in protest, metal grinding against metal. Then, the ceiling started to buckle. Feeling every muscle tense, he readied himself to run and dive clear should the worst happen. He had no doubt the others were doing the same. The floor slowly began to tilt. Praying that the rigidity of the base would hold out, Cal adjusted his footing and looked for something to hold onto. Then, the buckling eased, and the entire room rose up again as if spring-loaded.

Cal checked to see that none of the civilians were about to burst into a panicked run. He'd seen it all too often in situations like this—even in trained soldiers. The tension becoming too much and causing something in the mind to snap and demand action—any kind of action, anything to bring the waiting to an end, a resolution whether good or bad. Fortunately, Ebner and Campbell's expressions hadn't changed. There was still intense fear, but it was no worse than it had been previously. Cal was confident they'd hold it together. Weirdly, Christie now looked the calmest of the three. Remaining completely still in Becker's hold, her expression was one of pure exhaustion. Cal looked toward the scavengers. Durron had lost interest in him and was staring at the buckled ceiling, perhaps finally accepting the fact that there was something outside more worthy of his attentions. Pryce was doing the same, his bulbous eyes seeming in danger of abandoning their sockets.

Then there was Billy. The young addict's earlier indulging of the dreamwitch was clearly still causing him problems. He was staring dead ahead, breaths fast and ragged, profuse sweat beading across his face. Cal gritted his teeth and managed to hold back a cascade of curses. Billy was an expanding balloon of panic that was about to burst. Cal briefly berated himself for not remaining closer to the scavengers; if necessary, he could have rendered Billy unconscious. He thought about trying to alert Durron or Pryce to the worsening state of their skittish young companion, but based on the limited time he'd already spent in their company, he guessed their response would either be one of indifference or a complete overreaction that could make matters infinitely worse.

Fortunately, Cal was saved from having to make the decision.

Unfortunately, the intervention came in the form of chaos.

A sudden, sickening crack rent the air as if from a thousand lightning strikes. The room abruptly contorted, jostling every one of them off their feet to hit the floor hard. It was entirely likely that Billy had cried out in that moment—and he probably wouldn't have been alone—but the ear-splitting noise of the crack and the ensuing twisting and tearing of metal would have drowned out even the loudest of screams. Despite the room still shuddering and tipping, Cal managed to grasp a leg of one of the fixed tables and pulled himself to his knees. Sweeping his head around, he tried to assess what was happening and *where* the hell it was happening. At the far end of the room, the solid metal doors leading to the eastern corridor began to warp and crumple as if constructed from paper. A fissure appeared between them like the eye of a giant demon, rapidly widening to reveal the pitch black corridor beyond. Cal held on tight, his eyes fixed on that blackness, praying that no pale shapes would penetrate it.

None did, and eventually, the boiling chaos simmered to another still calm.

Cal looked to Becker. Although now on the floor, she still had a hold of Christie, who lay as motionless as a child's doll. Cal would have thought the girl asleep were it not for her wide, fearful eyes. Slowly twisting around, he looked back at Billy. The young man still looked like a potential flight risk, but Pryce had obviously noticed it too and was carefully crawling toward him. Cal wasn't entirely sure that stealth was going to do them much good at this point, but it certainly couldn't make their situation worse. He watched as Pryce looped his arm around his skinny young friend's neck and restrained him. Unlike Becker's firm but tender hold of Christie, Pryce went for an altogether rougher approach—more of a headlock than an embrace. Satisfied that the young scavenger wasn't about to put up a fight or start squealing, Cal once again fixed his gaze on the torn-open doorway at the far end of the room. As far as he could make out, it was the one and only breach into their little cocoon.

The corridor beyond was still black, still lifeless, but a

feeling descended on Cal that was cold and all-encompassing. A silent promise that poured out of the dark, assuring him that they wouldn't be alone for much longer. His bolt rifle gripped tightly in one hand, he reached over his shoulder to the spear-like weapon that was strapped to his back. He touched it once, more to reassure himself that it was still there than anything else, then used hand signals to guide everyone further back into the room, away from the skewed doorway. As they retreated, he laid his free hand on the chem-bomb at his hip and hooked his finger into the pin. He thought about activating it, throwing it at the foot of the breach. But what if the feeling that was tugging at his gut was just paranoia? What if nothing was approaching through the dark corridor? Maybe it was only an internal breach. Maybe the exterior shell of the base was still holding out. Then, the bomb would have been wasted, and they weren't exactly in ample supply. Not only that but the noise would well and truly announce their presence. He retracted his finger but kept his hand near the bomb.

As they continued to back up, Orisho and Wilson moved to the front of the group, swords gleaming, almost like some sort of energy weapons in the blue light. Franco moved a few paces behind them, bolt rifle leveled. Poots shuffled back with Campbell and Ebner's help, the scavenger's old pistol tight in her grip. Couter remained close to Becker while she practically dragged Christie. The girl's legs were moving, but they were weak and uncoordinated. Cal moved out to the side of the group; he wanted to cover his team as well as keep an eye on Durron and his cronies. Maybe he should have locked them in a separate room, let them fend for themselves. But it was too late for that now.

A loud thud sounded to Cal's right. With a pulse of adrenaline, he whipped his rifle around and almost let off a couple of reactionary shots. Fortunately, his training prevented what would have been a waste of ammo. A large dent had appeared in the center of the doors that led to the stairwell.

Thump. Thump.

The dent became larger.

Cal quickly retreated from the doors and used hand signals to guide everyone to the corner of the room.

Thump. Thump.

The sound echoed around the room as if it too was searching them out.

Christ. This visitor obviously wasn't the biggest of the brutes they'd seen approaching the base, but still, Cal didn't like to think of the creature that could do damage like that. It seemed that the hiding game was well a truly over. Something wanted in, and with the force it was demonstrating, it was going to get its wish.

Thump. Thump. Thump.

Cal detached the chem-bomb from his hip and signaled to the others to let them know he was pulling the pin. If the explosive heated the door sufficiently, it might discourage the creature. Silently, he began to count down the long detonation. *Fifty seconds.*

Thump. Thump. Thump.
Forty seconds.
Thump. Thump.
Twenty-five.

It was at eleven seconds that it all went wrong.

Having picked his spot, Cal was about to toss the explosive when a shriek pierced the air behind him. It seemed the sinister thumping had become too much for Billy's drug-addled mind. Cal turned to see that the young scavenger had wriggled out of Pryce's hold and was already stumbling away from him, straight toward the twisted breach at the far end of the room.

Trying his best to intercept him, Cal leaped back, dropped low, and spun, sweeping the fleeing man's legs out from under him. The move was effective, but it also caused him to fumble his hold on the chem-bomb. The little glass explosive bounced a few times before rolling away. Without waiting to see if Billy was going to get up again, Cal dove at the bomb and managed to give it a little push with his outstretched fingers.

The blast wasn't loud, but the sudden, yellow blaze was blinding in the near dark. Shielding his eyes from the worst of the glare, Cal was relieved to see that the detonation had occurred almost at the base of the dented door, the flames already licking up its side. There was a drawn-out pause as they all listened for continued thumping. None came, so Cal decided it was worth almost burning his face off for.

Rolling to his feet, Cal saw Billy demonstrating a

desperate scramble, his long limbs giving him the appearance of some strange insect. Hysterical words were spilling from his mouth. "Can't do it, can't do it, can't, can't, can't…"

Orisho took a single step in the young scavenger's direction, but with a glance at the dark, mangled breach at the far end of the room, he stopped. For a moment, Cal thought that his big teammate might run forward and chop the scavenger in two. But he moved back again, seeming to decide that the man wasn't worth the effort.

Billy's life was spared—at least for few moments.

CHAPTER TWENTY

Managing to find his feet, Billy rushed at the dark breach at the end of the room like it was his salvation. He didn't slow for a second, just burst through the gap as if en route to a haven of pure, incorruptible safety. The darkness swallowed him in an instant. Cal cursed the man's foolishness; he'd stewed his brain, and now, it seemed they were all to pay the price. With a steady breath, he leveled his rifle at the gap, which seemed to yawn back at him like the mouth of some giant ghoul. For a few seconds, there was nothing to be seen and nothing to be heard other than the popping of the little chemical inferno to his right.

Then, Billy cried out from the blackness, the sound cutting a sharp path through the gloom.

An eerie echo followed.

Then another cry, muffled this time and trailed by a high-pitched gurgling sound.

Then silence.

The first snake burst through the gap like a seeker

missile turned flesh. It was smaller than some they'd seen but larger than most. Cal shot it twice in the head, sending it into a contorted frenzy. Trained as they were, the whole team kept their eyes on the gap, not allowing the writhing snake to disrupt their focus.

A distant sound began to tumble through the gap: a strange, rough thrum that rapidly built in intensity.

Then they came, emerging from the black like a surging reptilian army. All had the same glassy, white scales, making them glimmer in the artificial light like creatures of the deep. But their proportions were not so uniform—some were no thicker than a wrist, but others appeared large enough to swallow a human whole.

Bolt rifles erupted into a popping tumult. Swords flashing, Orisho and Wilson roared battle cries. Usually more of a silent fighter, Cal joined his friends in making his presence known, unleashing his primal voice as well as round after round from his weapon—a welcome din after all that forced silence. One of the chem-bombs ignited in the center of the room, causing chaos among the attacking beasts. Cal didn't see who threw it, but he mentally saluted their aim. Many of the snakes burst into writhing balls of flame, and those that escaped recoiled, some attacking each other as they retreated from the heat. The bomb was proving as effective as Ebner had promised. But through the flames, Cal could see more of the creatures entering the room…a lot more.

Without removing his eye from his rifle's sights, Cal began moving carefully to his left, putting himself in front of the civilians. "Back up toward the western door," he shouted, barely pausing with his shots. Having learned marksmanship from a young age with a similar old-fashioned weapon, he wielded the bolt rifle with ease, each shot finding its mark. Some of the larger snakes, however, took the hits with little more than a brief recoil, their heightened aggression overwhelming any injury.

Fortunately, the attacking beasts didn't prove so resilient to the veterans' swords. The two men cleaved a circle of destruction around them, blue blood arching and spiraling through the air. Pale, scaly flesh pitching this way and that as it came apart to land twitching on the floor. But the snakes were countless now, legions of them swarming into the far end of the room. Another bomb went off, once again lighting up the room like a flare. Some of the beasts began evading Orisho and Wilson's defense. A large one came at Cal. He shot it three times before it died. Another passed him on his left. He twisted, rifle poised, but Couter was already there, stopping it with two fast, efficient shots. Confident in his new recruit's abilities, Cal took a second to assess their situation. Ebner, Campbell, and the two remaining scavengers were pressed into to corner of the room, their recent past seeming forgotten as the overwhelming threat closed in. All of the spite had left Durron's face and was completely smothered by cold, all-consuming fear.

Dispatching a relatively small attacker with a single shot, Cal looked up to see Becker practically toss Christie at Campbell. Spinning the make-shift spear once in her grip, she thrust it at a snake that seemed to have burst out of nowhere to attach itself to Couter's armored leg. Behind them, Poots used the old pistol to shoot two more with careful, considered aim. With no time to observe the outcome of these fights, Cal turned back into the room and almost fell into a trance as he fired shot after shot, reloading the old rifle with swift efficiency. Before long, the rifle's last mag ran dry. Without missing a beat, he threw the weapon aside and reached over his shoulder to seize his spear. Barely a second passed before he found himself having to swing it at another snake…then another. Trying his best to retain his defense, he continued to sweep his eyes over the chaos, attempting to put some order to it. Another bomb went off. *Five left,* he thought grimly. The explosive was well-thrown, and the collective heat of the burning chemicals was effectively keeping most of the writhing mass at bay. But heat wasn't the only thing being emitted; acrid fumes were fast filling the air and assaulting the senses. Cal could feel his eyes beginning to sting, tears fast turning the room into a blur.

Hoping it wasn't a trick of his failing vision, Cal allowed himself the hope that the number of snakes was diminishing. Moving forward to gain a better view, he saw that many of the creatures were abandoning the attack and retreating from the flames back through the twisted breach. But how long would the heat last? Glancing to his right, he saw that the intense chemical burn from his own bomb had already dwindled to a small spattering of lazy flames.

Wiping his eyes, he quickly joined Franco and jerked his head toward the western door. "Corporal, get that door unlocked." The fumes were starting to attack his throat, and the order came out more as a loud rasp than the shout he'd intended. "And save the rest of your ammo; we might need it later."

Slinging his rifle over his back, Franco nodded his understanding and backed up toward the door.

"Orisho, Wilson, fall back." Cal made the order as loud as he could while doing his best not to fall into a coughing fit. Then, he took his own advice and backed up. Slowly, the two veterans followed him. Both were breathing hard but still managing to defend against those beasts consumed with enough bloodlust to endure the heat. Cal glanced back. Franco was already working on the exit's pneumatic locks. The civilians were huddled next to him while Couter, Poots, and Becker stood facing outward, guarding them like lions protecting a pride.

Slinging his spear over his shoulder, Cal moved between them. "Ebner, Campbell, tear up some fabric for our mouths." Without waiting for an acknowledgement, he took hold of the door handle. "Pryce, make yourself useful, and grab that other handle."

Pryce didn't move. He just stared dumbly at the door with those bug eyes of his.

Durron hissed something at him and shoved him out of the way to grab the handle himself. He glared at Cal but appeared willing and ready.

"Let us know when, Corporal," Cal said as he braced

himself. The doors were heavy, designed motorized power, and took a fair bit of mus

"Ten seconds," Franco shouted.

"Just a few inches at first," Cal said t need to see what's going on before we burst through."

Durron didn't bother acknowledging the words, and Cal resisted the urge to plant his elbow in the man's face.

Some of the others had begun to cough. Cal could sympathize. His own throat felt like he'd swallowed an active plasma torch. Tears were streaming from his eyes, but he kept his blurry vision on the handle. He could hear blades swishing through the air, dull thuds sounding as they met flesh. Assuming their eyes were suffering like his own, Cal suspected that Orisho's and Wilson's strikes must be increasingly reliant on luck.

There was a clunk followed by an urgent hiss.

"*We're in,*" Franco shouted, his voice raw. "*Pull.*"

Cal heaved, and Durron grunted with effort as he did the same. A small wave of relief hit Cal as the doors began to move. He'd half expected the battering of the base to have left them jammed. "Okay, enough," he shouted to Durron. Without letting go of the handle, he quickly leaned forward to peer through the gap. An instant later, his heart almost breached his chest as a set of jaws slammed against the separated metal just inches from his face. The snake was definitely eager for a taste, and despite his blurry vision, Cal caught a glimpse of countless others waiting in line. "*Close it,*" he shouted, his arms straining as he desperately tried to push the doors shut. "*Fucking close it.*"

"It's our only bloody escape," Durron hissed, his rasping voice seeming to burn worse than the fumes.

"Durron, you bastard," Cal growled through the strain. The damn fool was still trying to pull them open.

Fortunately, the scavenger's attempts failed the instant Franco slammed his fist into his solar plexus and sent him reeling. The corporal quickly commandeered the handle, and together, he and Cal heaved the doors shut.

Both of them staggered back. Cal shook his spinning head, trying to clear it. Whatever the hell they were breathing was really starting to take its toll. If they didn't find another way out soon, the fumes would probably render them all unconscious within minutes. Trying to dab his eyes clear, he looked toward the other door that led to the stairwell. At its base, the flames from his bomb had become almost nonexistent. But the dent in the door didn't appear to have increased in size. Perhaps the snake responsible for the damage had gone, the robustness of the door having proved too much. Or maybe it had been put off by the escalating heat. Cal stared at the door for a moment, weighing up its viability as an escape route. Whatever snake had made the dent must have been far larger than any they'd faced yet. What if it was still lying in wait?

Someone gripped him by the shoulder, pulling him from the chilling thought. He turned to see Campbell holding out a small, torn cloth. She already had one pressed to her own mouth, as did the others, including, encouragingly, Christie. Gratefully accepting it, Cal shared a look with Franco that fortunately didn't require words. The corporal appeared grim but determined as they both glanced up at the services tunnel above them. The tunnel hung suspended from the high ceiling and stretched from one end of the room to the other. But it didn't stop there. During his earlier recon of the base, Cal had observed it running the entire circumference of the observation deck. Ironically, he'd ordered Franco to seal it up for fear it would act as a potential access route for the snakes. Now, it was perhaps their best chance of escape.

Detaching a small dispenser from his armor, Franco looked up to the tunnel's access panel situated directly above the door. The acid contained within the dispenser would dissolve the meld-glue in seconds. Seeing no chairs nearby, Cal quickly braced himself back against the door and, taking one last deep breath through his cloth, cupped his hands in front of him. Planting his right boot in the hand hold, Franco stretched up and just about managed to reach the panel. As the corporal got to work, Cal looked toward the blurred forms of Orisho and Wilson. Although the veterans had slowed, they were still managing a controlled fierceness in their swings. Cal was amazed how two men of advancing years could retain such momentum, particularly amid these fumes. But they weren't superhuman, and the signs of fatigue were unmistakable.

Moments later, a large, sizzling piece of metal clattered to the floor, and Franco climbed unceremoniously onto Cal's shoulders to pull himself into the tunnel. Cal remained in position, but much to his annoyance, Durron was the first to try and take advantage. The scavenger didn't get very far before Becker kicked him aside. Grabbing hold of Christie, she planted her foot in Cal's interlocked hands and, with Campbell and Ebner's help, lifted the girl up into Franco's reaching hands. The state she was in, the girl did little to help, but fortunately, she was petite, and the corporal pulled her up with ease. Placing her cloth against Cal's mouth, Becker allowed him another deep breath before deftly climbing the rest of the way in order to help haul up Ebner, Campbell, and Poots.

Pryce went next, clumsy in his movements and wheezing noisily. The man wasn't exactly a lightweight, and Cal had to use all his strength to heave him up.

"*Couter*," Cal said with a sharp, beckoning hand once Pryce was up.

Couter turned from the gesture and grabbed hold of Durron, pulling him bodily off the floor. The scavenger seemed to be having trouble breathing—unsurprising, not least considering the kick Becker had planted in his ribs. The young private roughly shoved him into position, and between them, he and Cal pushed him up to the hatch.

"Okay, Private, get your ass up there. That's an order," Cal said once Durron was out of his hands.

This time, Couter didn't hesitate. The young man was heavy but agile and had no trouble hauling himself up.

"*Orisho, Wilson, let's go.*" Cal grabbed his cloth from the floor and sucked in another breath before wiping his eyes. The two men were still putting up a good fight, but their strength and stamina looked close to failing them.

Barely missing a swing, Orisho took hold of an idle chair and flung it in Cal's direction. No words were necessary; Cal knew exactly what was meant by the deed, and he wasn't about to waste time debating. Planting the chair upright, he stepped onto it and launched himself toward the hatch—the quicker he was up there, the quicker the two men would follow. Multiple reaching hands grasped him and pulled. "*Okay, I'm up,*" he shouted as he twisted himself around in the tunnel and leaned as far out of the gap as he dared. "Now, get your asses in gear."

Orisho and Wilson began to fall back, but their movements were sluggish. Even with his worsening vision, Cal could see that both men had smaller snakes attached to their legs, aggressive in their attempts to breach the gaps in their armor. But the little attackers were inconsequential when compared to the sizable beasts that were now lingering beyond the dwindling fires.

Cal reached back and shouted for a chem-bomb. Almost immediately, one was pushed into his hand. Glad the giver had already had the foresight to pull the pin, he took a couple of seconds to consider his aim then tossed the explosive into the center of the room. The detonation countdown seemed to last an eternity, but then the flames burst out, and their effect on the remaining snakes was instant. He reached back again. "Your rifle, Corporal." Again, his request was fulfilled quickly, and moments later, he was peering through the weapon's sights and pulling the trigger. It was hard to know how much he was helping. His eyes were watering so badly that he suspected half his shots were hitting creatures that were already dead. The floor was literally covered with pale flesh and dark, blue blood. So much so that Orisho and Wilson were having trouble negotiating their retreat. They were breathing hard and staggering, seeming confused as they tried to orient themselves.

"*Here*," Cal shouted. "*Come on, damn it.*" He had half a mind to drop back into the room to drag them to the hatch, but he wasn't faring too well himself, and he suspected he'd only slow things down. He continued to peer through the sights, blinking away the tears and trying to master his overwhelming urge to cough up his burning lungs. All the while, he searched for threatening movement among the dead, pale flesh.

Then, something happened, something that confused his already muddled senses: two loud thuds followed by an almighty crash. The dented door leading to the stairwell burst off its runners and flew across the room. The huge slab of metal hit Orisho with the force of a wrecking drone and dropped him instantly. Cal barely had time to process what had happened before a huge snake, its head as wide as his arm span, erupted from the dark stairwell. The beast moved with frightening speed, lunging forward to clamp its massive jaws around Orisho's unconscious body. Cal heard Wilson roar, but he tried to remain focused on his own attack, unloading multiple shots from the rifle, doing his best to aim for the creature's eyes. But even if his vision hadn't been failing him, the shots were near impossible. The snake was in constant motion, ferocious in its movements. And already, it was retreating, barreling its way back toward the dark stairwell, taking its prize with it. Wilson charged forward, his sword biting into the beast's neck. But the weapon seemed distressingly ineffectual. The veteran rushed at it again, this time making a desperate grab for Orisho's limp arm, but one forceful jerk of the creature's massive head sent him reeling.

As abruptly as it began, it was over.

The snake was gone, as was Orisho, the stairwell now just a gaping, empty shell.

Cool air funneled through the broken doorway, sweeping away the fumes like some perverse consolation for the brutal tragedy. For a moment, the room seemed incredibly still and silent in the wake of the violence. The other snakes seemed to have suddenly disappeared, perhaps shying away in the presence of their far larger kin. Slowly, Wilson picked himself up and moved to retrieve his sword. He looked like a man whose bones had turned to lead, his head dropped toward the ground, forced down by crippling anguish.

"*Wilson...*" Cal was about to order him to climb up to the hatch, but the look on the man's face as he turned to look at him swept the order away. There was no anger there, just deep sadness. Cal knew what the veteran was going to do, and although he felt an overwhelming urge to persuade him otherwise, he completely understood it. There was no way that Orisho had survived—they both knew it—not in the jaws of such primal aggression. But the two men were brothers, a bond between them strengthened by a lifetime of events that Cal could barely imagine.

Cal locked eyes with his teammate for a few more seconds. Then, a simple nod was all that was shared in the way of farewell before the veteran ran to the stairwell and disappeared into the dark.

CHAPTER TWENTY-ONE

Cal held up his glow-tube and did his best to illuminate their escape route. Fortunately, the services tunnel had been designed with maintenance in mind, and even with their armor on, there was still space to easily crawl on their hands and knees. Franco was already positioning a heavy slab of detached grating over the open hatch while Couter readied himself with the meld glue. The patch up would set in seconds and, with any luck, would prevent pursuit. Awkwardly turning about in the tight space, Cal assessed the tunnel. There was a swathe of dark tubing and a network of pipes intertwined above their heads that had an unfortunate resemblance to twisting serpents. Doing his best not to make the tubes come alive in his mind, he glanced around at his companions. They were looking back at him questioningly. It didn't take long, however, before his expression and a shake of the head gave them all the answer they needed. They were fewer now, and if they didn't get moving soon, they'd likely be fewer still.

Detaching his water canister, Cal gave his throat and eyes a quick cleanse before passing it on. The water worked wonders, and soon, the gloomy tunnel became that much clearer. As far as he could make out, their choice of direction was clear-cut. The tunnel only ran in two directions, but the route behind them had been severely damaged, compressed to a point that would make it impossible to crawl through. Perhaps having seen this, Durron was already clambering off in the other direction. Cal wasn't bothered—if anything, the scavenger's impatience would simply alert them of problems ahead, an early warning system in the form of his screams. Pryce looked as though he wanted to follow but seemed reluctant to try and push his way past Becker.

"Okay, let's follow the idiot," Cal said as Franco and Couter finished their work on the patch job. "Poots, you okay under your own steam?"

"Not a problem," the private replied, her strange optimism born from disaster still holding out. "Doubt I'll manage while holding this though," she said, passing the old pistol to Franco.

Franco didn't look overly impressed with the little weapon but took it nonetheless.

"Okay, Corporal, lead the way," Cal said.

One by one, they set off, crawling through the tunnel like a procession of bugs through a drain. Cal hung back with the expectation of having to help Becker and Campbell with Christie. Fortunately, it wasn't needed. Cal couldn't say why, but for the first time, the girl seemed capable of moving without encouragement or aid. Perhaps the tight confines of the tunnel offered her some amount of mental comfort. Whatever the reason, Cal was glad of it. The girl wasn't demonstrating a fast crawl by any stretch of the imagination, but it was certainly faster than dragging her. Cal followed without relinquishing his grip on the rifle. He felt a touch of guilt at having *commandeered* the weapon from Franco, but the feeling was fleeting; there was no way he was going to be at the back of the line in a tunnel like this without a trigger against his finger. Sure, the corporal was at the front, which was arguably as bad, but he at least had Durron to use as a convenient shield.

For the first time ever, Cal found himself frustrated by their Corrian armor. In nearly every aspect of its design, the armor was exceptional and always lived up to its highly regarded name. When it came to stealth while crawling through a metal tunnel, however, it fell woefully short. Every clink and clunk and scrape sounded horribly amplified and seemed to echo far longer than was reasonable. Cal cursed the noise. At least his eyes were continuing to recover, and his throat had settled to a dull burn. The air in the tunnel was far from fresh, but it felt straight from an alpine vista compared to hellish fumes they'd just consumed.

Doing his best to keep track of their location, Cal took advantage of the monotonous crawl by assessing his next move. First and foremost, he wanted to get them a good distance from the last attack. Then, once they reached the next access hatch leading to one of the numerous stairwells, he thought it best to simply order a stop and restart their silent waiting game. So far, the tunnel seemed blessedly free from snakes, and he wanted to take advantage of the little miracle. Assuming their situation stayed that way, the wait would end in one of two ways. Either the warmth of day would roll in and banish the snakes or their rescue would arrive and it would be time to endure a little more chaos.

Even tucked away in this tunnel, Cal was confident they would hear the approach of a ship, especially an attack ship. They were damn loud, and a rescue team would hover close enough to shake the base like a rattle. But how long would it be until the craft succumbed to the atmosphere? Cal couldn't risk the loop starting again. If it arrived, they'd have to get to it fast and take their chances with the snakes. The rescuers would undoubtedly scan the base and track their movements. But even if the ship's location scanners screwed up early, a chem-bomb out in the open would be enough to alert them of their presence. The ship's weapons and the heat from its thrusters should keep any attackers at bay. Then, this damn hellhole could start to become a distant, painful memory.

Cal suddenly paused in his crawl. A creaking of metal had begun that was loud enough to pull him from his musings. It seemed too loud to be caused by the weight of a human. His heart began to quicken.

The noise had caused them all to stop, even Durron and Christie.

The creaking continued and soon amplified into a deep groan that reverberated through the tunnel, giving the impression they'd crawled unwittingly into the belly of some gigantic, metallic beast. *Christ, here we go again,* Cal thought bitterly. Nothing was moving in the darkness, but something was definitely close. Then the tunnel began to shift, slowly sinking downward as if subjected to some formidable magnetic force. Cal gripped his rifle hard and tried to calm his heart. Had the visitor detected them? Or was it just passing by? Ahead of him, Becker slowly moved forward to hover over Christie, ready to silence the girl should it be needed.

Cal tried to will the beast away, but the groaning and shifting increased exponentially, to the point where it hurt the ears and shook bones. Bracing himself against some overhead tubing, he felt a powerful need to shoot something. Not being able to see that *something*, however, was proving a serious antagonist to the urge.

Suddenly, the tunnel began to buckle—not simply above them or below them but everywhere, as if a great fist had clamped around its exterior and was squeezing it into submission.

Christie screamed then, but Becker didn't quiet her— she wasn't the only one making noise; this little game was up, and they all knew it. A mental picture of the snake that must have wrapped itself around the exterior of the tunnel flashed into Cal's mind. It had to be at least the size of the one that had taken Orisho to exert such force. He did his best to retreat the way he'd come. Becker followed him, awkwardly dragging Christie with her. Unable to help with the girl in the fast-shrinking confines of the tunnel, all Cal could do was give them room, but very quickly, it became a tangle of struggling limbs. Beyond Becker, Campbell and Pryce were also in a desperate retreat as a bundle of hard tubing was forced down on their heads. Cal heard Couter, Ebner, and Franco shouting as they retreated in the opposite direction, but seconds later, their voices were cut off as the tunnel was compressed into a tight thread of mangled metal that divided the team in two.

With the roof pressing down on him, Pryce began roaring at Campbell and Becker to move faster. Cal didn't blame him, but already, they were doing their utmost not to be crushed to a pulp. Frustrated in his inability to help Becker, Cal considered bracing his rifle in an attempt to slow the squeeze, but with the pressure being exerted, he doubted it would make any difference and may simply end up being one more obstacle. His mind raced in search of a solution. There was a bulkhead a little further back. Perhaps its structure would prove more robust.

But reaching it was not their fate.

The metal beneath Becker and Christie began to tear as the stresses on the abused tunnel took their final toll. Lunging forward, Cal grabbed Becker's armored shoulder plate a mere second before both her and Christie fell through the rupture. Determined not to relinquish his hold, Cal grunted in pain as the weight of the two women pulled him partway through the gap and almost separated his arm from its socket. Fortunately, the spear strapped to his back became wedged into the side of the tunnel, preventing him from spilling out headfirst. Partially suspended, he crooked his neck to see Becker swinging in his grip. The sergeant was struggling to retain her own hold on Christie, who was wriggling in panic. The space below was a wide, dark corridor. Thankfully, its smooth floor appeared blessedly free from snakes.

As he tried to haul the two women back into the tunnel, Cal felt a gentle breeze of cool air tease his skin—somewhere, the corridor was breached, exposed to the outside world. As this realization hit him, he also became aware of pale scales slowly undulating in his peripheral vision. It seemed the snake that had wrapped itself around the tunnel was as big as its ridiculous strength suggested. His heart thudding, Cal doubled his efforts and did his best to ignore the massive predator next to him. If he'd had the inclination to do so, he could have easily reached out and touched the beast. Fortunately, it was barely moving, seeming in no great hurry to uncoil itself and seek them out—perhaps recovering from its herculean effort of crushing its perch.

Again, Cal tried to pull the two women up, but the angle at which he was suspended meant he couldn't reach Becker with his left hand, and with his right, it was all he could do just to keep a hold of them. He turned his head to view the corridor. They were close to its end, and he could see that the snake had quite literally pinched off the tunnel just before it entered the next observation room.

There were doors leading through, but they were shut tight and were unlikely to open in a hurry; not without Franco's expertise. Cal heaved again, trying to remain silent as he did so. Their best option was to get back into the tunnel, but try as he might, each effort was falling further short of the last.

Then, Campbell was by his side, stretching through the gap as far as she dared. "I can't reach her," she said in a panicked whisper. "If I lean any further, I'll fall."

"Pryce, help us," Cal hissed. "Hold onto Campbell."

They only received an unintelligible grunt in reply.

As Campbell tried to reposition herself, the tunnel began to vibrate. The snake was on the move, gradually shifting along the shaft like it was some sort of giant branch.

Cal looked for the creature's head, but most of its long body was enveloped by the darkness. He closed his eyes and gritted his teeth, his arm trembling under the strain. "*Pryce, damn it, help us.*" Whether frozen in fear, trapped in the wreckage of the tunnel, or simply unwilling to risk himself, Pryce still made no move. Cal cursed the man, strongly suspecting the latter reason. "Help us, or I swear I'll—"

Cal's threat was cut short as the weight on his arm suddenly lessened. Then, he watched helplessly as Christie fell through the air, the torn fabric of her clothing still tight in Becker's grip. The girl hit the floor hard.

God damn it. "Becker, try to climb up." Cal said the words but knew they were futile. There was no chance

Becker would leave the girl even if it meant facing a snake that could easily swallow her whole. She confirmed this by reaching up and digging her fingers into the appropriate pressure points on Cal's wrist, forcing him to release her.

She dropped, silent as a stone.

The body of the huge snake almost rubbed against Cal's face as he pulled himself back up into the tunnel. Wasting no time, he opened a compartment on his armor and began to unwind a length of smart cord. Unsurprisingly, the nano-tech in the cord had become inert, but it was still strong and flexible; he'd just have to rely on old-fashioned knots and brute strength to pull them up. He glanced down to see Becker staring back up, but she wasn't looking in his direction. Instead, her attention was on the looming threat. As he tied one end of the cord around a thick pipe, part of the snake's pale body began to pass over the hole. Campbell cautiously leaned forward and peered at it then flinched back as it rapidly narrowed to a tip and disappeared. "That was its tail," she whispered.

"You have a chem-bomb?" Cal asked, glancing at the woman.

"No, I already used it."

Silently, Cal berated himself for not ensuring they'd had one of the little explosives at the back of the line.

"Let's get the hell out of here," Pryce said. "They're screwed. Forget them."

As he looped the tied-off cord over an overhead tube, Cal glanced at the scavenger. If he'd seen terror in the man's eyes, he might have found it within himself to forgive the comment. But Pryce's expression was hard and cold. Just like Durron, he wore the look of the man obsessed with his own survival. Cal dropped the rest of the cord through the hole. "Go your own way if you want," he said, jerking his head toward the long, dark tunnel. As he suspected, the man didn't move a muscle. He was weak-minded and unable to do a damn thing unless he had someone to lead him. Cal shook his head. How could such a man recognize the advantage of safety in numbers yet be incapable of grasping the logic behind working together for survival? *Ignorant, bloody fool.* "If you want to stay under my protection, you'll pull your damn weight and help me pull them up." Cal took a second to fix his eyes on the scavenger, but the man's expression only triggered an urge to garrote him with the remainder of the cord.

Cal looked back down through the hole expectantly, but the cord hung idle. Becker had started to move away, her spear clenched tightly in one hand as she used the other to guide Christie back.

Time's up, Cal thought grimly as he grabbed his rifle. "Hold on to me," he said to Campbell. Half expecting to be bitten in two, he knelt and leaned through the gap. Unwilling to remain a blind bit of prey, he saw that Becker had tossed a spare glow-tube down the corridor. The soft, blue light revealed a large, ragged tear where the cool, outside air was entering. But the breach didn't hold his attention for more than a second. As he'd suspected, the snake was as big as the one that had taken Orisho.

This beast, however, seemed far more relaxed in its methods, turning itself around at the end of the long corridor almost lethargically—perhaps so assured in the inevitability of its kill that it was unwilling to expend unnecessary energy.

Cal peered through his sights, anxious in the knowledge that only five rounds remained. After that, the weapon would be nothing more than a half-decent club. At least the snake's slow approach allowed for careful aim. The first bullet struck the creature's left eye, and Cal wasted no time tugging on the trigger again and again. All the shots found their mark, but only after the fourth did the snake recoil. Then, it went completely still, as if paralyzed. It wasn't easy to see in the dim light what sort of damage had been done, but Cal found it hard to believe that the beast wouldn't be hurt. As the seconds passed, he found himself holding his breath, fearful that even the tiniest movement might entice the snake forward. *Retreat, you bastard... Retreat...*

But the snake didn't retreat. Instead, it surged forward in a sudden burst of kinetic fury.

Cal made his last shot, but this time, the creature was moving too fast.

He pulled himself back up, his eyes flicking toward Becker and Christie. The pair had retreated to the door at the corridor's end. Becker stood in front of the girl, grasping her spear like a gladiator facing the opening gates.

The snake would be on them in seconds.

The mass of pale scales became a blur beneath Cal.

With a surge of adrenaline, he tossed the useless rifle aside and unslung his spear. With the weapon grasped tightly in both hands, he dropped through the hole.

CHAPTER TWENTY-TWO

Cal slammed into the snake's back hard, driving all of his weight into his spear. Even so, the weapon barely pierced the creature's hide, and an instant later, a violent bucking reaction launched him through the air to collide with the corridor's wall. Despite his armor protecting him from the worst of the impact, Cal dropped limp to the floor, and it took him a few moments to regain any semblance of being. Aware that his weapon had been wrenched from his hands, it came as a great relief to realize the snake was no longer close. Finally, it had retreated and was now coiled up at the other end of the corridor. Cal stared at the beast for a moment and, through the gloom, could just about make out his spear protruding from its back. Again, the snake was completely still—hopefully now injured enough to dissuade it from further attacks.

Climbing painfully to his feet, Cal saw Christie curled in a ball at the foot of the door. She was sobbing quietly. Becker's spear and glow-tube were on the ground in front of the girl. Cal swept his eyes desperately across the scene and saw Becker lying a good twenty feet away, a splatter of dark blood spread up the wall beside her. She was completely unmoving. The thought that he might have lost yet another friend unleashed a dread in Cal that weakened him more than any physical battering. Trying to overrule his protesting limbs and spinning head, he ran over to her stiffly. There was more dark blood on her face and pooled around her head. His legs giving way, he dropped to his knees and tried to work out whether the blue sheen to the blood was simply a cruel trick of his glow-tube. He could see her breathing, and as he laid his hand on her neck, the feeling of her pulse against his fingers seemed to reignite his own heart. Running his hands over her head and neck, he couldn't find any obvious trauma, but there were definite teeth marks gouged into the chest plate of her armor. Whatever she'd done with her spear, it seemed she'd strongly discouraged the snake from its meal. Her head then moved of its own accord, and her limbs began to shift. Slowly, she was coming around.

"Come on, Sergeant, I won't have you sleeping on duty." Cal didn't quite achieve the light tone he'd been aiming for, and the relief at seeing Becker's eyes flicker open made his voice crack. "That's it, you can—"

"*Lieutenant, it's coming. It's coming at you again.*"

The shout came from above—from Campbell. Cal's brain had barely taken in her warning before some primal part of his being shocked his body into action. Without so much as a glance in her or the snake's direction, he seized Becker's arm and began to drag her back toward Christie. Her armor slid easily on the smooth, blood-soaked floor.

Campbell shouted again, but this time, Cal barely heard it over the deafening roar in his ears—the resulting sound of his body and mind desperately fighting in unison to keep him and his companions alive. The floor was vibrating; the snake was close. With his adrenaline pumping and no time to be gentle, he heaved Becker toward Christie with as much force as he could muster then twisted on the spot and made a lunge for the idle spear.

The snake was there. Right in front of him. Jaws wide and moving fast.

As he wrenched the spear off the ground, the beast crashed into him like a runaway cargo hauler. His vision flashed as if lightning had struck him, but somehow, he held onto consciousness. The corridor's door then made for an unforgiving barrier as he was barreled into it. The world span. He couldn't see Becker or Christie, only moist, pale flesh and a distorted view of big, sharp teeth. A rancid stench hit him, making him wretch. He was in the bastard's mouth at least partially…but the huge jaws hadn't closed. Thick, hot liquid ran over his hands and splattered at his feet. Weird, guttural noises came from deep in the beast's throat as if it were attempting *suck* him in. The spear was juddering in his grip but not for long. As the snake snapped its head back, the weapon went with it, and Cal found himself dropping to the floor like a tower of loose bricks.

Shaking his head in a desperate attempt to retain focus, Cal awkwardly pushed himself upright, his hands slipping on the slick floor as he tried to keep his attention on the snake. Again, the creature was retreating down the corridor, the walls trembling as its powerful body clumsily smashed into them. The spear was protruding from the side of its mouth like a badly hooked fish.

"Sergeant?" he said, risking only a very brief glance behind him. The two women were slumped against the door, just to the left of the dent that he and the snake had left. Despite appearing barely conscious, Becker was once again doing her best to protect Christie—one hand gripping the girl while her other held her knife.

"We're okay," she said with a weak nod.

For now, Cal thought grimly as he looked back to the snake. The beast was slamming its head against the floor in an attempt to drive the spear from its mouth. Gradually, it was succeeding. *Don't these bastards feel pain?* Surely, it had had enough by now. Surely, the three of them couldn't be that appetizing or that much of a threat to its territory. Without attempting to get to his feet, Cal dragged himself back so he could lean against the door alongside Becker and Christie. He glanced up at the rupture in the tunnel. Campbell was watching them, wide-eyed, and even Pryce was peering through. Campbell wore a look of desperate concern while Pryce seemed as though he were being torn in two by anger and fear. Cal was surprised that the scavenger hadn't made a run for it yet, but perhaps he was afraid of the inevitable noise he'd make if he went clambering off down the tunnel.

Cal stared at the cord that still dangled from the rupture. It didn't seem like the most promising of lifelines anymore. Even with its tech inert, the cord had thousands of micro spines protruding along its length like those on the placoid scales of a shark. This grip aid would make the climb easier. But he seriously doubted whether either he or Becker could manage it—not in their current state. Ironically, Christie was probably the most physically able of the three of them at that moment. Perhaps they could be hauled up, but the expression on Pryce's face didn't fill him with hope on that front. The scavenger was more likely to try and appease the snake by leaving them as a dangling offering.

The sound of a spear clattering to the ground was a disturbing one to say the least. The snake had finally succeeded in bashing it free. Just as Becker had done, Cal pulled out his combat knife. The blade was large, but considering the size of the opponent, it seemed little more than a toothpick.

The snake began to advance. This time, there was no sudden burst of fury, but neither was it demonstrating the steady, almost lazy approach from earlier. Instead, the creature moved in a swift, controlled manner that seemed completely unhindered by its injuries. Cal gritted his teeth as it neared, determined not let the fact that they were hideously outmatched cloud his focus. Christie pressed her hands tight against her ears and tried to mute her senses to the deathly approach by burrowing her face into Becker.

Then something happened, something that almost made Cal fumble his knife in surprise: Pryce dropped out of the tunnel and fell through the air right in front of the snake's lethal maw. The look on the scavenger's face as he hit the ground was one of such shock that Cal was certain the move wasn't a miraculous act of self-sacrifice—the piercing scream that followed seemed confirmation of the fact. Perhaps mercifully, Pryce's shock was short-lived. The man barely had time to peel himself from the floor before he was snatched up in the beast's great jaws. Without the benefit of armor, his death, although grisly, came fast.

Then, just as had happened with Orisho, the predator swiftly withdrew, taking its victim with it.

Still feeling stunned, Cal watched silently as the creature squeezed itself through the large, twisted tear at the end of the corridor and completely disappeared from view.

"What the hell?" Becker mumbled.

Cal had no answer. The two of them looked up to the rupture in the tunnel to see Campbell once again leaning through it. There was some small vestige of shock on her face, but mostly, her expression had returned to the hard, no-nonsense look that Cal had seen numerous times earlier.

Campbell shrugged at them as best she could without falling from her perch. "He slipped," she said in a tone that not even a gullible child would believe.

Cal felt his darker side almost laugh at that, but there was something about almost being eaten that smothered a person's humor. Instead, he slumped back against the door and finally allowed all his pains and exhaustion to present themselves. He wasn't entirely sure how he felt about Pryce's demise. The man was far from an innocent, but did he deserve to die in such a way? The alternative would have been that either he, Becker, or Christie would have been killed or possibly all three of them. There'd been mere seconds for Campbell to make her judgement, and in the heat of the moment, he wasn't convinced that his would have been different.

The three of them remained slumped at the base of the door, breathing hard for what seemed like hours but was likely no more than a minute. Then, quite suddenly, the door was no longer there. Their backrest having slid apart, all three of them fell back in surprise.

Figures loomed over them.

"Taking a rest?" Franco asked, looking down at them, one eyebrow cocked.

Again, Cal felt a strange urge to laugh rise up in him. "You need to work a little harder on your timing, Corporal."

CHAPTER TWENTY-THREE

"You hear that?"

Cal turned to see that Poots had paused in her one-legged shuffle and was cocking her head to one side. The private had impeccable hearing. The sound was barely perceptible, but just as Cal had predicted, the thrum of the arriving ship soon reverberated loudly though the walls.

"Is that our rescue?" Campbell's voice sounded hopeful, but the look in her eyes remained skeptical—as if to fully embrace the hope might somehow jinx it.

Cal nodded. "It is."

"About damn frickin' time," Franco said. The corporal had his hands buried in an open panel and was doing his best to disable yet another set of pneumatic locks within.

"Thank God," Ebner said as he leaned heavily on a nearby storage container, his relief almost seeming to overwhelm him.

Cal could understand the emotion. The sound of the ship was akin to a life raft being tossed to a shipwrecked crew in a dark, turbulent sea. But they weren't safe yet, not by a long shot; the storm was still raging, and the sharks were circling.

"Our rescue has arrived, which is obviously very good news," Cal said, making sure he had the attention of Campbell and Ebner. "But it's only one ship and possibly has no more than one team on board. We can't simply rely on them to land and pull us out of here. From what we've seen, at least two of the snakes out there are large enough to pose a serious threat to the ship. The rescue team will likely remain airborne."

"What do you mean *airborne?*" Campbell asked sharply. "How the hell are they going to rescue us if they don't land?"

Aware that fear was fueling her anger, Cal did his best to remain calm and patient. "We can only try and predict the situation by what we've experienced so far," he explained. "Our rescuers won't be any good to us if the ship becomes badly damaged, or worse, they get themselves killed…two distinct possibilities if they try and land. Right now, the tech on that ship is probably still operational, but we all know that won't last. We're in a race against time, plain and simple. I can assure you that they will have scanned the base and pinpointed our location already, and they'll continue to track us until we reach a suitable extraction position." Cal took a pause, his eyes still fixed on Campbell and Ebner. He was well aware how exhausted they were, but he hoped his words were hitting home. He needed them as alert and mobile as they could be. "Our one and only objective is to get to that extraction point as quickly as possible."

"We understand," Ebner said quietly.

Campbell said nothing, but she nodded an acknowledgement.

Guess that's all I'm going to get, Cal thought as he turned to observe Franco's progress on the pneumatic door locks. "How long, Corporal?"

"Any moment," Franco assured him.

"Okay, everyone, stay sharp," Cal said as he felt his tension rise again. The thrum of the ship's engines had brought a great deal of relief, but it was an emotion buried beneath frustration—obstacles had arisen that were proving difficult to overcome. This would be the third stairwell they'd tried. The first had become home to so many snakes that they'd have needed twenty more chembombs to clear a path, and the second had been so badly warped that they'd found it impossible to even get the doors open. Cal hoped this one would prove third time lucky. The fact that their rescue had arrived was a huge blessing, but it wouldn't be worth a damn if they remained trapped on the observation deck.

Although he couldn't be sure of the exact time since the suns went down, Cal knew for certain there was a good deal of night left. The snakes wouldn't be leaving them in peace anytime soon—a fact supported by the numbers they were still encountering. None too keen to subject them all to the cramped confines of the services tunnel for a second time, Cal had instead taken a chance at moving through the corridors and observation rooms. Snakes had attacked, weapons had clashed with teeth and flesh, and a couple more chem-bombs had been ignited. Fortunately, unlike the first attack, the numbers of snakes had been manageable, and none of them were anywhere close to the size of the beasts that had killed Orisho or Pryce. But now, they were almost out of bombs, and fatigue throughout the entire group was taking its toll.

Cal himself was doing his best to ignore his failing body—not an easy thing to achieve during the quieter moments when the heart calmed and the adrenaline eased. That big snake had treated him like a child might its least favorite toy. Every part of him throbbed in pain, and he suspected that he had a number of broken ribs. He turned back to check on Becker; the sergeant looked as tired and as battered as he felt, but she was forcing her posture straight, and her eyes remained alert. Understandably, Christie had worsened, her blank stare and her need to be practically carried having fully returned. Still appearing strong, Couter had taken up the mantle as the girl's minder although Becker never strayed far from her side.

Durron lurked nearby. Like Pryce, he seemed to recognize the advantages of sticking together, but also like Pryce, he was about as helpful as a sulking teenager. The scavenger hadn't once asked about the whereabouts of his comrade and seemed completely indifferent to his fate. Of the group, Ebner looked worst of all and appeared ready to drop at any minute. Fortunately, Campbell was doing her best to help him both physically and mentally.

"Okay, we're in," Franco said as he moved toward the big, sliding doors.

Cal stepped forward, and together, he and Franco heaved the doors open just enough to take a cautious peek inside.

"Shit." Franco moved back from the door but didn't elaborate on his assessment.

Cal took up position and had a careful look through the gap. The corporal's one-word reaction summed up the situation pretty well. The stairwell lacked half of its stairs, and those that could be seen had been crumpled beyond recognition. Also, there was a good deal of moisture dripping. Cal supposed it must be rainwater as he awkwardly twisted his neck to look up. Wherever the breach was, it was shrouded in darkness. All he could see was more crumpled stairway. The beast that had pushed its way up through the shaft must have been seriously big and strong as hell. Igniting a spare glow-tube, he dropped it into the darkness and watched as the circle of blue light briefly illuminated multiple levels of wreckage on its way down. Eventually, the little tube landed, but rather than hitting hard metal, it thumped onto a bed of pale, writhing flesh. Cal bit back a curse, the sight of the distant snake pit instantly upgrading Franco's assessment to an altogether harsher word.

He backed away from the doors, letting Becker take a look as he turned to meet the questioning eyes. He wished he had better news. "The stairs are severely damaged. It might be possible to get down, but it won't be easy."

"I'll take difficult over dead," Poots said, glancing at the doors.

Cal rubbed at his chin. "I'm afraid there's also a pit of snakes at the bottom that looks deeper than your average swimming pool."

Franco let out a quick, humorless laugh. "So a nice soft landing if we fall. Does our luck know no bounds!" The corporal shook his head and after a moment looked back at Cal. "So on to the next one?"

"No," Cal replied. "Time's not on our side. And I doubt the other stairwells are going to prove any more promising."

"So what are you proposing, Lieutenant?" Campbell asked.

Cal looked back at the doors and considered for a moment. "We go up."

"*Up*," Campbell repeated incredulously. "Just how damaged are these stairs? We're not exactly in the best shape right now."

"It won't be an easy climb," Cal admitted, "but the wreckage above looks far less severe than below. And the damage at the bottom seems to be preventing the smaller snakes from ascending."

"And the big snakes?" Campbell asked. Her tone made it clear that she had little admiration for this plan.

Not used to having to explain every decision, Cal again did his best to keep his cool. "The big snakes will be a risk no matter what we do or where we go. If we go up, we can attempt an airborne rescue."

"Sounds like our best chance." Surprisingly, this came from Durron. His tone was far from friendly, but it held no sarcasm.

"No one asked your opinion, scavenger," Becker said, turning from the doors to shoot the man an icy stare. It had the desired effect and froze his mouth shut. "We're wasting time," Becker continued as she turned sharply on Campbell. "How many of us have to die trying to protect you before you put your fears and judgments aside and start trusting? You may have a problem with the lieutenant's past decisions, but we're deep in the shit now. Our team's become one of the most respected in the fleet, and it's mostly down to him. There's a good reason he's in charge, and you need to start accepting that. Either you can keep endangering us all by analyzing and arguing every decision he makes or you can start trusting and acting fast."

Looking a little startled, Campbell silently stared at her for a moment. Taking a deep breath, the older woman's eyes finally softened a little and she nodded. "I apologize," she said somewhat reluctantly. She looked at Cal and then toward the dark gap in the doorway. "Okay, Lieutenant, up it is… So who goes first?"

CHAPTER TWENTY-FOUR

Cal had been right; the climb wasn't easy. This time, he'd decided to lead the way. If they were going to be attacked, it would likely come from above, and it felt only right that he should bear the brunt. Having lost his spear to the big snake in the corridor, he'd been grateful for Becker's insistence that he arm himself with hers as she helped Campbell aid Ebner and Poots with the tricky ascent. Fortunately, everyone was faring surprisingly well with the climb. Poots was managing better than most could with two good legs, and Ebner was a more competent climber than his frail frame would suggest. Christie had proven more of a problem, but in the end, they'd decided to simply strap her to Couter's back. Despite his youth, the private was proving quite the powerhouse, and even carrying the weight of two didn't slow him a great deal. Unwilling to go last, Durron had insisted on climbing ahead of Franco, who guarded the rear. Cal had been close to physically forcing the scavenger to reconsider his demand, but in the end, time pressures had prevented any costly arguments.

Rain was still falling into the stairwell. The cool moisture felt good against Cal's face as he peered up into the looming darkness. As yet, he could see no sign of moonlight penetrating a breach, but the raindrops seemed sparse and heavy as if they'd accumulated and dripped off an edge rather than fallen directly into the shaft. Although he didn't really need it, he was tempted to light up another glow-tube. In the gloom of the wreckage, every handhold he reached for felt like a game of chance—one he may well lose if he unwittingly grabbed a handful of scaly flesh instead of metal. But so far, their climb had been blessedly free of snakes. He allowed himself the thought that these beasts were somehow afraid of heights, but it seemed unlikely. Up to now, they appeared to be afraid of very little, pain included.

As they slowly continued to ascend, the deep, resonating sound of the rescue ship came and went. Cal guessed the pilot was performing sweeps of the area. Assuming they'd flown here directly after entering the atmosphere, it stood to reason that their tech should still be in good working order. But it was raining now—more moisture, more potential exposure to Ebner's disrupting particles. How long would the rescue ship remain in the air? Cal pushed the question aside; he could have no possible influence over its outcome, and mulling over it would do little good. So far, he hadn't heard any evidence of a landing, but considering the local wildlife, this was hardly surprising. Occasionally, he would hear the ship's rail blasters hammering out rounds, which he guessed were attempts to ward off or lure the large snakes away from the base. He just hoped to God they were having success.

After what seemed a mammoth climb, they eventually arrived at the point Cal had been aiming for: the entrance to a huge strut that ran horizontally high above the central dome, linking to the central communications tower. Each of the stairwells were linked in this way, the struts acting like a set of spokes on a huge, horizontal wheel. Their purpose was for structural integrity, but each had an accessible passageway within, which offered plenty of room to comfortably walk along. From what could be seen under the light of the glow-tubes, the passageway still appeared intact. Cal had considered continuing upward and trying to exit onto the roof of the stairwell tower, but the thought had been a brief one. The stairs above were still mangled, suggesting that the huge creature that had caused the damage had continued up and was perhaps still lingering. It was a suspicion rather than a certainty—one they could easily confirm by continuing their climb. But Cal was finding his curiosity on the matter unsurprisingly muted. He felt good about leaving the huge beast in peace.

Bracing himself at the mouth of the strut's passageway, Cal reached down to pull Ebner up. The older man was breathing heavily and had a bad case of wobbly climber's leg.

Becker came up close behind. "We there already, boss?" she asked, a touch of her usual playful tone having returned. "Ebner here was only just getting into his stride."

The older man managed a small smile. "To be honest, I think I'm game for a bit of horizontal climbing," he said, looking at the new passageway with obvious relief.

"With any luck, we won't have to go far," Cal replied, squeezing his glow-tube to its brightest setting and directing it toward their new path. "How well do you know the structure of this base?"

"I know it inside and out," Ebner replied, sounding a little affronted that the question had to be asked. "What do you need to know?"

"Overhead access panels to the outside world." Cal nodded down the passageway. "If we can get out onto the top of this link strut, it might make a good spot for an airborne rescue. It'll be far clumsier than meeting the ship on the ground, but if our climb so far is anything to go by, we may have no snakes to deal with."

Ebner smiled at him, his eyes regaining a tiny spark of enthusiasm. "Well, for once, luck is on our side. I've never been to them myself, but I know for certain that there's an exterior hatch halfway along every link structure." He glanced at the passageway. "No more than a hundred feet."

Cal was encouraged by the man's conviction. He nodded appreciatively and looked down to confirm that everyone was ready. Not only were they ready but they appeared eager to keep moving, perhaps an underlying paranoia that the rescuers would decide to leave without them. Gripping Becker's spear tight, Cal took a breath then ventured forth into the new darkness.

They only made it a third of the way along the linking structure before they were faced with yet more destruction. A twisted tear in the floor had created a gap wide enough that it reached both walls. Cal cautiously crawled over the torn metal toward its edge. Peering through to the outside world, he took the opportunity to breathe in a lungful of fresh air. It was still raining, and he could see the vast roof of the base's main dome a good fifty feet below him, its silvery surface glimmering in the wet. Keeping his weight as evenly distributed as possible, Cal shifted himself back toward Becker. The rest of the group was further back still, huddled within the last intact portion of the passageway.

"Well, there's not much to see," he said to Becker as he detached the safety cord from his armor and began to loop it around his hand and elbow. "It's a fair old drop to the main dome. Too far to lower ourselves onto with cord. I still think our best hope is to climb onto the roof of this strut."

"If Ebner's right, it can't be far to the hatch," Becker said.

Cal nodded. "Not far if only we could all miraculously float over this gap." The two of them held out their glow-tubes and once again studied the gap in question. Crawling through it and trying to scale the outside of the structure was out of the question. Some of them might make it, but that wasn't good enough.

"Would have been nice and convenient if the ceiling had been torn open instead," Becker pointed out. "Could have just climbed out to the rescue ship right here."

Cal looked up and surveyed the damage above them. The metal had definitely been stressed, but there wasn't even a hole large enough to stick a hand through let alone an entire person. "That would be too much to ask, Sergeant."

"Seems so. I suppose a flying carpet might be too big an ask as well," Becker said then sucked at her teeth as she stared back down at the gap. "Just a bit too far to jump, especially with this unstable floor."

"A bit too far for you maybe but *way* too far for most of our group. We do have this cord though," Cal said as he finished looping it up. "You ever play out in the woods when you were a kid?"

Becker smirked. "I grew up on Galdon 3: a flat, dusty, desert colony on a back world. Closest thing we had to a tree was a rickety old water tower."

"I didn't have much better...except when I was on Mars."

"What are you thinking?"

Cal shrugged. "I met some kids on Exon a few years back who'd rigged up a swing rope in the surrounding forest. Let me tell you, all tech entertainment goes out of the window when you have a good length of rope and a decent tree." Cal pointed to the ceiling over the center of the gap. "I could climb up there and traverse along that exposed buttress. If I can tie one end of this cord around it, we could swing over one at a time."

Becker shot him an enchanting smile and tilted her head. "How sweet. I get to live the childhood I always wanted…if but for a moment."

Cal weighed the cord in his hand and surveyed the buttress. "When we get back to the starship, Sergeant, remind me I need to have words with you about your sarcasm."

"Will do, boss. I'll write a reminder on my ass right now."

CHAPTER TWENTY-FIVE

Cal decided that tying a knot while clinging upside down to a buttress that was stretched over a sixty-foot drop wasn't an easy job. Nor indeed was it a quick one. And to top it off a creaking sound had started just as he finished securing the cord. The creaking was intermittent at first then gradually increased in volume and tempo. It was a noise with which they were all becoming terribly familiar—the sound of something large slowly moving across metal, stressing and disrupting its structure with its great weight and power. A noise that instantly set their hearts pounding and their adrenaline pumping. Trying not to let the implications of the sound distract him, Cal continued to focus on the job at hand. Making sure that his grip was good, he double checked his knot then tossed the other end of the cord down to Becker, who was waiting with an eagerly reaching hand at the edge of the passageway's torn-up floor. Twisting his neck as far as he could, Cal had a quick glance through the gap beneath him. It was a long drop, and retaining his grip while practically hanging upside down wasn't easy. It didn't help that rain dribbling in through the fractures in the ceiling was making the metal dangerously slick. Carefully, he continued his horizontal climb until he had cleared the gap. He felt like a bug trying to defy gravity—except he lacked the confidence that he'd bounce harmlessly if he fell. Even with his armor on, such a fall would likely be fatal.

The creaking continued to grow louder. He tried to decipher whether the threat was approaching from inside or out, but he couldn't be sure. Trying to ignore the ominous sound, he instead listened for the rescue craft. The roar of its engines sounded distant, but it was a fast ship, and he knew it could be hovering over them within seconds. They just needed to get outside. Then, the ship's firepower would hopefully deal with the threat. *Just a matter of timing,* he told himself as he twisted around to assess the floor beneath him. Satisfied that the metal grating at least *looked* solid, he dropped down and was happy to find it wasn't simply an illusion. He unslung his spear from his back and shone his glow-tube down the dark passageway, holding it up like a cave explorer clasping a lantern, desperately hoping not to meet a hungry bear—or a big-ass snake. Taking a steady breath and a few steps forward, he further peeled back the darkness and, with relief, found the passageway promisingly intact and empty.

Turning back to the gap, he saw that Becker already had Ebner ready to swing across. The older man had one foot in a loop at the bottom of the cord and was gripping it with both hands in front of his chest, knuckles as white as his face.

The structure shuddered for a moment then gradually settled. It seemed that whatever was closing in on them was becoming more enthused. Taking that as his cue to hurry, Ebner dropped forward and let the cord carry him in a smooth, inverted arc over the gap. Having attached his glow-tube to his shoulder, Cal thrust out a hand and grasped the older man's skinny arm. Hauling him close, he made sure that Ebner had his footing before sending the cord back over to Becker. Campbell came next, seeming about as keen on the activity as Ebner. Then, Poots crossed. She was fast, confident, and altogether more graceful despite her injury.

The creaking became a deep groan—that familiar change in tone and intensity that acted as a proximity gauge. Cal swung the cord back then quickly glanced over his shoulder. Still nothing to be seen. *Must be outside,* he decided as he again listened for the rescue ship. It still sounded some distance away, its rail blasters firing. Whatever beast was holding their attention was proving an unwelcome diversion from the snake that was closing in on them.

Cal turned back to those on the other side of the gap just in time to see Durron aggressively barging his way forward and barking something as he made a desperate grab at the cord. In the blink of an eye, Becker thrust her knuckles into his throat, simultaneously knocking him to the floor and instantly silencing him. For what seemed like the hundredth time, Cal felt despair at the man's foolishness. When it came to words, the scavenger could be quite shrewd, but when action was required, he became nothing short of an imbecile who seemed keenly unwilling to learn from his experiences.

Wasting no more time, Becker unceremoniously grabbed Christie around the waist and quickly swung across the gap with the dazed-looking girl clutched tightly to her side. Grabbing hold of the pair, Cal hurriedly pulled them to solid ground and swung the cord to Couter. The new recruit deftly caught it then looked back toward Franco. The corporal shook his head and frantically indicated for him to cross with a wave of his hand.

Come on. Cal clenched his jaw, his heart thudding. The young man's willingness to put others first was admirable, but it wasn't always helpful. He was going to have to learn to follow orders without question. "Swing over now, Private. That's an order," Cal said, keeping his voice as low as possible.

Without further hesitation, Couter turned back and obeyed. Within seconds of him reaching the other side, the structure shuddered again. Then, it began to shift, the resulting stresses on the metal screaming out like a thousand angry harpies.

His vision somewhat distorted by the vibrating floor beneath him, Cal readied the cord and looked over the gap to Franco. The corporal was grabbing the still-floored

Durron by his collar and yanking him to his feet. "*Move it, Corporal.*"

Franco practically dragged Durron to the edge of the gap and looked up with an outstretched hand. Sorely tempted to order him to leave the scavenger behind, Cal carefully swung the cord over. The floor lurched again, almost causing Cal to tumble over the edge. He wobbled for a moment then took a generous step back. Whatever snake was trying to get at them, it seemed worryingly close and was stressing the already damaged structure to its limits.

Franco shoved the cord into the scavenger's hands and, without giving him time to put his foot in the loop, roughly pushed him over the edge. The structure lurched again, even more violently this time. The sharp movement jolted Durron's journey mid-swing to the point where it flung him off the cord. Fortunately—or perhaps not—the man's forward motion was enough to send him the rest of the distance over the gap on a collision course with its jagged edge.

Unwilling to waste time observing whether Durron had fallen to his doom or was perhaps skewered on a jutting piece of sharp metal, Cal thrust out his spear in an attempt to hook the now weightless cord. He missed it by an inch, and the cord's momentum rapidly slowed. Cal cursed, his mind reeling over solutions. But, looking over to Franco, he was reminded that the corporal wasn't one to hang around or indeed miss an opportunity to save his own life. Having already backed up, Franco began sprinting toward the gap, his face more a mask of desperate determination than true confidence. Acutely aware that his Italian friend would never make the jump, Cal was relieved to see that he was instead aiming for the slowly swinging cord.

Cal found his own stomach lurching as Franco flung himself out over the gap. But the aim and timing proved true, the corporal's hands closing around the lifeline with outstanding accuracy. His impressive velocity, however, was woefully overcooked. His legs whipping forward, Franco crossed the remainder of the gap at speed and barreled into Cal like a charging bull. The two of them crashed clumsily back into the passageway, their armor thudding loudly on the hard floor.

Quickly rolling to his feet, Cal saw that Durron had been awarded far more luck than he deserved and was still clinging onto life—quite literally. Somehow, he'd avoided being skewered, but only his face and arms were visible as he grasped the ragged edge of the ruptured floor. His expression was one of animalistic fear and desperation—a look that didn't seem tempered by the fact that Couter was already kneeling before him in order to haul him up.

The structure let out a deep moan and seemed to sag as if the metal had taken on the consistency of rubber.

Then, the beast was on them.

No sooner had Couter pulled Durron to relative safety than the snake's head smashed its way through the gap and slammed into the ceiling with terrifying force. It was a monster that made the previous creatures seem small in comparison. The impact of its sudden attack knocked every one of them cleanly off their feet. Then, metal tore and buckled as the snake withdrew its wide, blunt head only to ram it forward once again, bucking the sagging structure as if a bomb had gone off. Couter and Durron tried to back away from the turmoil, but the floor beneath them had become twisted like the roots of some ancient, metallic tree.

Feeling like a bug caught inside a child's rattle, Cal shouted at those behind him to retreat further into the tunnel before lunging forward to retrieve his spear, which had been torn from his grip when he'd hit the floor. The crude weapon's shaft felt a pitiful reassurance as he looked toward the snake. The beast was slamming its head from side to side, its jaws snapping in furious determination to sink rows of teeth into something living. Couter was horrifyingly close to becoming that target. The private was almost on his feet, but instead of retreating, he was grasping at Durron's arm, pulling the scavenger up from the contorted floor.

Managing to get his own feet more or less steady under him, Cal hefted his spear into a horizontal position and launched it at the snake with all his might. The combination of the effort and the quaking floor brought him back to his knees. At this range, he could hardly miss the huge target no matter how violently it thrashed about. But to his dismay, the spear deflected off the creature's head like a blunt stick hitting an armored tank. Cal grimaced. He'd already suspected that the larger—and presumably older—the snake, the tougher its scales, and this was perhaps proof. At least the beast's immense size was preventing it from fully squeezing its way into the structure.

"*Move, Couter,*" Cal shouted as he surged back to his feet. The private had succeeded in pulling Durron up and was urging him forward. But gratitude wasn't on the scavenger's mind—a fact made clear by the look on his face. There was of course fear and desperation, but it was infused with a sadistic ruthlessness that turned Cal's heart cold. He rushed toward them, but it was too late. Durron had a poisonous core that demanded self-preservation no matter what was required. The scavenger turned with a snarl and shoved Couter hard toward the snake. To say that the young private wasn't expecting it would have been a gross understatement. He was so full of untainted goodness and sense of duty that he was blind to the ruthlessness that could arise even in those he was trying to protect. As Cal surged forward, Couter fell back, his expression more one of surprise than fear. The snake's huge, thrashing head hit him with such force that his instantly limp body was smashed through the air, flying past Cal as if shot from a starship cannon.

The sight hit Cal like a bullet to the chest.

Feeling in a sudden daze, he stumbled clumsily back from the raging snake, and as he moved, came to the realization that Durron's throat was tight in his grasp. He had no memory of seizing the man, his body seemingly having acted without conscious thought. Cursing and forcing himself out of his stupor, he threw the choking scavenger aside then turned and ran to Couter's prone form. Franco was already there, his face grim. The private's armor was crushed down one side, blood already seeping out. Without a word, Franco carefully helped him drag Couter further from the raging snake before kneeling by his side to assess the damage.

"Campbell, I need your help," Cal shouted without looking up. "Sergeant, find that hatch, get it open, and get that bloody rescue ship over here. Attract their attention with a chem-bomb if need be. We're getting the hell out of here. All of us."

Cal had barely finished shouting the order when he heard the familiar thrum of the ship's approaching engines and the distinctive din of the rail blaster. *About fucking time.* He turned to see bright, orange flashes bursting up through the gap in the floor, illuminating the snake's glassy scales. Some of the gunfire tore through the structure to thud into the beast's body. Seconds later, the snake was gone, its head violently wrenched from the gap as it went to face the threat.

"You hear that, Couter?" Cal said, turning back to look at his young recruit. "The ship's—" His words suddenly failed him, the expression on Couter's face extinguishing them in an instant. The young man's eyes were full of confusion and fear. But there was also a glimmer of hope—hope that his commanding officer might somehow be able to fix him, to reveal some previously unseen trick and turn back the tide. The look was almost too much for

Cal to bear, and he had to force himself to retain a steady gaze. He was aware of Campbell by his side, but no matter how much he wanted to deny it, he knew that there was no fixing this. Couter was already as pale as a ghost. Too much blood was leaking through the grating, and his armor was far too damaged to remove. It was done. Death would close in fast, and there'd be no fighting or denying it.

The world seemed to go quiet as Cal gently put a comforting hand on the side of his young friend's face. "You did well, kid. You did really well."

Couter continued to look at him, managing only very slight movements of his eyes. There were no last words, no final requests like those seen in the holo-drome movies or acted out in the pleasure pod games. His young friend simply stared at him, his expression conveying infinitely more in only a few seconds than limitless words ever could. Cal felt guilt closing in on him like a merciless, all-consuming vice. No matter how much he wanted to blame Captain Decker or Durron or even this planet and the snakes, in the end, it had been largely his decisions that had brought them to this point in time, his actions that guided them all but in the end failed them. He stared at Couter's face—the youthful, fearful visage—and watched as unfulfilled hopes and dreams slowly leaked away. Cal did his best to remain calm…composed. He owed his recruit that much. But the vice was tightening, fast threatening to overwhelm him and throw his mind into turmoil.

Then, something changed, like a small light that flickered to life within his darkening awareness. Couter's eyes had begun to glaze over, but his terrible look of fear seemed to melt away and was replaced by something Cal couldn't name—just a glimpse of something that seemed beyond the comprehension of the living, a sort of peaceful wonderment. Cal stared at him entranced and wondered where his young friend was in that moment? What was he experiencing?

Then, as quickly as it had appeared, the strange moment was gone, closed off to the mortal world to leave nothing but a broken body and lifeless eyes in its wake.

Cal felt Campbell's hand on his shoulder. Things were being said to him, shouted even, but he was finding it hard to understand the words and even harder to tear his eyes from his dead, young friend. The floor of the passageway was still shuddering beneath him with varying degrees of intensity, and blasts of gunfire still lit up the dark and reverberated through the walls. But everything felt strangely muted—or perhaps drowned out by the war that had started up within his mind. He felt as though he was being torn in two by sorrow and rage, the two emotions seeming worlds apart yet eminently coupled.

Finally, he broke his gaze from Couter's body and looked toward Durron. The sight of the man instantly sent a sickening coldness flooding though him. The scavenger was breathing hard, his eyes wide but calculating as they flitted between him and the rest of the group. Driven by pure impulse, Cal was on the man in the blink of an eye, slamming him against the wall of the passageway, his hand wrapped around his neck, gripping him mercilessly.

"Think what you're doing, Lieutenant," Durron said desperately, rasping the words through his constricted throat. "The rescue ship's here...probably scanning your every move. If you—"

Whatever the man was going to say was forever silenced as Cal yanked him away from the wall, dragged him half a dozen steps toward the ruptured hole, then flung him headfirst into the open air.

CHAPTER TWENTY-SIX

Durron's scream was quickly stolen away by the long fall.

Cal stood for a moment, breathing hard. Then, feeling his rage start to ebb, he turned back to the others. All eyes were on him. None of them appeared disapproving. Indeed, Becker and Campbell wore looks of approval, even hints of an overdue satisfaction. Cal briefly wondered whether he'd ever regret killing the man, but he doubted it, and right now, he didn't much care. What would their situation look like if he'd killed him earlier? Even in his current state, Cal knew that the thought was a dangerous one, and he pushed it away. His eyes flicked down to Couter's body, but he didn't let them linger. He felt as though something had broken inside him, torn apart with no chance of repair. He'd lost friends and comrades before but not like this. Not so many in such a short period of time. Not when they were all under his command.

He felt a numbness seeping into him, smothering the pain like a mental anesthesia administered by his subconscious. A natural intervention to help ensure focus and ultimately survival. He had to get the others out of here. He had to get them on that ship. *I can't lose any more.* The thought echoed in his mind and coalesced with his anger.

He looked at Becker. "Sergeant, the hatch?"

She shook her head. "It's jammed shut. The structure's too twisted."

Cal suspected as much; Becker wouldn't have been idle if the hatch had been successfully opened. He could still hear the rescue ship kicking out rounds. It seemed like the snake wasn't easily tamed. Perhaps the beast's huge scales, which had deflected his spear so easily, were even holding out against the rail blasters. The structure was still protesting noisily under the weight of the creature, but Cal was encouraged by the fading din of the fight. At least it was being lured away from them.

He momentarily turned his eyes back to his dead recruit and forced himself to retain his steady resolve. Then, he moved back to the ruptured hole and studied the walls and the ceiling where the snake had inflicted its rage. There were plenty of holes and tears, but search as he might, he couldn't see one that was large enough for them to climb through.

As he continued to look, he found his gaze snapping back up to his right. There was a tear in the top edge of the structure that was perhaps large enough. But why hadn't he already seen it?

Suddenly, the tear grew larger, and the floor started to tip.

The structure was coming apart.

Cal almost cursed, but in the end, there simply wasn't time.

"*Go, go, go.*" He turned as he shouted and did his best to negotiate the fast-pitching floor. Fortunately, the others had had similar reactions, their collective glow-tubes a bubble of blue, juddering light as they all fled into the darkness of the passageway.

Without slowing for a second, Cal grabbed hold of Poots, whose injured leg was causing her to fall behind. She didn't protest but instead threw her arm over his shoulder, and soon, they managed a half-decent pace. Up ahead, Franco and Becker were practically dragging Ebner and Christie.

But then, the running stopped.

The supporting structure failed in its duty. The floor dropped out from beneath them like some kind of amusement park ride with a complete lack of restraints. Cal did his best to protect both his and Poots' head with his armored arms as they hit the ceiling. That was the last action that he had any real control over for what seemed an eternity. He and the private were forcibly separated as the collapsing structure violently tipped further, throwing them into a tumble. Moments later, it lurched again but this time began to level off. His head spinning, Cal realized that the structure's other end must have been ripped free. For a moment, it was relatively still, suspended by persistent support cables. Then, the cables began to tear, and a chaotic battle with gravity began. Fortunately, that battle held out, the threads of cables slowing the structure in a juddering decent until it crashed into the great, domed roof of the central hub.

There were a few seconds that came tantalizingly close to a still calm. But, ever the persistent adversary, gravity took hold again. Despite friction doing its best to oppose it, the structure began to slide down the domed roof, causing a metallic maelstrom that showed no mercy to those caught within. There were moments when Cal thought he'd managed to achieve a purchase on something solid, but those moments were soon torn from him as he was flung elsewhere. In the end, he decided it best to ball himself up, throw his arms around his head, and wait for the structure to find the ground.

It took Cal a while to realize the chaos had stopped.

Lying completely still in the near dark, he eventually managed to gain a little more awareness and carefully began to uncoil his arms and legs. Thankfully, all four limbs obeyed, leaving him hopeful that none were broken. He wasn't so sure about his skull. The way it was throbbing, he felt certain he must have cracked it open. His hands felt numb as he carefully ran them over his head, but there was enough feeling to confirm that, although he was covered in bumps and cuts, he was still mostly intact. Stiffly, he pulled his glow-tube from his shoulder and climbed to his feet. Peering into the dark, he tried to pinpoint the other blue lights.

"That you, sir?"

Cal recognized Franco's voice. He was close by, and Cal stumbled over to him. "You in one piece, Corporal?"

"I have no frickin' idea. But for the sake of getting the hell out of here, I'm gonna say yes."

Cal could see a fair amount of blood on the corporal's face, but he still seemed compos mentis. As he helped him to his feet, other voices rose up in the dark.

"Ebner's hurt." The voice was Campbell's.

Cal and Franco made their way over to her as fast as their battered legs could carry them.

"He's alive," Campbell assured them without looking up. "But he's seriously injured and out cold."

"What about you?" Cal asked.

"I think I've broken my arm…maybe some fingers too."

Cal bent down to look at the injury. It probably hurt like hell, but there simply wasn't time to do much about it. "Are your legs okay?"

Her face a mask of barely controlled agony, Campbell nodded.

"Okay. We need to get the hell out of this death trap. Corporal, secure Campbell's arm while I check on the others. Then, pick up Ebner. You steady enough to carry him?"

"Sure; there's not a lot to him," Franco replied confidently.

"Good." Cal turned and was about to move toward the next blue light when Campbell caused him to stop mid-step.

"I trust you, Lieutenant."

Cal turned back to face her. She'd climbed to her feet. Her face was pale and full of anguish, but her tone was sincere.

"I trust you to get us to that rescue ship...all of us." Her voice was remarkably steady. "And I'm truly thankful that you're here."

Cal nodded, her simple statement seeming to revitalize some of his strength. "I appreciate that. Just stay strong for a little longer. We're almost there."

Poots was attempting to get to her feet when Cal reached her.

"Busted my wrist and my damn ankle on the other leg. You believe my luck?"

Cal grabbed hold of her and helped haul her up. "That all that's wrong with you?"

"Few bumps and scrapes," she replied. Her voice was calm, but it was clear she was struggling to conceal her pain.

"Then I'd say your luck's holding out," Cal said as he helped to steady her. "Franco's back there seeing to Campbell and Ebner. Stay put. I need to check on Becker and Christie."

"No need."

The voice was Becker's. Cal looked up to see her emerge into the blue light.

"I was just coming to check on *you*," she said. Christie was by her side—a wide-eyed, ghostly waif swaying gently in the dark. Both appeared miraculously unhurt. "You mind spotting me a fresh glow-tube?" Becker said almost casually. "Seems I mislaid mine."

Cal tossed her his spare.

"Jesus, Sarge," Poots muttered. "How the hell is it that we look like we've been rolled through hell and you look like you've just been for a quick jog in the park?"

Becker shrugged. "Managed to jam us under a support strut before it got too manic. Made for quite a painless ride."

"Right, so the idea is to jam your entire body under it rather than just your foot," Poots said as she leaned heavily on Cal and painfully adjusted her stance. "How I wish I was as smart as you."

"Perhaps one day, Private," Becker replied, managing a brief smile.

"Talking of smart," Cal said, getting a good grip on Poots' armor before shining his glow-tube back toward Franco. "Let's get the hell out of here and onto that damn ship."

The statement was accompanied perfectly by the soft rumble of approaching engines.

CHAPTER TWENTY-SEVEN

"Here comes another." Poots fired a single shot from the old scavenger pistol that she'd reclaimed from Franco. "This one's bigger," she said as two more shots rang out.

Cal didn't look back at the snake she was referring to. What would be the point? It wasn't like he could scare it to death with a hard look. Instead, he continued to drag her over a series of twisted bulkheads that were too mangled to carry her over. It was her job to cover their backs while he did his best to haul both their asses to the outside world. Ahead of him, Franco was lifting Ebner back onto his shoulders, having already negotiated the bulkheads. The older man was still unconscious. Thankfully, Christie was managing under her own steam while Becker led the way, spear in hand. Already, the weapon was dripping with blue blood, but fortunately, none of the attacking snakes so far had been that large. Campbell followed, clearly struggling with her injured arm. The pain was exacerbating her exhaustion, but

Christie stayed close by her side. It might have been a trick of the dim light, but Cal could have sworn he'd seen the girl actively helping her older colleague.

Cal was certain they were nearing the end of the ruined structure. Unfortunately, the end in question had turned out to be a mangled network of upended grating, compressed metal, and torn cables. Gusts of cool air teased their perspiring faces as they pushed forward, the rumbling sound of the circling ship outside encouraging every step. Now and again, Cal heard the rail blasters hammering out rounds, then the engines would fade away only to return a few minutes later. It seemed the rescuers weren't being left in peace, and he suspected that they were repeatedly attempting to lure the larger beasts away.

Another single shot went off behind Cal's back then a couple of sharp clicks.

"Shit… Gun's run dry."

Cal cursed but didn't pause in his efforts.

Ahead of them, Franco stopped and looked back.

"*Don't wait for us, Corporal. Get the others out,*" Cal shouted as he shoved aside a tangle of hanging cables and climbed onto the last of the smashed bulkheads. "Forget the gun," he said to Poots as he reached down to get a better hold of her. "We're almost there."

"I'm not sure *almost* is going to cut it."

Cal heard her unsheathe her knife as he dragged her up, his arms exhausted and burning under the strain. It seemed adrenaline could only sustain a body for so long.

"*Oh Christ—*"

This time, the urgency in Poots' tone couldn't be ignored. Letting go of her, Cal reached for his own knife just as a large snake—its body twice as long as he was tall—smashed into the private's legs. The creature's thick head was only a few inches from her face when she brought her knife up. Holding it horizontally, the long blade ended up in the beast's jaws. Despite the immediate damage and deluge of dark blue blood, the snake was still determined to drive forward its attack.

Cal brought the point of his knife down hard just behind the creature's head. The strike did its job, and moving as quickly as he could, he heaved the dead weight off her. Poots was breathing hard, sucking in air through gritted teeth. She was incredibly tough, but her pain was getting the better of her.

"Get your ass out of here, Lieutenant." Her words were labored.

"Shut the hell up, Private," Cal replied as he turned to assess the mangled tunnel ahead. "And keep your eyes peeled for more of them."

"*Goddamn it, Cal, I mean it*. My legs are fucked," Poots replied angrily. "You've got thirty seconds."

Cal looked back sharply to see that the private was grasping the last chem-bomb tightly in both hands. There were tears in her eyes, and she was trembling. The pin was already pulled.

"They're closing in," she said, her voice raw. "There's too many of them. I'll buy you some time."

Cal didn't answer. Instead, he grabbed her wrists and

forcefully started to prize open her fingers. Within seconds, he had the bomb out of her grip and was tossing it in the direction they'd come. In its place, he quickly pushed her abandoned knife. "*We're getting the hell out of here, right now, both of us.*"

Poots only stopped protesting once Cal had pulled her up over his shoulder. Dropping off the smashed bulkhead, he pressed on, a new burst of adrenaline doing its best to enable a reckless pace in the dim, blue light. Seconds later, the darkness wasn't a problem. The chem-bomb ignited like a bright, orange flare, creating a harsh pattern of jagged black shadows ahead that flickered in a way that seemed to beckon him forward.

Cal resisted the urge to look back. The heat in their wake would protect them to an extent, but snakes were finding their way into the wreckage from countless small breaches—a fact quickly confirmed as a little beast dropped on them from above and latched onto his right arm. The creature instantly began to gnaw at his armor. Poots bashed at it with the butt of her knife, and moments later, it was coiled on the floor. More came at them from further down the passage. With no chance of outmaneuvering them all, Cal brought his boot down hard on one of their backs and did his best not to lose his stride. The impact felt damaging. But the creature was far from deterred and somehow managed to wrap part of its body around his ankle. The snake wasn't large enough to bring him down, but its weight slowed him. Poots slashed at it, but her reach was insufficient, her knife clashing ineffectively against his armored thigh.

"Lieutenant, over here. We're out."

The shout came from Franco. Cal couldn't see him, but he had a good idea where the call had come from. Altering his direction, he stumbled on some loosened grating and almost went down. His tired legs were barely fit to hold his own weight let alone Poots' as well. He could see movement all around, seeming to fill his peripheral vision—long, pale smudges closing in under the fading, orange light. He didn't look at them, not even a flick of the eyes. Afraid of the consequences if he lost his focus, he just surged on toward Franco's voice.

"Here, over here."

Twisting his body slightly to protect Poots' head, Cal barreled his way through a mass of service tubing that hung limply to his right. The tubing gave way far more easily than he'd anticipated, and his extra momentum sent them crashing toward the floor. Before he hit the deck, however, Cal glimpsed Franco leaning through a tear partway up the wall, his arms reaching, waiting to pull them to the outside world.

A snake snapped at Cal's face as he pushed himself to his feet. He bashed it away with a savage swing of his arm. His heart was thumping hard, a new reserve of adrenaline surging through his veins. He suddenly felt like an overcharged machine, all thoughts pushed aside, only instinct left. The sound of rail gun fire was loud now. They were close. Ignoring the snake wrapped around his leg, which was relentless in its efforts to get its teeth into him, he righted himself and moved to get a fresh hold on Poots. She looked barely conscious. Another snake was slithering over her shoulder. He took a swing at it and succeeded in knocking it aside. Then, he yanked the private off the floor, and together, they half stumbled, half fell over to Franco. Fortunately, the rupture that the corporal was leaning through was only chest high and was wide enough for the flashing gunfire outside to make a silhouette of him before it spilled past to invade the darkness.

Without hesitation, Franco grabbed Poots and pulled her roughly through the gap, speed taking priority over care. Cal was set to follow when a sharp pain lanced his side; his aggressive passenger had found a gap in his armor and was taking full advantage. Gritting his teeth, he seized the snake with one hand and unsheathed his knife with the other. The blade put a quick end to the attack and instantly diminished the pain. But the relief was barely realized before he found himself being tugged violently to the ground. In a desperate fury, he slashed out with the knife, not even fully comprehending where the new attack was coming from. The weapon's edge met flesh, but his vision had become a muddled mosaic of scales and teeth, confusingly illuminated by the flashing gunfire above his head.

Tearing his knife free, Cal thrust it down again. The snakes were small, but they were fast swamping his legs. He kicked at them, trying to match their ferocity. There was another shout from Franco…also Becker. As he desperately fought to free himself from the swarming beasts, he became aware of reaching hands grasping his arms and shoulders. He kicked as best as he could to get his legs free, but it felt as though they were immersed in quicksand. The hands grasping him pulled hard, but the collective weight of the snakes had become too great, and the efforts seemed futile. Then, a spear came down over his head only to be drawn back and thrust again…and again. But it was only one blade against what seemed like hundreds of attackers. Soon, they were coiling around his torso, then his chest. Anger overwhelming any fear, Cal continued to fight with everything he had, even resorting to biting one of the beasts that attempted to coil around his neck.

Then something happened—something nothing short of a miracle.

The snakes withdrew, inexplicably uncoiling from him to rapidly disappear back into the darkness of the structure. Before he had much chance to question the strange development, the grasping hands hauled him up toward the gap. Then, he was outside—pulled from one chaotic tumult into another. There was a brief, clumsy fall before he hit soft mud. A number of small snakes came with him, but most were dead, and those that weren't quickly slithered away.

"*What the hell?*" Franco shouted, sounding confused.

Cal shook his head and blinked his eyes. Rain was lashing, cold and sharp in the blustery wind. The sky above was ablaze, and the gunfire was loud. It was that familiar din of war and destruction, but right now, it sounded more like a blessing—rail blasters, pulse rifles, and then the wholly welcome sound of a pressure grenade.

Climbing to his feet, Cal saw Becker, spear in hand, climbing up the side of the ruined structure's exterior to get a better vantage point. Turning about, he swept his eyes over the chaos, quickly trying to give it some order. The ship was close by, hovering near to the ground, but the pilot seemed reluctant to land and was actively moving further away from them. The hover was standard procedure when the threat level was high. Taking off took time—only seconds, but often, seconds was too long. Cal could see soldiers ready and waiting through the ship's open side hatch. Two were already on the ground, outfitted in full armor and large, ten-click pulse rifles pulled in hard against their shoulders. They were lit up brighter than day under the ship's thrusters and were probably regretting the fact they'd jumped out early. There were dead snakes everywhere, their corpses a grisly mess, but the number of live beasts seemed amazingly few and, just like those in the structure, they were fast retreating. At first, Cal thought the heat from the engines was causing them to flee, but then he suspected something else—the same something that was suddenly dissuading the pilot from landing.

Quickly, Cal turned back to his own people. Ebner was now conscious, slumped in the mud at the base of the mangled structure. Christie and Campbell were next to him, thankfully both on their feet. Poots was in a similar position to Ebner, but her knife was still tight in her grip. He looked back to Franco, who was keeping an eye on the hole through which they'd come, ready to deal with the appearance of any snakes. But the hole remained a dark void, the beasts seeming reluctant to emerge.

"Forget the hole, Corporal; they're not coming out," Cal shouted. He was starting to understand the nature of these beasts—and their hierarchical instincts. Whether due to fear or some sort of respect, the smaller snakes seemed to retreat when their much larger kin came close. "There's a big bastard closing in on the other side of the structure. Get ready to carry Ebner."

Franco nodded and moved without hesitation.

Cal looked up to see Becker making her way back down to them. She was moving fast.

"How close is it, Sergeant?"

"*Too close*," Becker yelled as she leaped off the structure to land semi-gracefully by his side. "*We've gotta move. Now.*" She moved to grab hold of Christie.

Cal knew Becker wasn't one for dramatics. The fact that she hadn't taken the time to brief him on the exact proximity, speed, and location of the beast meant they were in even more trouble than usual. Running over to Poots, he again hauled her up and over his shoulders just as Franco was doing with Ebner.

"Everyone run," Becker shouted as she made a beeline out into the open. She was forcefully dragging Christie along while Campbell stumbled close behind. Although his rational mind was screaming at him to stay close to the structure, Cal trusted Becker implicitly and on this occasion ignored his instincts. The fact she was heading in the direction of the two soldiers and their ten-click pulse rifles certainly didn't hurt her cause.

As they ran, the rescue ship flew directly over their heads, the combination of its thrusters and another eruption from its rail blasters a deafening roar. But even that noise wasn't enough to drown out the massive boom that sounded close behind them.

"*What's going on, Private?*" Cal shouted to Poots as he continued to run.

"Something hit the structure," Poots replied, her voice strained. "Something big as hell. Don't stop."

But moments later, Cal did stop—not by choice but as a result of colliding with Franco, who'd skidded to a halt in front of him. In fact, all of them had stopped. The two soldiers were running out of the darkness toward them, yelling something unintelligible as they tried their best to shoot over their shoulders without breaking pace. Something huge was looming out of the wet, windswept night behind them, its ghostly scales increasingly brighter under the flashing discharges from their pulse rifles. It was one of the two monstrous beasts they'd seen emerge from the lake earlier in the night. And there was no doubt in Cal's mind that the rescue ship was busily occupying its twin that had smashed into the other side of the structure.

Cal didn't need to look back to know that the ship wasn't about to come to their aid; its railblasters were going ten to the dozen and were becoming more distant as they attempted to deal with the other huge snake. He briefly wondered whether the two snakes coming at them from opposite directions was a coincidence. Or was it a tactical maneuver that suggested intelligence? Either way, it didn't really matter now. He lowered Poots to the ground and ordered Franco to do the same with Ebner. Bitterly, he realized there was no running from this. There wasn't much chance of a fight either, but the least they could do was face their enemy. Never one for defeat, Becker moved forward a couple of steps, spear held tight. Cal almost moved to stop Christie as she shuffled forward to join her, but the girl had pulled something from her torn clothing that caused him to stop—one last chem-bomb, which she held out almost tenderly on her open palm. Becker's look of surprise as she scooped the offering out of the girl's hand mirrored Cal's own. The girl must have been concealing the little bomb since before they'd even arrived, probably having swiped it during Billy's drug-addled watch. Perhaps she'd been more aware than they'd known, just paralyzed by fear. But now, it seemed that after all they'd been through, that fear had run dry.

Becker didn't hesitate in pulling the pin. The soldiers were almost on them, and the snake wasn't all that far behind. The beast's size was becoming terrifyingly apparent, probably able to swallow the lot of them in one go if they were good enough to bunch together for it. Becker pushed Christie back as she readied herself to the throw the bomb. Cal moved to her side, as did Franco. They were under no illusions that the bomb was going to be particularly effective out in the open against such a large foe, but it was something, and something was always better than nothing.

In a strange symmetry, Becker threw the bomb just as the two approaching soldiers withdrew their sidearms and tossed them in their direction. Cal snatched one of the pulse pistols out of the air and knew Franco would be doing the same with the other. A second later, Cal had adjusted the weapon in his grip and was tugging on its trigger. He'd been expecting the move, knowing that the team in the rescue craft would be fast thinkers and trained just like his own. The two soldiers skidded to their knees right in front of them, turning as they did so in order to blast out round after heavy round from their ten-click pulse rifles.

Christie's bomb exploded a dozen paces in front of the snake and instantly slowed its attack. Rearing up and twisting away from the flames, the beast retreated a little distance then altered its course, its long, glassy body reflecting the little inferno as it efficiently maneuvered in a wide arc around it. The bomb had bought them some time, a handful of seconds, but inevitably, the beast was coming at them again, regaining its pace quickly. The feel of the fully operational weapon shuddering in Cal's grip accompanied by the blaze of surrounding gunfire filled him with hope. But it didn't last. Their defense was clearly doing the snake some damage—its pale, blunt head blackening to the point that it would soon be indistinguishable from the darkness surrounding it—but still, it was advancing, demonstrating that same reckless ferocity seen in its smaller kin.

Cal prayed for the beast to open its jaws, his past experience telling him that its insides were far more vulnerable than its near indestructible scales. But the beast didn't oblige. Again, Cal found himself having to ignore his instincts, which were urging him to spread out from the group and attack the creature from different sides. But half the group were unarmed, and some couldn't even move. No, they would stand fast and unleash everything they had until the very last. Either they all made it or none of them did. Even though the latter was fast seeming inevitable, none of them retreated—even when the monstrous beast was a few meters away, its pace and bulk like a wrecking truck. Cal held his trigger down, the weapon growing hot in his hand. *Open your jaws, you bastard.*

But the snake didn't open its jaws...at least as far as he knew.

The beast was suddenly gone.

Something had hit it hard and fast—*very* hard and fast.

Cal eased off his trigger, confused and a little shocked as he stepped back and looked to his left. Max was there. The big battle robot had rammed into the side of the snake's head, smashing it away from them, and was now furiously grappling with it. He seemed far smaller than usual, pitted against such a massive foe, but he was fierce, almost savage, as he repeatedly crashed his fist into the side of the snake's head. All of them watched, barely moving, the sudden fight having thrown them into a stunned silence. Normally, Cal would have fancied the robot's chances, but Max had multiple malfunctions and was already struggling as a result. One of his mechanized arms became caught within the monster's jaws, and his left leg was juddering violently. It seemed the fight wasn't going to last long. The snake was drawing its long body in, beginning to coil up and roll over, taking Max with it.

"Let's move," Cal shouted, turning to grab hold of Poots. But one of the soldiers was already there, perhaps realizing that fresh legs were better suited for the job. Cal didn't argue. And likewise, no one argued with his order.

Their pace as they fled from the fight proved that much quicker now that they had two more able bodies in the group. As they ran, Cal again looked for the ship. From what he could make out, the link structure had been turned over and almost torn in two near one end. Becker had definitely been right to get away from it. Beyond that, there was a great deal of fire and a huge amount of smoke, dark and billowing against the gleaming surfaces of the base. But search as he might, he could detect no sign of the other snake or the ship—none, that was, but a faint thrum of engines that he hoped to God wasn't just in his imagination. They ran on, but his attention never strayed far from the smoke.

Then, the thrum increased, gaining credibility in his mind the louder it became. "*Come on, come on*," he whispered under his breath. Suddenly, as if in answer to his quiet plea, the ship burst out of the smoke and immediately altered its course to head in their direction.

"*Here's our ride*," Franco shouted.

The corporal yelled something else, but the ship was incredibly swift, and already, the increasing sound of its thrusters drowned out his words. The pilot flew low and set down far closer to them than was considered safe. Thruster burns, however, were the least of their concerns.

Despite the relative proximity of the landing, they still had a little way to run. Without breaking his stride, Cal looked back to try and catch a glimpse of Max and the now distant fight. His eyes battling the dark, he peered through the sweeping, stinging rain and after a moment confirmed his fears. The clash between monster and machine was over. Max was nowhere to be seen. Only the snake was emerging, once again sliding relentlessly toward them. The huge creature was slower than it had been, clearly injured in its battle. But still, it pursued them, seeming entirely mindless in its need to attack…to *kill*. Cal had to wonder which of them was truly the machine: Max or the beast.

There was a familiar change in pitch as the ship's thrusters prepared to take off again. *Don't you bloody dare,* Cal thought, shooting a fierce look toward the cockpit window. Whoever sat at the controls was nowhere near as ballsy as Sinclair had been. "Corporal," he shouted, "get on that ship, and stop that bloody pilot taking off again. Not before the civvies are on board."

Franco put on a burst of speed. Cal, on the other hand, slowed to a near stop and turned to fire his weapon at the approaching menace, gradually backing his way toward the ship as he did so. Maybe he could slow it just enough.

Seconds later, one of the soldiers joined him.

"The bitch refuses to die, eh."

A ten-click pulse rifle was shoved at him. Cal grabbed it and managed half a grin as he thrust it forward and tugged on its trigger. The soldier was Becker. Somehow, she'd acquired two of the pulse rifles—probably forcibly. He refocused his attention back on the snake. The beast slowed under the fire, but it was close. Too damn close.

Without relenting his defense, Cal glanced back again to see Ebner, Campbell, and Christie being pulled into the folds of the ship. "Okay, Sergeant," he shouted, confident that Becker would know his intentions as well as he did. "Let's go." Together, they spun and bolted for the ship, doing their best to gain momentum on the wet, muddy ground. The ship was already beginning to rise. Abandoning their weapons, they leaped for the opening, crashing into its hard edge and scrambling for a decent hold. The soldiers reached down to help them, but the look of horror on their faces was enough to turn Cal's head. The snake had increased its speed, and as the ship continued to lift, the beast arched its body, raising its head in an attempt to smash into the underside of the hull.

Cal stared, transfixed, the passing seconds painfully stretched. He was now completely incapable of affecting the outcome one way or the other. For a terrible moment, it seemed the snake was going to achieve its goal. But suddenly, its massive head jerked in midair as if hit by an immense electrical surge. Then, it was dropping, having inexplicably lost all of its lethal drive. Something long and sharp was protruding from the top of its head—a huge blade, shining bright under the fierce light of the ship's thrusters, blue, glistening blood coating its length. The snake's impenetrable scales were upended where the weapon had pushed them apart from the inside.

Cal could scarcely believe his eyes. Dragging himself forward, he leaned out of the ascending ship's hatch and watched as the lifeless beast pounded into the dark mud. The killing blade had already been retracted, no doubt automatically sheathed back into Max's big forearm. It seemed that being eaten simply wasn't enough to prevent the robot from saving their lives one last time.

Cal became aware of hands grasping him, pulling him back as questions were being asked. Climbing to his feet, he shrugged the hands off and called out for whomever was in charge. A woman stepped forward, deactivating her night vision visor as she did so. Cal recognized her immediately; he'd worked with her on a couple of missions a few years back. She was a good officer and thankfully at this moment appeared entirely composed. She had to shout to be heard over the noise of the thrusters. "Harper, what the hell happened here?"

"Lieutenant Shaw. I've no time to explain," he shouted back. "How long have you been in the atmosphere?"

Shaw didn't hesitate and tapped a control on her data pad. "One hour twenty-seven minutes."

Cal nodded, satisfied. It hadn't been long. "Any

trouble with the engines?"

Shaw's brow creased as she shook her head. "None."

"Any other technical problems?"

"Our targeting's started to play up. Made it near impossible to use our Jago cannons."

"What about other signs of life…*human* life?" Cal knew full well that neither Orisho nor Wilson had survived, but he wouldn't have been able to forgive himself if he hadn't at least checked.

"You lot are it," Shaw replied. "We've done multiple scans."

Again, Cal nodded and turned to look out of the open hatch. The pilot had brought the ship to a static hover, ensuring an altitude that posed no risk from predators on the ground no matter what their size. Fire still burned near the base, fierce despite the rain as it continued to billow thick, black smoke. The area was becoming increasingly hard to see. "And the snake? The other big one by the base?" he asked without turning from the hatch.

"It finally retreated. We managed to fire a helix bomb at it…but with the screwed-up targeting, it took some doing…"

Thank Christ for that, Cal thought as he took hold of an overhead grab rail. Leaning forward, he looked directly down to get a bird's-eye view of the huge beast that had almost been the end of them. The ship's thrusters were casting a bright light, which illuminated the entire length of the dead snake's body. It was undeniably an impressive sight, but he didn't waste time gazing at it. His attention was on the relatively small, hard-edged form lying a few meters from the creature's massive, gaping jaws. A tangle of twisted parts that now lay inert bar the odd, juddering, cybernetic spasm. Even under the bright light, Max would have been barely recognizable were it not for the domed head and those unmistakable round eyes that still retained a soft glow. Never one to give up, the battle robot had crawled free from his opponent's jaws, leaving a trail of blue gore in his wake.

Cal felt transfixed by the sight of the robot. The move to crawl away from his defeated opponent was one last demand from his AI protocols to ensure the ease of retrieval at a later date. Or perhaps there was more to it than that. Cal couldn't deny those little spikes he'd seen in Max's system, the ones that occasionally caused something akin to a personality to flash into existence. Maybe the big combat robot had crawled free deciding that he didn't want to be left—didn't want to be abandoned on some hellhole by his team. Cal struggled with the thought. It seemed impossible. Maybe he was losing it. Maybe this mission and all its tragedy had proved too much for him. His rational mind was screaming at him to just get the hell out of there. To leave this damn planet in their wake and let it become someone else's problem. But those round, glowing eyes seemed to be staring up at the ship, staring directly up at *him,* imploring him not to forsake a teammate.

Shit, I really am losing it.

Cal continued to stare—seconds feeling like long

minutes, those round, glowing eyes staring right back.

Damn it.

He turned back into the ship and did his best to appear entirely sane. "Shaw, we need to get out of here; this is not a friendly planet. But first, I request a quick retrieval of my last teammate."

Shaw looked puzzled. "Like I said, Lieutenant, the scans showed no signs of—"

"I mean our combat robot directly below us."

Shaw hesitated. Understandably, she appeared surprised by the request, but she seemed to be weighing it up nonetheless.

"I'm referring to the same robot that just saved every single one of our lives," Cal added. He considered elaborating with some bullshit about critical data stored within Max's system which was imperative to retrieve, but in the end, just as Max had done, he let his eyes do the talking.

It took some moments, but eventually, Shaw activated her comm. "Paulter, retrieve the combat robot below us. Do it fast, and use the grasper. Be ready on the emergency release in case there's any trouble."

"Copy that," the pilot replied.

"Once it's done, take us on a fast track out of the atmosphere."

Cal felt himself relax, Shaw's words seeming like a mild sedative. He held the woman's gaze. "I appreciate that."

She gave him a brief, consoling smile. "It seems like your team's already suffered enough loss."

Cal nodded. "It's been bad," he replied. The statement sounded woefully inadequate, but now wasn't the time to start baring his soul and certainly not to a fellow officer. He glanced over at the civilians, then at the last of his team. The sight of them alive and mostly intact went some way to banishing the sorrow that was already trying to creep its way back into his mind. "To be honest, Lieutenant, it's nothing short of a miracle that any of us made it out alive."

"Gotta be grateful for that."

"I am," Cal said more to himself than Shaw. "I truly am."

Epilogue

Cal breathed a long sigh of relief as the ship's juddering came to an end. Finally, they were clear of the planet's atmosphere. Clear of its hellish dangers and ominous secrets. Soon, the ship would reattach to its bulky Slipdrive, which lingered idly out of orbit. Then, they'd make the long journey back to the starship—back to debriefings, a shit load of questions, and some hard decisions. Cal would say his piece, draw up his reports, and make damn sure they were given the right attention. If he could help it, no more lives would be claimed by Capsun 23. Then, he'd pay a visit to Captain Decker—*force* a visit if necessary. As he'd suspected might happen, Decker hadn't even bothered to send a backup rescue ship. If Shaw and her team had failed to retrieve them in time, the cycle would have started over again. Cal found himself wondering how many times that would need to happen before the idiot captain saw sense. How many lives needed to be lost? He decided it would probably be best to give it some time before he confronted Decker—not a lot but enough for his anger to dissipate to a degree where he was less likely to cause the man serious damage.

Resting his head back, Cal was pleasantly surprised to find that this ship actually had decent smart-gel padding. He felt a wave of gratitude for that little element of comfort—to a level that was probably completely disproportionate. Right now, however, he'd happily grasp whatever blessings came his way no matter how small and seemingly insignificant. Perhaps unsurprisingly, he felt as though his body had been pulled through a meat grinder. On top of that, it probably wouldn't be long until the unpleasant aftereffects of all the stim drugs he'd consumed kicked in. Fortunately, he was fairly adept at disconnecting from such physical pains. A part of him wished he had equal talents for pushing away the mental pain, to numb his mind until the passing of time inevitably lessened the impact. But there was another part of him, a far more dominant part, that allowed it in. *Forester, Malloy, Orisho, Wilson, Sinclair, and Couter.* He needed to remember the loss. He needed to learn from it. Bad decisions had been made, most notably his own.

Beside him, Becker deactivated her restraints and climbed to her feet in order to strip off her armor. In truth, he felt like doing the same himself but couldn't even come close to rustling up the energy or the will. For a moment, he wondered how she was managing it. But as he watched her unlock and peel off her chest plate, he noticed her battle-scarred arms trembling under the effort.

"Sergeant, sit down before you fall down. That's an order," Cal said, his tired voice lacking any real authority.

Letting the chest plate drop to the deck, Becker collapsed heavily back into her seat. "Just had to get out of that fricking thing. Felt like it was crushing me."

Cal looked down at the armor, the blue blood stains and massive teeth marks reminding him just how lucky he was to still have his sergeant with him.

"Thanks for having my back down there, Becker."

"Ditto, boss. I think we made it out just about even on this occasion."

Cal smiled. No matter how many times they saved each other's lives, Becker never made a big thing out of it.

Letting out a small groan, she pressed her head back into the smart-gel. "When we get to the starship, remind me to ask for some time off."

"Consider it already asked and approved," Cal replied.

The request and answer were both made in jest, but in truth, Cal doubted whether any of them would be fit for duty for quite some time, especially Poots.

"You think Max will be fixed up again for service?" Becker asked.

Cal shifted in his seat and rubbed at his eyes. Max's retrieval had thankfully gone without a hitch. If it hadn't, it would have been a tough one for him to explain. Now, the combat robot was secured in the hold where Franco had set him to recovery mode; he needed to recuperate just as much as the rest of them—probably more. To say he was a malfunctioning, mangled mess would be an understatement. "I hope so," Cal replied. "The big guy deserves it. And we'd have been screwed without him."

"You got that right," Becker mumbled in agreement. "What about the four of us?" she asked after a moment. "What do you think we can expect?" Her tone was tentative, as if afraid to hear the answer.

Cal knew exactly what she was asking. When a team lost a member, or even two, they were promptly replaced. But to lose six…it was entirely possible they'd be disbanded and absorbed separately into other teams. Cal turned to look at her. "To be honest, I really don't know. I'm afraid it's possible they'll break us up." Now perhaps wasn't the best time to give her bad news, but she'd asked, and he couldn't keep the truth from her.

Becker wordlessly reacted to his answer by heaving her right leg up and yanking off her thigh protector. Allowing the piece of armor to clatter to the floor, she threw the leg back down and sat quietly.

Cal turned to his right. Franco was already asleep a couple of seats down, and beyond him, Poots was being attended to by the rescue team's medic. On the other side of the cabin, Ebner and Campbell were both horizontal, strapped down, and fully sedated. Christie was sitting between them, awake but staring at nothing, face still and pale as a ghost.

"You ever get the feeling you have absolutely no control over your life?" Becker asked after a time. "Just getting bounced around like a bug in a storm."

"All the bloody time," Cal replied, and he meant it.

Becker sighed and lethargically tugged at the armor on her other leg. "I guess it's our choice to be in the storm in the first place."

"I guess so."

Succeeding in freeing her left thigh, Becker leaned forward and turned to look at him as if she'd suddenly plucked a thought out of his head. "You're thinking of getting out of the storm, aren't you?"

Cal shrugged. "Maybe," he said, deciding there was no point trying to hide this from her either.

"Because of this mission?"

Cal gave her a melancholic smile. "I know what you're going to say, Sergeant, that death is part of the job, that you can't always make the right decisions or give the right orders all of the time."

Becker raised an eyebrow. "It may be cliché, but it doesn't make it any less true. You told me yourself that it's impossible to protect everyone."

"That's true," Cal agreed with a nod. "But it's not that I can't accept it or that I doubt my ability to lead. I just don't know whether I *want* to. I'm not sure if I want an entire lifetime of having to endure those inevitable consequences." If he were to stretch his honesty a little further, he might have told her that his faith in the military's motivations had also started to crack.

Becker looked disappointed but nodded understandingly and settled back in her seat.

"It's far from a definite decision," Cal admitted. "I know it wouldn't be an easy thing, starting a new life from scratch. I mean, what the hell would I do with myself?"

"You'd just end up finding yourself another storm," Becker replied with a smirk. "Probably an even bigger one."

Cal smiled at that, and deep down, he suspected she was probably right.

"Just do me a favor, will you, boss?"

Cal rustled up enough energy to lean forward and look her in the eye. "Of course."

"Just make sure to remember all the lives saved as well as those lost."

Cal nodded. "I will," he said sincerely.

Settling back in his seat, Cal sunk his head deep into the smart-gel, closed his eyes, and tried his best to quiet his mind. It wasn't easy, but for a while, he achieved a state that could almost be considered restful. When he finally roused himself, he noticed that Christie was looking directly at him. The girl still looked as pale and fragile as ever, but perhaps for the first time since meeting her, she seemed fully aware of his presence. Then, she smiled at him. The gesture was small and gentle, but it held real power and seemed to sweep through him like some sort of miracle elixir, instantly dimming a great deal of his pain, physical and emotional.

The smile said a lot, but mostly, Cal suspected it was a simple thank you. She was glad to be alive.

Cal didn't blame her one bit.

I hope you enjoyed Harper's Ten, the prequel to the Fractured Space Series. Read on for the first chapter of Star Splinter, book 1 of the Fractured Space Series…

Star Splinter

Fractured Space Book 1

Chapter One
GUILT AND REGRET

Lieutenant Callum Harper felt no satisfaction from the punch. He watched grimly as the big man stumbled back across the office, his arms flailing like some sort of faulty windup toy before a collision with a hefty metal desk bounced him face first to the floor. The man lay still, seemingly out cold. Cal cursed. Violence had never been his intention, but now that the time had come, he'd found it impossible to hold back. In truth, he was surprised it hadn't happened sooner. Patiently, he waited for the man to come to. It started with a confused shifting, which before long turned into a clumsy panic. The man was bordering on obesity, and getting to his hands and knees was proving a struggle. Then there was something close to a whimper as he caught sight of his tooth set neatly in a little pool of blood beneath him.

Oh bloody hell. Cal felt his jaw tighten as well has his

fist. He could take raging expletives, violence, or even arrogance and spite, but not self-pity and blubbing. There was no way he could put up with the man crying, not *this* man. He'd just have to knock him out again. Fortunately, the tears didn't materialize, and Cal relaxed his fist.

The floored man was Captain Laurence Decker, someone whom, to Cal's utter bewilderment, had been deemed worthy of commanding a Class One Military Starship. Even more confusing was the fact that he was the son of the highly revered Admiral James Decker, a man who'd worked his way up the ranks with unrivaled determination, wit, and charm. How the hell could such a great military leader have produced a son who fell so short of the mark? The only logical explanation was that the Admiral's greatness simply didn't stretch to his parenting skills. There were, after all, plenty of rumors to back that up, talk of inflated grades at the Admiral's hand and echoes of disgust relating to his son's absurd leapfrog from academy to starship command. Cal had started military training shortly after Laurence Decker had graduated, but the rumors had lingered on. He had even heard talk of a discreet bodyguard being hired in the early years to deal with bullies.

Laurence Decker had more than a few bodyguards now, and they were far from discreet. The sound of multiple cutting lasers on the other side of the sealed office door pulled Cal away from his thoughts, and he briefly turned to the sound. "It seems your guards are finally coming to your rescue, Decker. But they won't be getting through that door seal anytime soon."

Decker didn't react to the words; he was still staring at his front tooth, seemingly struggling to come to terms with the fact that it was no longer in his mouth.

"Stand up and face me, Decker."

As if trying to prevent any more teeth from spilling out, Decker placed a hand over his mouth and finally looked up at his attacker. There was unmistakable fear in that look, fear that this man who'd punched his tooth out might not be finished with him. Cal had never considered himself a particularly imposing man, and the level of the Decker's dread took him by surprise.

Good, let the bastard be scared.

Clumsily, Decker shifted back against the same desk that he'd recently bounced off, his eyes darting wildly about the office no doubt in search of an escape from his nightmare. But there was no escape. Not unless you counted the exterior viewing panel, which, even if he could break through it, would make for a rather messy, unceremonious exit out into the cold vacuum of deep space. There was only one exit, and Cal had activated the door's heavy duty punch locks and placed himself between that exit and the captain.

"Are you going to stand up and face me, or am I going to have to come over there and haul you up?" Cal hoped for the former. He didn't relish the idea of lifting that much weight.

Leaning back against the desk to steady himself, Decker managed to struggle to his feet. "Anything you want. I'll give you anything, just name it."

Here we go. "Let's dispense with the begging and bribing," Cal replied evenly. "You know why I'm here." *Why the hell am I here?* Would pounding his fist into this man really do any good?

"Open that door, Lieutenant. Open it now, and your career will remain intact." The shaking in Decker's voice drowned out any inkling of authority it might once have contained.

"My career ended when I failed to stop you sending good soldiers on yet another suicide mission." *I'm here to try and knock some sense into you, you useless bastard.*

"But I had no choice," Decker reasoned weakly. "I had to send at least one squad in. The pirates—"

"They weren't the threat. You're a weak, dim-witted fool, Decker, but even you should have seen that."

"You're wrong… There were orders… I—"

"Shut your damn mouth," Cal shouted more in frustration than anger. All he wanted was to get through to the man. He wanted him to realize what a fool he was. He wanted him to realize the weight that his command carried and the cost of his foolishness. He also wanted to punch him again. "The order came from you. You know it, and I know it." The lazy bastard probably hadn't even read the mission brief. "I can't let you do it again, Decker."

Decker didn't reply. He gripped the desk behind him and shot nervous glances between Cal, the exit, and the exit's locking mechanism. Cal could still hear the guards battling furiously with the sealed door, but he wasn't concerned. There was still time. He stared at Decker, reading the man like a book. The pathetic excuse for a captain had tried begging, making excuses for his actions, and of course pulling rank. They'd all failed, and now, Cal saw a level of desperation that suggested a last ditch effort at physical action. It seemed that apologizing and admitting his guilt would never occur to such a man.

"Don't bother—" Cal began, but the captain was already launching his ample weight forward.

Swiftly, Cal twisted aside, easily tripping the man and once again setting the arms flailing. Decker's journey was a short one that ended abruptly as his head connected with the rear wall.

Cal rubbed his face and eyes. What the hell was he doing? He'd never get through to a man like this, not with fists and certainly not with words. Stepping towards the crumpled captain, he was amazed to see that he'd somehow remained conscious. Reaching down, he clamped a fist around his collar and dragged him up onto his knees.

Decker pawed at the fist with weakened fingers. "I'm sorry... I'm sorry they died." The words were quiet but clear.

Cal paused, not quite trusting his ears. He stared into the man's terrified eyes, searching for some sincerity, some truth. Releasing his grip, he allowed the captain to slump to the floor. "Is there none of your father in you?" he asked, his brow creased in frustration.

After a few moments of silence, Cal shook his head and

turned away. Maybe it hadn't been a complete waste. Maybe something had made it through. "You can take this as my resignation," he said as he walked slowly over to the office door and activated its release mechanism. The military would have to do without him from now on. He'd had enough of foolish orders and bullshit missions. He'd had enough of men like Captain Laurence Decker. And he'd had enough of being responsible for people. From now on, he'd be responsible for himself and leave it at that. *No more taking orders, no more giving orders, and no more responsibility.* With that in mind, Cal almost smiled as Captain Decker's guards burst in and surrounded him with pulse rifles raised.

"What d'you want done with him, sir?" asked the guard who had taken up position directly in front of Cal. His voice was aggressive, and the muzzle of his weapon was practically touching his nose.

Suddenly feeling much calmer, Cal looked down at the crumpled man.

Remaining on the floor, Decker took a few moments before answering. "Earth," he said simply, his voice sounding as broken as his face. "Send him back to Earth."

As the guards escorted him from the office, Cal caught a glimpse of an unfamiliar expression on Captain Laurence Decker's face. It was the unmistakable look of guilt and regret.

Star Splinter is available now in kindle and paperback on all Amazon online stores. It is also available as an audiobook on audible.com and audible.co.uk

If you'd like to be notified of the release dates for my new books please feel free to sign up to my news letter at www.jgcressey.com/news-letter/

Author's Thanks

Firstly, I'd like to thank you, the reader, for plucking Harper's Ten from Amazon and delving inside! I hope you enjoyed it and are hungry for more! I'd be incredibly grateful if you'd take a moment to leave a review on Amazon (even a very brief one). For a new author like myself, those reviews act as firepower in the great battle to be seen among the hordes of novels lining Amazon's shelves! (Also, I really like reading them!)

I'd like to send out a big thanks to my family and friends for their continued, unwavering support. And to Mark Evans who went above and beyond the call of duty, offering me invaluable advice and aid when it came to bashing this book into shape! Also to Donald and Paddy whose thoughts and comments were a huge help. And I'd like to say a special thanks to my wife, Liz for her editing and typo hunting!

As always, many thanks to my wonderful editor, Amanda Shore for your hard work and support. Massive thanks to the incredibly talented Linggar Bramanty for his amazing cover art, and to my good buddy Andrew Hall for the brilliant cover design. Also, huge gratitude to Polgarus Studio for the stella formatting.

About the author

John G Cressey was born in 1976, and grew up on the south coast of England where he enjoyed an active childhood involving swing ropes, tree houses and homemade go-carts. In his teens the interests became scuba diving, rock climbing and martial arts. At the end of his teens a spanner was thrown in the works in the form of a car crash in which damaged his spine. Deciding that University was too dangerous for a young man in a wheelchair, he decided to travel the world for a decade or so, taking in some of Africa, Brazil, Cambodia and Australia. He also lived in New York and San Diego for a time. But always looked forward to heading back home to England.

Seeing a documentary that showed Roald Dahl sitting in a little garden shed sharpening pencils and scribbling away first piqued John's interest in writing. Soon after, it was Star Wars that began to influence his imagination. But it was much later down the line when viewing the TV show, Firefly that he finally decided that writing was for him. The show's balance of light hearted humor, sometimes dark, emotional drama and kick ass action really hit home and the idea for his first book 'Star Splinter' began to take shape.

You can learn more about J G Cressey and his upcoming books at his website: www.jgcressey.com

Made in the USA
Charleston, SC
29 November 2015